SPIRAL

SPIRAL

JAMES M. FISHER

LUMINARE PRESS

WWW.LUMINAREPRESS.COM

Luminare Press
442 Charnelton Street
Eugene, OR 97401
www.luminarepress.com

LCCN: 2018968505
ISBN: 978-1-64388-009-9

For Baw

BOOK I
The Crane Trilogy

I am moved by fancies that are curled
Around these images, and cling:
The notion of some infinitely gentle
Infinitely suffering thing.

T.S. Eliot

TABLE OF CONTENTS

Chapter 1

MY GENERATION

I woke in a pool of my own blood. The last thing I remembered was the sound of bullets whizzing by my head like metallic bees. I opened my eyes; they burned from the acrid smoke and explosive flashes. I did a personal inventory. Head and neck, check, arms and hands, check, M-16, check, torso… I'd been hit in the side. Blood trickled, pulsed, *lub-dub, lub-dub*. My legs overlapped, paralyzed in a mannequin pose. A large piece of shrapnel protruded from my side. I lay face up at the edge of a pear-shaped swamp. The stench and blood, smoke and disease of the war collected here drip by drip, drop by drop. Death stew. It was raining poison; the only thing the heavens could do was cry. Flies spun around my head, and though I saw leeches attached to my exposed leg, I couldn't feel them.

Cleverly camouflaged Viet Cong soldiers had ambushed my platoon. Nine of us were down. I heard the rattle of artillery fire in the distance. Large black shadows, bombers sucked the horizon, shook the ground. Fighter planes whipped the sky overhead. The worst of it all was the helpless screams of my buddies. Most of us were around eighteen, barely more than kids and here we were, dying in a swamp half a world away from home.

I was choking on my own blood and knew the next breath could be my last. My thoughts flickered, "I'm going to die here." I tried to remember something beautiful, but couldn't. Overhead, an army of napalm bombs were spinning toward us, spilling across the sky like dominoes.

With my last breath, I raised my M-16, emptied the magazine toward the rattle of gunfire and yelled, "Bring it motherfuckers, bring it!"

Just before impact, I awoke drenched in sweat.

Since I was in eighth grade, I had had this theme to my dreams—nightmares, really. Growing up in the middle of the Vietnam War had been pretty scary. The daunting coverage on the TV and radio, the images in *Life* magazine, which was on every newsstand, not to mention on our living room coffee table, combined with the anti-war marches on Main Street and at the local colleges in our community, found a corner and set up camp somewhere in my brain. When I turned sixteen, the military draft was still in place. I hated the war and the lies that went with it.

My uncle John and several guys from my neighborhood got drafted and never returned from Vietnam, not even in body bags. The news called them MIA's. Their deaths had been ordered by politicians' manicured hands. They'd been sent to an unknown land against their will, left unprotected, taken prisoner of war, trapped in sheet music made of barbed wire, the black notes in someone else's badly written song about freedom.

My parents, relatives, friends, nearly everyone I knew, had silver bracelets with their names engraved on them, and the date they went missing. Eventually the bracelets became just another item clanking in the kitchen junk drawer, rotting and fading like stannic bones.

I internalized the fear of dying. I was desperate for the chance to experience life outside the grip of Trophy Wife and Jock Dad before that last great wipeout. Hell, I hadn't even had a girlfriend by the time I was old enough to get drafted. President Reagan had joked about bombing Russia and the media had a field day with it. Stuff like that angered me even more. I was pissed. I couldn't forget those guys, what they did, how they died. Our government's Frankenstein machine, with its weapons, collateral damage, cover-ups, scandals, blind arrogance towards its own people, the slaughter of others. Time will tell the story. For me, the machine needed to be rebuilt and this time not on the bones of kids too young to have been on a date.

In the end, no amount of wishful thinking or rage kept the nightmares away. After one of those dreams, I ended up with a familiar, overall sense of relief, feeling that I narrowly escaped death. This one had been worse, in full color. It was also the first time I had tried to fight back in some small way.

I rubbed my eyes and sat at the edge of my bed. The petrichor smell of the swamp was still on my skin and flowed through my veins, filled my nose. My alarm buzzed and vibrated on the nightstand. I slid over and silenced it. The damp, wet earth smell dissipated without a trace as if by a kill switch. My nose was clear, nothing.

The phone rang.

I flinched, but was too dazed to care. It rang again. I pulled off and balled up my sweat-soaked shirt, buried my face into it and inhaled. "Only me," I said, taking a half breath, carefully chasing the stench of the swamp. It was gone—like gone. I threw the shirt at the hamper. It banked off the wall and landed perfectly on the lid. "Two points," I also said.

There was a knock on my bedroom door. Trophy Wife. I knew by her knock. It was a sad knock, two quick taps followed by a slow fading peck on the wood.

"Michael, are you in there? Dave's brother is on the phone, and it sounds important," Trophy Wife said, loudly, through the door. My head kicked back, and my eyes raced up to the ceiling as soon as I heard her voice. I took a deep breath. I do that when I sense her nagging coming on. It sounded like she was yelling through a megaphone full of gravel. Dave's brother? Why would my best friend's brother be calling me?

"Okay, thanks, I got it." Still in my boxer shorts, and foggy from the nightmare, I rolled across the other side of the bed to reach the phone extension on my nightstand, pulled it towards me. Dave's brother had never called me before.

"This is Michael."

"Hey Michael, it's Dana Stark. Uh, I got some bad news. Dave's had an accident, man." His words were slow and he sounded lost. A dozen possibilities raced in my head. Images of fire, turbulent water, were first in line.

"Oh my god. Is he gonna be okay? What happened?" I grabbed the corner of my pillow and bit down hard as I braced myself for the news.

"He was riding his bike along the Santa Ana River Jetty and…"

"Yeah, and?" I pulled the pillow out of my mouth and threw it across the room.

Chapter 2

TEENAGE WILDLIFE

A little over three years earlier, regardless of how I felt, to everyone else, it was just the first day of high school. Butterflies from Hell flitted through my flesh; their wings etched under my skin—nettles and pins. Abduction, unlawful restraint, freedom hanging from the gallows, walking the line—the themes played out in my head during that morning's drive. The only thing to calm Satan's butterflies would be the sound of an afternoon bell. The hellish wings vibrated like cicadas as my new high school nestled in Santa Ana, California came into view.

Jock Dad and I approached the intersection of Bristol and Edinger Street. I pressed my foot into the floor on the passenger side hoping to brake, but the light turned green. I was a little nervous; being forced to do something without my consent made me crazy. It didn't help that I didn't know a single person, either. Up until then, I'd always gone to public schools, cheap, harmonious. The idea of going to a private high school so far from home seemed cruel and harsh. Trophy Wife was behind it all. She wanted to separate me from my neighborhood friends and she succeeded. Sure, I got into a little trouble with my friends, smoking in the boy's room, playing hooky and going to the beach. We'd been caught with a Playboy magazine we had found in a trashcan on the way to school, but nothing I'd done would warrant a call like this. There was more to it. It was no coincidence that not a week after Trophy Wife's tennis club friends had gathered for some fancy brunch at our house, boasting about why they sent their snooty kids to private high schools like Bishop Amat, Our Mother of God, and Servite, she suddenly developed a deep concern for my education. I had overheard the whole thing. After a glass or two of wine, the group had gotten really loud. Then Trophy Wife comes up with the plan, pretending it to be this wonderful idea to send me to "a good school".

No surprise, predictable, status and image on rye, cackle sandwich. The next thing was her and Jock Dad arguing over the money, which was miraculously solved a few days later. Come to find out, Trophy Wife's daddy was a wealthy real estate broker and he kicked in a few bucks as the saga developed. In the end, Jock Dad threw his hands up and caved. Sure enough, without even asking me, I was registered and inundated with brochures.

The fifty-minute commute with Jock Dad everyday was arduous. The day began with waking up at o-dark-thirty (as he put it), losing two hours of sleep compared to my public school friends who would never think about getting up before dawn. Instead of a calm, quiet ride to school, we listened to jazz all the way down the 405. It was bumper-to-bumper parts of the way. Billboards advertising Black Velvet and the Marlboro man, restaurant signs with banners "All you can eat," "Free Happy Hour Buffet," blocked the many lines of palm trees and rolling hills, the majestic face of the San Bernardino mountains was choked by smog most of the time. Sunrise was often blinding as it broke through the overcast morning sky. The further we drove away from the house, the more chaotic things seemed to be. Jock Dad turned the Jazz volume up too, and along with it, my anxiety level. The drive would have given us an opportune time to talk; instead, Jock Dad created a wall of music between us. The sounds of Dave Brubeck, Herb Alpert, Stan Getz, and other jazz greats were the soundtrack of our time together. Don't even start singing "The Girl from Ipanema."

The fun just wouldn't relent. I had Jock Dad and jazz in the morning but when the afternoon bell rang, it was off to the bus stop. My afterschool ride home was the Orange County bus system, the OCTD. I felt like such a loser having to ride the bus, which continued for almost two years until I was licensed to drive. While I cruised home on the bus, I met hookers and gang bangers, commuters, drug addicts and crazy people. While I waited for the bus at various points of transfer these people swirled around me in a haze of stale smoke, body odor, and nameless unwashed funk. I listened to their conversations, though not by choice. It was, 'motherfucker this', and 'motherfucker that'. I hadn't thought my first taste of these outer areas would be characterized by such words. *Is this how these people really communicate with each other?*

They dispersed somewhere along the stops between Santa Ana and Garden Grove. I was mostly alone on the bus by the time I reached my stop—a tiny corner in my neighborhood, white suburban, middle class, safe, and where teens would most likely be put on restriction or told to eat a bar of soap for even thinking of using the word 'motherfucker'. It was the same walk Monday thru Friday, the bus doors would swing open, same black diesel smoke would billow from the bus as it left me on the curb, frozen. I would stand there, take a deep breath to jump-start my brain, and ask myself, "What am I doing?" Only to arrive at the same conclusion day after day: I had no options, I just had to proceed.

I jaywalked the busy street of Chapman Avenue avoiding the safety of the fading lines of the crosswalk and into the mouth of my neighborhood. I tried to guess the aromas and spicy flavors of suppers cooking as I made my way along my dimly lit street. Garlic-tomato, beef stews, the distant scent of tuna casserole, bacon, and fried fish permeated the air from the cookie cutter houses on my block.

That first morning of high school as Jock Dad and I neared the entrance of Mother of God, I noticed the school was surrounded by chain link fencing. Four rows of barbed wire were strung along the top and suspended at an angle that pointed in, toward the campus. Odd, as that would prevent people from climbing out. There was a rolling chain-link gate complete with barbed wire at the entrance of the parking lot; it slid on a rail. There was a sign on it that read, "This gate will be kept locked from 8:10 am until 2:45 pm."

To be locked in like POWs until the final bell rang was hellish and creepy. Los Alamitos High School was a five-minute walk right down the street in my own neighborhood. Seniors could leave for lunch and come back. There was no chain-link lock up or barbed wire. Most importantly, my friends were there. This place was going to be Hell.

The butterflies in my chest were at full-metal-flit as I stepped out of the car and onto the tarmac that led into what looked like a place too old to care. This might be the spot the word "institution" was born. Anyhow, there was nothing cool about getting out of your parents' car as a

 James M. Fisher

freshman on your first day. I assumed I wasn't alone. There had to be others like me, who were too smart to fall for the fake hoopla and rah rah hype of being in a prestigious high school, rated in the top ten for college prep. The brochures and letters had arrived shortly after Trophy Wife sent in the first tuition payment. They all blathered on: *You have been handpicked, specially chosen, carefully selected to join one of the premier high schools in the nation.*

I imagined the sugary, Kool-Aid elixir of institutionalized academia, fused with religious philosophy that would be forced down our throats in the years to come. It would be administered in small spoonfuls, daily, hourly, and most of the student body wouldn't know what they were swallowing. Maybe a couple of people shared in the context of my cerebral demise, maybe not. What I did know was this would become known in my personal dialogue as "my Catholic damage".

One newbie like me would have sufficed on that first day of dread. It was obvious a few of the students in the crowd looked punished, forlorn. Not knowing a single person made it feel like a jail sentence. At least Dante had Virgil and Beatrice to guide him through the Nine Circles of Hell. The morning trudged along on its knees, the sun was swallowed, a light rain began to fall, and the world turned into a sketch by Doré. Forgiving my parents for this would probably never happen. I chanted to myself, "It's only temporary, it's only temporary." Four years was a stretch on temporary; the math failed.

I was aware that I was a little awkward, a late bloomer, whatever the hell that was supposed to mean. Not ten minutes after entering the school, some jerk came running along and knocked the books out of my hands. It was totally reminiscent of my experience in middle school.

For five years my classmates had called me "Crane." I was taller than most and skinnier. My body was a cruel joke at times. Just when I would start to fill out and put on a little weight, I would grow two inches almost overnight. My pants rose above my ankles, which was not cool, my shoes wore fast and holes formed. My parents couldn't keep up with the cost of new clothes every couple months.

I tried to play basketball with the other kids at recess. I was getting better, too, and could make some shots. My favorite shot was the Kareem Sky Hook, at least my version of it. I didn't know how ridiculous I looked when I attempted it until it was pointed out to me at recess in front of half the student body by my arch nemesis, Mark Richardson, who yelled out from the sideline, "Hey, Price, you look like a crane out there!"

The crowd laughed. I overheard someone say, "Yeah, he does look like a crane."

Mark began to commentate on my every move. "Crane has the ball. Crane shoots and misses. Everyone knows cranes can't play, so why does he bother?"

After ten minutes of ridicule and mockery, I turned and stared him down.

"What are you going to do now, Crane? You gonna cry?"

"Up yours, Richardson," I said, and flipped him off—full on, Johnny Cash style. I loathed that guy. It was all I could come up with. I remember swallowing, and in seconds he was on me like a football linebacker—the lights went out. I woke up in the nurse's office with a bloody nose, a black eye, and a slight concussion from my head hitting the pavement. Apparently, Richardson had kept on hitting me after I was knocked out. To this day I cannot recall the beating, just the memory of Richardson's body eclipsing the sun, his catcher's mitt hands, the pain of healing, mine and Richardson's suspension from school, and my nickname, "Crane." That name stayed with me all through middle school to the point that my teachers started calling me Crane. Whenever something was out of reach and I was near, someone would say, "Have Crane get it." To no surprise I stayed with baseball and eventually became a first string pitcher—my long lanky arms aided my fastball and my teammates were cool. But even with all the good times, my clearest memory was the fear, how I cringed every time I heard Richardson's voice echo in the hallways.

My time at high school did not start off well, either. At least in this instance I wasn't alone. Most of us freshmen were carrying four or five newly purchased textbooks since our lockers hadn't been assigned yet. That was to be the second piece of business on the homeroom orientation agenda, following the "Welcome to Our Mother of God" speech. The book-knocking asshole moved on and repeated his attack on other new arrivals. I could hear books dropping and students yelling, "Hey!" and "What the hell?" from down the corridor until the homeroom bell rang. The jerk's letterman's jacket, red, white and gray, and buzzed haircut disappeared in the bedlam. A trail of victims remained, kneeling on the floor in dismay. It was us versus them; a line had been drawn, leaving us to drown in our own perturbations.

The brochures had failed to mention the warm and welcoming part of the student body that was the pride of "Our Mother of God." My books had hit the ground and scattered like oversized cards. The new three ring binders I had put together the night before, with new paper and dividers, were launched into the crowd to be kicked and trampled. I was in the way, hunched over, gathering my things, like a hideous rock in a stream. My hands moved quickly and carefully as I picked up the papers between the waves of the stampeding feet and knees. I felt uncomfortable, uncoordinated, and upside-down. Was this what being fifteen was supposed to look like? I needed a new perspective because the view from down there sucked.

We hear about the awkwardness of our early lives until our bodies fill out and grow hair. Only then can we begin to start shoving back the jerks that bullied us in freshman year. Simple evolution, really. Later, you pass that reality on to your kids, or maybe not. Perhaps it depends on what type of father you have. In my case, there was this day of shame that still seems to stick in the corner of my mind and prick me from time to time. It's when I least expect it, too. Just when I think that memory is gone forever into some discarded nightmare vault, never to be heard from again, there it is, like a brand new pair of shoes.

The day began beautifully, a few families from the neighborhood met up with us around 10 am at Huntington Beach, just south of the pier. The waves were glassy, perfect for body surfing. It was a California postcard-picture-worthy-day. That's when I met Charlene. I saw her standing on the shore while I was in the water holding for the next set. A clean wave approached, I kicked my Churchill fins and positioned myself inside the peak and rode it in to where Charlene was standing. She was a genuine California beauty with long blonde hair, strands bleached by the sun, and a tan: orange marmalade and honey.

"Wow, that was a great ride," she said. I felt like a stud.

"Thanks, the waves are perfect today."

"I'm Charlene; your dad's my dad's best friend."

"I know, I've seen you around. Good to meet you finally."

I was so glad I hadn't eaten it on that wave. I had wanted to say something to her for a long time but the shyness always got the best of me and I avoided her.

That day, the stars seemed aligned in my favor. We started talking and before we knew it, we walked passed six lifeguard stations and ended up at the pier. We were almost a mile from our beach towels.

"We better get back, our parents are going to freak out," Charlene said.

"Let 'em freak," I thought.

"You're right. I'll race you," I said.

Charlene giggled and took off running before I could count to three. I caught up to her and let her win. She looked so confident in her stride, long hair bobbing in the wind. Her laugh was intoxicating. I'm not sure why I slowed, but it felt right.

At the barbecue that followed the trip to the beach, Jock Dad referred to me as a 'late bloomer'. I was having the time of my life with Charlene. It was, and always will be, a memory of such innocence between us.

Jock Dad, hovering next to the grill, used words like "skinny," "puberty-stricken," "probably won't play sports in high school," in his slurred comments to Jock Neighbor, Charlene's dad. They were random, thoughtless statements. The two men chuckled and laughed about whatever the other had to say. Jock Neighbor was busy cracking beers and cooking. His skills matched his IQ. The burgers on the grill were beaten to death; he flipped them like they were trying to get away. His extra long spatula never stopped moving, every turn made them catch fire. Between stabs and flips, the flame height increased to eye level. With all the beer they chugged, neither noticed that Jock Neighbor eventually had one eyebrow missing. By the time the burgers were assumed finished and removed from the grill, the place where his eyebrow had been was a red blister in the shape of Florida.

A delicious smoke, smelling of charred meat and ash, permeated the air. It wound around the backyard trees and shrubs like a ghost. Trophy Wife sipped a daiquiri, talked about her recent boob job and how much more Jock Dad did around the house and what a better listener he had become since the day of the surgery. It sickened me really. He was always attentive to her, he saw nothing else after meeting her. She loved doing the social thing, talking about daily soaps, tennis club events, her, her, her, with the other imbibing Trophy Wives. They gossiped about the women who couldn't make it to the party and complained about all the things they didn't have but would soon attain. I stood behind them all, in my saggy swim trunks, dripping wet, thin, and insignificant, hearing the whole thing. It wouldn't have been so bad if Charlene wasn't standing next to me at the time.

She seemed so innocent and good. We had sat by the pool earlier and talked about stuff we liked to do. She said she played piano and promised to teach me Beethoven's Für Elise sometime. I thought, cool, we have a future date. She must like me. We talked on about how much we loved the ocean and the problem with pollution along our coast. Both of us hated the tar that stuck to our feet that we picked up on the shore that morning. We might have kissed that day as things were progressing. I could really make her laugh

     James M. Fisher

and would do anything to make her lose it. Charlene was my first crush, the first girl that ever got me. But after what Jock Dad announced to everyone about me and puberty—the pitying, unforgettable look on Charlene's face, I was done.

Under my breath I whispered loudly, "Screw this! I'm out of here."

I grabbed my soaking wet T-shirt off the lawn chair. Someone's fat ass had sat on my shirt after cooling off in the pool. The cheek marks told the story.

"Don't go," Charlene said. "It's okay."

I ignored her and didn't look back, contorting and pulling the wet T-shirt over my head. Seconds later, any dignity that might have been waiting around to see what might happen next ran for its life, when the collar of my T-shirt completely ripped its way out, into the perfect shape of a zero. For a second, it stuck to the circumference of my head. I wore it like a halo.

Jock Neighbor yelled, "Hey St. Michael, come get a burger."

The adults laughed. I unbolted the side gate, hopping over the decorative gravel and onto oval shaped pavers that merged into the sidewalk. My shame quickly turned into anger, and loneliness. I regretted not saying goodbye to Charlene after having such an incredible day with her. The self-esteem I'd felt when I was with her was gone, consumed in a fire of drunken slurs. The tears infiltrated the back of my eyes like an army of stinging ants, but I didn't cry. That would have made me feel even more like a wuss. I tightened my jaw and clenched my fists and tore off, leaving my ripped shirt and halo in the street. I headed home, skudding through streets of burning asphalt and the concrete pathways of the suburban wasteland. The crows on the wire seemed to look the other way; I took my chances as I walked beneath them.

"Shit on me! I dare you, everyone else has!"

My face flushed with embarrassment. I looked around to see if anyone heard me. The crows let me pass. I was angry like them with their dead eyes and black jackets. The neighborhood was quiet, the heat was intense, and everyone was probably at the beach. The scorching heat of the Santa Ana winds coughed and hacked through town in a deliberate huff. It reminded me of our crazy neighbor down the street, old man Decker, clearing his tobacco-road-of-a-throat.

Fifteen was a bitch, I decided.

I never asked Charlene out, even after my own metamorphosis a couple years later. In fact, as a result of that day, I never even got up the nerve to talk to her again.

Just before turning seventeen, I was no longer the skinny cockroach of a man becoming, standing around poolside dripping wet. I grew five inches in the summer between sophomore and junior year, gained weight and filled out. Everything had become an exciting challenge. Call it whatever you want, new energy, confidence, renewal. Like a stray cat, it just showed up.

Along with my body, my interests grew. My surfing and athletic abilities improved. Learning how to fight was mostly due to my cousin Frank, who took karate. He would come over on the weekends just to demonstrate his newest move. During our bouts, I was usually the victim. I pretty much resigned myself to Frank kicking my ass until we started sparring on a regular basis.

I have to say, with my new confidence, a little payback

was due to the bullies I put up with in freshman year. I swore I would get back at those guys, but never really got the chance to pummel anyone. There were just a couple of instances where I was tested. In those moments, chests were bumped, eyes glared, and those bullies from freshman year backed off without a punch. It was a little disappointing, actually.

The most important thing to me was that my surfing took off as I became stronger. I entered a few surfing contests and was picked up by a local board shop and got sponsored. After competing for a year, I quit. Somehow the thing I loved the most became something else when I competed. The peace of my early morning sessions returned when I let go all the pressure of competing and the bullshit that went with it.

Towering over Jock Dad felt great too; not being the puberty-stricken kid felt even better. He loved the fact I was on a surf team, but when I'd had enough of it, he was irritated and called me a quitter. He would say over and over again, "Team sports and competing are good for your character. Surfing is in your blood, you're a natural." Trophy Wife would stand there, arms folded, just nodding her head in agreement.

"Trophy Wife, kiss my ass," I said from a deep cave inside my head.

When I was a kid, I used to sit and listen to my grandfather play guitar, Southern blues and Johnny Cash. He'd sit on the back porch and play next to a bottle of Jack Daniels and a deck of cards, smoking his Chesterfields one after the other. I would sip a Coke with a red licorice whip hanging out of my mouth. I'd pretend it was a cigarette.

Grandpa taught me a couple chords and how to sing, "I Walk the Line." I told Jock Dad and Trophy Wife that I wanted a guitar for Christmas. Trophy Wife insisted it was just a phase. Instead, I got some really lame clothes for school. *Thanks, Trophy Wife.*

At the close of my freshman summer, two months after the poolside barbecue incident, I watched Grandpa die of lung cancer at his house. He was unrecognizable, but had kept his sense of humor and wit intact until the end.

"Cancer is not going tell me I can't smoke," he said. All the procedures and chemo had only given him six extra months. He sent me to the kitchen for cigarettes. When I returned, my Dad lit up and slipped him what would be his last Chesterfield. Dad had to hold it in place for him. Grandpa took a big drag and said in a toothless voice of passing and pain, "Big Mike, take care of that ol' guitar for me."

"I will, Grandpa."

That was fifteen: another death, a crush, and poolside humiliation. The good-byes were stacking.

A couple years later (during my metamorphosis), I picked up that old guitar and learned to play. Every chance I got, I played. I woke up with Grandpa's guitar in the morning and sometimes fall asleep with it at night. It became an extension of me, my soul. Soon I was trying to sing and play at the same time.

Since I was ten-years-old, I had been writing in an old logbook Grandpa had given me. He said it was a place for my thoughts to go, even the scary ones. It started out as a journal and then soon it became much more. I wrote stories, poems, letters, and dreams in it. In time, that old guitar would help me find a way to lift the words off some of those pages and make them something else. Poetry, stories, letters, transformed into different types of songs, even an occasional outlaw love song would pop up. I kept all of it private and hidden from everyone. I didn't even tell Dave about the poetry, much less the love songs.

Losing Grandpa and Charlene made me relive again the loss of my real mother. It was the darkest summer for me. Having a place for my thoughts to go kept me sane. However, the memory of that shameful day at the poolside barbecue has never left. Like a bad skip on a vinyl record, it played over and over, with its needle etching itself into my being, never shutting the hell up.

I found out twenty-one years later that Charlene had had a crush on me, too. Her sister, Karen, mentioned it during a brief conversation at Charlene's wake.

"I just can't stop thinking how different her life might have been if she'd told you how she felt. We used to joke about you two getting married someday. Maybe she wouldn't have ended up with him. Maybe she wouldn't have gotten hooked on those damn pills. Maybe…" Karen trailed off and wiped her eyes.

"I thought of calling her many times," I said, standing there, remembering how I always assumed she was dating someone else and not completing the call.

"Thanks for coming, Mike. You didn't have to make the

trip, but I know it would have meant a lot to Cherry."

I stood at Charlene's graveside and wondered, could I have saved her? She had died at thirty-six from a heart broken, by a broken man, in a broken town, and an accidental overdose.

Chapter 3

ONCE IN A LIFETIME

Once I hit my junior year, I crossed over to other youthful priorities, like a job. Working to get a car with a stereo to blast my favorite songs was big, but to be able to surf as often as possible and whenever I wanted was living the dream. The freedom of coming and going as I wanted was pinnacle.

MY DAD WAS AN AVID BODY SURFER AND WATERMAN. HE loved the Wedge in Newport Beach and thrived on seeing my terrified, six-year-old face when he would vanish in the waves. I watched him slice through fifteen-foot shore pound with his Churchill swim fins, black and yellow, tearing through the green summer barrels. Real Mom would have both arms around my waist to keep me from getting too close to the outgoing tidal flow. As the chaotic walls of whitewater exploded on the shore, I felt the immense power resonate through my young body and align with my beating heart.

My dad's shit-eating grin that used to terrify me at six became mine by seventeen. The only difference—I was paddling out on the newest technology surfboards, a Harbour Rocket-Fish. Rich Harbour, the owner and shaper of the boards, invited me in to watch him make it. I was there for every moment of its creation, from the transformation of the foam blank to the final glassing. I was in another world. This was my personal thing. My business. Rich was really cool and included me in every step.

The Rocket was my vehicle to carve out my own place in the waves. It enabled me to separate myself from the life on land and allowed me to exist in the space beyond the shoreline, sublime.

As I paddled out, I could look back and see the world disappear more and then more, the further my hands dug into the water. For the first time in my life, I felt something in the universe that was bigger than me, extremely personal, and mine. It saddened me that Real Mom wasn't around to see me surf, but I found some friends who felt the same as I did, and we became a brotherhood of sorts.

We started night surfing under the lights at the Huntington Beach Pier, usually on Friday nights. A few of us would have to lie to our parents and tell them we were staying overnight at each others' houses. None of our parents would approve of surfing the pier at night. Could you imagine saying, "Hey Mom, we're going to surf the pier in the middle of the night in head high waves and occasionally surf between the pylons. See you in the morning."

Surfing the pier at night was extreme to most people. Paddling out with only pier lights reflecting off the water made the experience surreal, dangerous, exhilarating. On occasion, having glassy waves and a full moon looming overhead was like paddling through "The Starry Night". Elongated beams, sea foam exploding like sparks, stars on the water, majestic. Back-crack creaking of the pier, waves bashing the pylons, the ocean's hiss on the shoreline while the city slept, glorious. Dropping in on waves I couldn't fully see pushed my senses to a new place until it became natural.

Onlookers standing along on the pier rail above would point and sometimes yell:

"Nice wave."

"Where'd that guy go?"

The Huntington Beach cops had a reputation for being a little rough, especially towards punks. Long Beach cops up the road were worse. Some of the skinhead hard-core punks were beginning to make their violent entry onto the scene and the media made it look like we were all that way. A recent article showed a picture of an HB cop beating a punk with a nightstick down on Main Street. The title of the article was "Keeping Our Neighborhoods Safe," not police brutality, or an explanation for the beating. Articles like these were showing up across the nation.

One Friday night a few of us were walking down Pacific Coast Highway around eleven o'clock. We had parked the car and slipped on our wetsuits and were headed toward the pier. A police car pulled up alongside us and rolled down the window and turned on the spotlight. We kept walking.

"Oh, fuck," Dave said.

"Just be cool," I said. Our other two friends remained silent.

"You guys headed for the pier?" said the officer in the driver's seat.

"What a stupid fucking question," whispered Dave.

"Just be cool. We'll make a run for it at the hedge coming up," I whispered.

"We are done for the night and heading home," I said.

"Not one of you has sand on your feet and you all are completely dry. Violating curfew is serious, fellas," the cop said.

"Run for it!" Dave yelled, diving head first into the hedge.

"Fuck!" we all said, laugh-running through the hedge and darting across the parking lot adjacent the pier. The cop sped to the stop light at the corner, turned his lights on to clear traffic, and finally entered the parking lot. By the time he got remotely close to us, we were in the water. Later that night, the cop had a couple other officers with him on the pier. They all had stern looks on their faces as they peered out over the rail looking for us. There were at least twenty of us in the water. We all looked the same, sea lions bobbing up and down in waves.

Sometimes we would flip them off as they yelled for us to get out of the water, but we knew they couldn't touch us. They were trapped on land and could only go out as far as the pier's end. They could get really nasty when the curfew was violated and so could we.

"Come in and get us," we yelled. Other surfers in the water followed our lead, making it more confusing to home in on the minors in the water. "Yeah, come in and get us," they shouted. Most guys out there were older than us and didn't have to worry about the stupid curfew. Though we were locals too, all of us younger guys had to respect them. As long as we didn't drop in on their waves and gave them the right of way, they looked out for us.

It all felt purely natural too, like a second home. I could not imagine a life without the ocean. For a time, she was mine. Many others felt the same—she was theirs. I didn't

     James M. Fisher

mind sharing and the ocean didn't either. Each of us had our own special bond, and yet we shared a common love for our dangerous, glorious mistress.

⸺⸺ ⧢ ⸺⸺

REAL MOM DIED WHEN I WAS TEN. HER NAME WAS MARIE. She loved gardenias, planted the seeds, harvested the blooms and put them in vases. Her hands always smelled like them. A devout Catholic woman, but you would never know it. She wasn't preachy or judgmental. She just had a compassionate, peaceful way about her. Everyone loved her. They say that only the good die young, and it was totally true in her case.

We lived in a humble home on a block with down-to-earth friends and neighbors, happy. I remember only one time when my parents argued. It was about work or money, maybe both. I was sitting in a chair in the living room, watching TV, and they were standing just inside the kitchen.

"Dammit, Marie. It's never enough! I'm working my ass off and finishing school, I want more for you guys, this living check to check crap is getting old" Dad said.

"We have everything we need," Mom said.

"You deserve more," he said.

"I don't need or want more. That's what they want you to think, darling," she said. "Is that what you need, more?"

"I'm not sure. I'm not making sense am I?" Dad said, voice slowing, feather falling.

"Let's not let the world tell us what we need or who we have to become or impress. We have the dream now. The rest is just…stuff." Mom's tone was soft, and gentle.

"You're right. I'm being stupid, aren't I?"

"A little." I could almost hear them smile at each other.

Mom giggled, took Dad by the hand and headed toward their bedroom. "Mikey, don't stay up too late. We love you," she said.

They never went to bed angry and as far as I remember, Dad never slept on the couch. The world was safe. We could get through anything. Oddly, the sun always seemed to shine inside our house or wherever we were with Real Mom. Her arrows were always out, and not just for us, but towards everyone. The woman was a beacon, our lighthouse, and probably a saint. Because of her, we had it all.

Sometimes I forget what she looked like and it breaks my heart. I have a picture of her that I carry for those moments. It was taken on the shoreline when I was eight. The way she looked at me in that picture makes me miss her even more. In her eyes, I was perfect, I could do anything. Everything was always going to be okay when she was around.

I am compelled to talk about the holidays. They were crazy-amazing. Cra-mazing. Real Mom made Christmas such a special event—special and exciting. I would get so revved up, so committed, that every year since I was five, my excitement would go off the Richter scale, and I would throw up on Christmas Eve at about 9 pm, like clockwork. It became a little embarrassing. The excitement would start on December first. An advent calendar with chocolate squares behind each window would appear, mounted to the fridge. That's when it started. We began to pray again at dinner and did the advent wreath. For whatever reason, we didn't really pray much during the summer, and by fall almost not at all.

My dad was different, too. He was happy and he played with me and my cousins. He would tell us stories to make us all laugh, or terrify us depending on his prerogative. Like my throwing up, the storytelling stopped after the last Christmas with Real Mom.

She passed on the first day of spring. When she went into the ground, I didn't think I would make it. The house was different, cold, hollow, desolate, the type of silence that only existed in space. It rained for days after. I rained for years.

The house smelled like gardenias long after Real Mom died. My dad and I never talked about it. I was superstitious; I thought if I mentioned it, she would go away like the petrichor in my dreams. I believed Real Mom was still trying to comfort us and make everything all right. When I think of her, I remember light.

Chapter 4

UNCONTROLLABLE URGE

Real Mom looked saintly, angelic, incorruptible, lying in her casket. Not even Death could steal her beauty. A rare heart disease took her without warning. I had assumed she was just sleeping on the couch when I had come home from school that day. I tried to be quiet so as not to disturb her and went right to my room to do my homework. She rarely slept on the couch unless she was sick or tired. The Hollywood Squares was on the TV, and Paul Lynde was laughing at one of his own jokes. It felt like any other day and I had no idea she had died. When my dad came home from work, I heard the front door close; it rattled the windows like it always did and there was a pause. I waited for some sort of eruption of laughter between the two of them. He liked to pick her up and give her a good kiss or tickle her. They were always glad to see each other.

"Jesus, God, no. No!" he cried.

It was a frightening voice, a scream really. He arrived too late to make a deal with God. I had never heard such a sound come out of my dad before or since. I ran out of my room to the living room. My dad held my mom in his arms. Tears poured from his face to hers. I knew she wasn't just sleeping. My knees hit the floor.

 James M. Fisher

THE FUNERAL AND THE WAKE ATTENDEES CONSISTED mostly of women from Mom's prayer group, many people from church who I recognized but didn't know, their families, a few of Dad's work associates and close friends, and my grandpa.

I went into a black place, a void of sorts, when the bagpiper began to play at the funeral procession. It was a place where I could no longer cry, like my tears were denied, no matter how much I felt the need to sob. I had run out of tears. Was that possible?

Real Mom's coffin had heather and gardenias draped over the sides. I was one of the pallbearers: the smell of the gardenias made this seem more real than it should have. I clung tightly to the pewter rail of her silver-blue coffin with one hand, the other moving militarily in time with the bagpipes, my swollen eyes fixated ahead on the green drape over the hole in the ground. Saying goodbye to Real Mom would linger way beyond the blackness of that day.

AT THE WAKE IN THE CHURCH HALL, THE ONLY THING I could remember were the random comments. She was such a beautiful lady, kind, generous. They had no idea of how wonderful she was.

The men drank while music that Mom had liked played in the background. "I Can Hear Music," by the Beach Boys came on. Dad broke down when he heard it. One of his buddies grabbed him like he was about to fall.

Grandpa was having a beer and saw me sitting in a corner. He was in shape, had a golfer's tan. The silver hair and crow's feet around his eyes made him look like a wise old cowboy. He looked at me from across the room, caring and puppy-eyed. His head and his left thumb pointed at the door. I nodded yes, and mouthed the words, "Get me outta here, please." He gave me a thumbs-up, finished the last swallow of his beer and placed it on the counter. He had a wet circle on his khaki slacks where his beer rested and it showed itself as he got up, like a happy face sticker but without the face. Grandpa walked over to the counter where my dad was leaning and took his car keys from him. Dad reached into his pockets and looked at me; both nodded their heads in agreement. They hugged each other and Grandpa escorted me to the car.

On the way home he said, "It's going to be all right, Mikey. You're going to be all right," and patted my leg. He reached into his shirt pocket and grabbed his Chesterfields. He shook the soft pack until one slipped out, one hand on the steering wheel, one eye on the road and the other on the cigarette lighter that popped inside the ashtray. We drove in silence until we arrived at the house; I went straight to my room.

"I'll be out here watching TV if you need me, Mikey," Grandpa called in the doorway, taking the last drag of his cigarette. A couple hours later my dad came home and knocked on my bedroom door. He cracked the door open.

"Mikey, are you okay?" His voice slurred a bit, I could hear beer swish around in the bottle as he sipped it. I was on my bed, face down in a pillow; he stood in the doorway, lost. It went quiet as he stood there. My shoulders shrugged, he closed the door. We could have used a shrink.

COMMUNICATION BETWEEN DAD AND ME NEARLY stopped after the funeral. My daily ablutions, food, clothing, books for school were the exceptions. The concept of living without Real Mom felt impossible, unfair, cruel. It seemed like my heart had shattered, then refused to beat. Life as we knew it died, along with Real Mom's gardenias.

Dad started dropping me off at my grandpa's house. At first it was 'just for the afternoon' then 'just overnight' and soon it became a regular thing. He would leave me for weeks, sometimes. When I wasn't at Grandpa's, Dad and I would eat together in front of the TV. After I would rinse the plates, do homework, take out the trash, and go to bed. It was our ritual for weeks on end.

Months passed, dust formed over the pictures along the walls, the living room tables, and nightstands in the bedrooms. A hazy film reflected off those faces, our faces, frozen in magical moments, monochromatic and Kodachrome, now distant, now dreamlike. The sun imposed its rays through the windows of the house as it crawled over the roof from east to west. Real Mom, Dad, and me in the light again, I thought, as I watched from the couch where she took her last breath. Our lives masked, in a handful of dust. Weeds thrived in the garden, and in our hearts; the house became a place where joy used to live.

TROPHY WIFE AND JOCK DAD STARTED DATING SIX months after Real Mom died. He kept it a secret for a while, had his reasons. The two of them met playing tennis during a singles round- robin at the Newport Beach Racquet Club.

Jock Dad had a complimentary trial membership; Trophy Wife was a socialite with a personality only money could buy. Her daddy was in real estate and liked to talk about how much he spent on his new car, his boat known as 'the forty-footer', and his shoes.

Just over a year after Real Mom died the big day came. For those two, I mean. Jock Dad wore a tuxedo jacket with a black bowtie and white tennis shorts. Trophy Wife wore an all white tennis skirt with baby's breath in her hair when they exchanged vows. The ceremony was on the indoor tennis court where they played their first match. Super cheesy, right? Yeah, even twelve-year-old me knew that.

The Justice of the Peace, also a club member, wore a referee outfit as he officiated. As a token best man, I was dressed in white shorts and a white polo shirt. It would be the first and last time I would wear such a thing.

After they said their I-dos, somebody with a sports announcer's voice congratulated them over a loudspeaker. Their recessional song was a choir of volleying green tennis balls.

TROPHY WIFE BECAME MORE CONTROLLING THE FUR-ther I walked away from my little boy shoes. She was obsessive, always cleaning, straightening and organizing the house.

That included my room.

One afternoon, when I was in the eighth grade, she dug through my drawers and came across my journal. I had been writing in it daily, since Real Mom died. It was full of poetry, songs, and short stories. It also contained a lot of random free writing; my most profound ideas about everything were contained therein, like science fiction, sex, fantasy, ecology, religion, but most importantly, private letters (conversations really) I had written to my mom, even though she was dead.

I think Trophy Wife read it all, because ever since I walked in on that particular day, there was an even weirder vibe from her. She just looked at me, staring at me with her judgmental eyes and kept on cleaning. Not even her usual nasally, dry greeting, "Hey Michael. How was school?"

Nothing.

I had an impulse to say, "What? what are you looking at?" but refrained. I knew she had read my journal because of the obvious way it had been left splayed out on my bed with various pages sticking out of it. I normally kept it hidden, buried in a drawer.

I confronted Trophy Wife on it in the middle of her vacuuming. She hated to be interrupted by anyone while in her "zone". To be stalled or stopped during her precious arpeggio of rhythmic glides over the carpet would get you the death look or the guillotine wince of disapproval.

"Did you read my journal?" I yelled over the vacuum noise.

Trophy Wife's head was down in careful glide formation. She paused, huffed, and flipped the switch off. Her head came up, she tossed her hair back and glared at me. I swallowed, and pushed forward.

"You don't have to yell, Michael," she snapped.

"Did you read it?"

"You should send some of your poems off to John Denver. Maybe he could make a song out of them," she said mockingly. She knew I hated John Denver. She would make us listen to his albums over and over at Christmas time.

Trophy Wife flipped the vacuum back on and was making her way to my room. The vacuum might as well have been a shark in her hand.

I followed. "What? You had no right to do that!"

She turned her back and kept the vacuum on to drown me out. She went on doing the housework like she had every right to invade my privacy.

How could anyone think like that?

I don't know why I wrote the things I did. I just woke up one day and started doing it. Moments after Trophy Wife's invasion, my frustration turned to shame as I realized that she must have read my story about an alien abduction. It was obvious from the way the story had been jammed into the journal upside down. I wasn't sure why I had even kept that one, but I had. It been inspired by a weird dream, and I had simply, secretly, converted it to a story.

Blame the dream on Captain Kirk. In one of my favorite Star Trek episodes he had this romantic moment with a female alien, humanoid in appearance except her skin was a turquoise green, at least on our TV. It was pretty awesome and I obsessed about it a little. Maybe more than a little.

In my story, the protagonist was captured and forced to have sex with several beautiful aliens. They were female, also humanoid, and had three breasts each. Their sole purpose was to copulate and save the Earth. The precise reason for such an undertaking was unknown. I didn't ask questions; I was mesmerized by three pairs of emerald blue eyes and nine naked breasts. The balance of the planet had to be restored. It was the ultimate sacrifice, but I was glad to do it for the sake of Mother Earth, so it read.

I was ashamed and angered to think Trophy Wife had read any of this. I felt violated, like my mind had been raped. She knew my secret thoughts, notions, feelings, stories, my life, my conversations with my dead mom. I was exposed, cast out along some roadside, naked, like a discarded corpse. My anger swelled, an oil spill, a black crude effused my bloodstream; my heart, my brain, imbibed. The dam broke, I yanked the cord out of the wall. The vacuum made a gasping sound.

Trophy Wife spun around.

"You're going to listen to me!" I yelled.

"Michael, put the plug back in the wall."

I threw the cord to the floor, my eyes fixed on hers. "You invaded my privacy, you read my journal."

"So what if I did? Plug the vacuum back in, now!"

"Kiss my ass."

"Michael!"

"How could you do this to me? This is mine, and only mine, this is all I have, and you had no right to go through my things and invade me like this."

She snorted and put her hands on her hips. "You take yourself too seriously Michael, really. Now plug me back in."

"Are you stupid? You're not hearing me." I stormed towards her. She huffed and quickly moved around me. She bent over, her slender arm reached for the cord. I stamped my foot down over the cord, denying her access.

"God dammit, Michael, move out of my way!"

"You need to apologize, now."

"For what? Reading your little book?"

"You're a bitch!"

"You little asshole!"

I was in a dangerous place. I wanted to strangle her. My heart pumped, fire. I had to get away from her. I shook my head and turned to walk towards the door.

Whack!

A flash of extreme heat and pain strapped my back, like a fire alarm going off under my skin. I was in total shock, endorphins rushed in like Hitchcock's birds. My brain stopped to gather information.

"Fuck!" I wheeled around to stare at her. "What the hell?"

She had whipped me with the cord. She whipped me with a fucking cord! The strike shocked me. Neither of my parents had ever hit me before.

"You hit me with a fucking cord!" I said. I reached for the newly torn skin to rub out the pain but I couldn't quite reach it. Trophy Wife began to coil the cord in her hands like she was arming herself to hit me again.

I charged.

Her shoulder length hair bobbed as she clung to the cord. Her pink fingernails slipped nervously along it as she swung it a second time.

I took another strap to the face before I managed to yank the cord away from her.

"It's different when you're not holding the weapon, isn't it?" I yelled. "You hit me when my back was turned. You're a coward." I took a step toward her.

"Get away from me, Michael!" she shrieked, looking at me like I was the psycho.

"Get out of my room and take your vacuum with you!" I threw the cord past her into the hallway.

"Your father is going to hear about this," she yelled, with her hand on the shark's tail pushing it awkwardly out my door.

     James M. Fisher

"I hope so, you fucking bitch! You whipped me! You invaded my privacy! My dad's not going to put up with your crap. He's going to divorce your ass!"

"You're going to military school, you bastard!"

"Fuck off!" I slammed my bedroom door and locked it. Who am I? Where am I?

The situation was foreign and horrific. I must have said the "F" word a hundred times. I thought of saying it before to the bullies at school, but never had the guts to say it out loud before. My parents had never hit me, either. That woman was insane.

Immediately, I began to rehearse the dialogue I was going to have with my dad. He would understand what she did and be appalled that she had hit me with a fucking vacuum cord.

MY DAD WAS HOME RIGHT ON TIME: 5:30 PM ON THE DOT. This would give us the opportunity to start over. I imagined our conversation, me comforting him after we booted Trophy Wife's skinny ass out the door. I would tell him it was the right thing to do and we'd go and get pizza. We hadn't been close since Real Mom's death, but this would be our chance to make things right again.

5:30 pm became 6:30 pm.

I could hear their voices in the living room but not a word of what they were saying. I could hear Trophy Wife's crying and my dad's monotone, then silence.

It was 7:15 pm when a firm three knocks tapped my door. I was sitting on the floor with my back against the bed.

The locked doorknob jiggled. I stood up, pulling my

T-shirt down over my jeans. I felt my skin tear where the blood had dried.

She had drawn blood. She was going down.

"Michael, you in there? Open the door," my dad said in a foreign tone.

I turned the lock and stepped back. He walked in.

"Hey, Dad."

"Really Michael? 'Hey, Dad'? Did you really call my wife a fucking bitch?"

"Whoa. I can explain the whole thing. She came into my room and-"

"Did you call my wife a fucking bitch?" He cut me off, his eyes fixed on mine, his neck red. He lowered his head slowly until he was inches from my face. I could smell the Scotch on his breath.

I tried to back up, but my bed was in the way. "Dad, I can explain."

"Answer my question!"

"Okay, yeah it happened, but—"

Whack!

He slapped me in the face with his open hand. I flew over the bed and landed on my feet, well sort of.

"Are you serious?" I stood up and walked back, to explain. I could taste the blood on my lower lip. "She's a bitch, Dad. She-"

Before I could finish my sentence, he back sided me again. I fell to the floor. I wanted to get up and swing at him, but how could I hit my own dad?

"Don't you ever talk to my wife like that again. Ever. And don't count on dinner either. You need to think about what you did."

"Yeah, but Dad—"

He walked out and slammed the door.

Tears stung my eyes, but I refused to let them flow. I brushed them away, anger swiped. At that moment, both Trophy Wife and Jock Dad became dead to me.

I wrote everything in my journal and would continue to do so. I had never imagined that somebody would ever see it, or see me through my own words, like some creepy voyeur, or that I might get a beating because of it. Like everything else we avoided, we didn't talk about that day either. I ate many meals alone until eighth grade ended.

Time heals all wounds, they say. That's fine if you're a cliché. Time is the vessel to remember, time never sleeps. It became a Band-Aid, more of a Halloween mask, really, to hide such an ugly chapter of our lives. One could only hope to forget such an awful day. The prong shaped scar left from Trophy Wife's Hoover vacuum, model U2002, made it impossible to forget.

In the following months, I felt like I was a pain in the ass most of the time, or an unwanted guest in my own house. I assumed most kids my age were probably going through the same thing. Did I mention how much I hated high school?

My salvation in high school was the windows I peered out of during lectures in that concrete and brick prison. Most teachers would recite the words from the textbooks, jargonized and sterile, without soul, empty, vacuous, passionless. Their words made my brain hurt. I got headaches if I listened too long. The incredible amount of time I had to think, dream, plot, and plan was unlike any other time in my life up to that point. I tried to live in the moment, but often the moment sucked.

High school was my Jungian rock, a springboard into the void and mystery of life. It was my mystery, my light, my darkness. When sitting in class and my own thinking turned to drifting away into a blank page, my mind defaulted to the beach. I would draw pictures of waves on a piece of scratch paper, or hide the latest Surfer magazine in my textbook and pretend to follow along in class. I'd flip through the pages and read about the surfers who dared to leave their normal lives and venture to distant lands to find the perfect surf.

One day, in September of my junior year, I was lost in such a reverie. The class had gone silent, like everyone stopped breathing at the same time. I sensed expectant eyes on me. I looked up from my book. Shit. Father Bernacki had apparently asked me to recite the five points of quantum theory he had listed on the board last class.

"Well, Mr. Price, the five points please." His voice was impatient, monotone like it had risen from the depths of a brown paper bag. The entire class was still not breathing, and most everyone behind me knew I was into my magazine (Gerri Lopez getting barreled at Pipeline).

Fortunately for me, I actually loved physics, and before the entire class passed out, I replied, "One, energy is not continuous but comes in small discrete units. Two, the elementary particles behave like particles and like waves. Three, the movements of these particles is inherently random. Four, it is physically impossible to know both the position and the momentum of a particle at the same time. The more precisely one is known, the less precise the measurement of the other. Five, the atomic world is *nothing* like the world we live in."

Father Bernacki looked astonished. "Very good," he said from somewhere inside his brown paper bag. He walked slightly out of step back toward the blackboard.

He scowled a little, like a disappointed henchman. Father Bernacki thought he had me. I was bored to death in most classes, but I wasn't stupid; not knowing the answer was, for me, unacceptable.

The bell rang.

⸎

Inside Dave's van in the school parking lot, I packed the bowl of a miniature wooden pipe with some pot Dana had given us, and told Dave about my narrow escape in physics class. I grabbed his lighter out of the glove box and torched the solid weed pack. It glowed red then crackled and popped. I took a nice long drag as he loaded a cassette tape. "Psycho Killer" by the Talking Heads. The intro began to play. I passed him the pipe and exhaled my smoke. That pungent primordial smell of the first hit, like Earth's armpit before a shower, Pan's hooves maybe, gecko sweat, granite perfume, sex and sage, charred loincloth, all the above. Weed has its own vaporous fingerprint. Dave's stereo illuminated the dark cavern of the van and reflected off his eyes at the end of his toke.

"Man, that was close, Mikey…that physics stuff is cool. It's cool you love it, even if it is kind of nerdy. You really covered your ass, man." He chortled, like he did about everything.

"Yeah, it was a close one, man…don't you marvel at this universe we live in, bro?"

"Uh-oh," he said, passing me the pipe.

"I feel like I'm a visitor just passing through, bro. I also like that the atomic world is nothing like the world we live in. But is that true? We are so limited by our simplistic thoughts that we fall and stumble inches away from the most profound truths. We constantly find ourselves in the state of 'I can almost put my finger on it,' only to give up like Schrödinger and his half dead cat. I think our world is atomic indeed. We are made up of multi-microcosms." I took another hit and held it in.

Dave was fried and clearly not listening. His eyes were focused on the window, like a bird in a mirror.

"Let's get out of the parking lot before some priest catches us," he blurted, starting the van.

"Yeah, they'd expel our asses for sure. That was some nice red hair in that bowl, bro," I said, feeling mellow. "Hey, I heard there's a southwest swell. Let's go to the beach and check it out."

"Sounds like a plan, Mikey." He put the van in reverse.

The music and smoke poured out of the van windows as we headed down Edinger Street. We sang the chorus of "Psycho Killer" at the top of our lungs. We drove to our home break, the Huntington cliffs, to check out the surf. It was four in the afternoon, and the September sky was showing signs of its newborn pumpkin skin. The tide was going out quick, like it needed to catch happy hour, and the waves were slightly blown out, but ride-able. We slipped our wetsuits on, grabbed our boards and scampered down the cliff, following an eroded path of busted concrete, rebar, and broken glass, to the soft salt and pepper sand of the beach. It was getting cold; there were no tourists and only a couple surfers had paddled out. Salt and seaweed brined the air. The waves hit the shore, fizzing and hissing, then retreating in a hush back out to sea.

Dave pointed out at a dark licorice blob about a hundred yards down the beach.

"Let's check it out," I said.

   James M. Fisher

"It's probably just an oily kelp bed," Dave said. "I hate that shit, man."

We walked toward the dark patch. As we approached, I realized it was a sea lion. It looked old, like it might have recently died.

I felt overly sad, still a little buzzed from the pot. "Aw, damn, man. I read somewhere these guys choose the beach they want to die on when they hit old age, because somehow they know it's their time."

"Thank you, Mr. Science," Dave said, ripping on me. He bent over. "I want to get a closer look. I think he's still alive."

"Nah, let's paddle out and then go eat, bro," I said. "Let's let him be."

Dave would have no part of that. He approached the sea lion, and I trailed behind him. He whispered, "I think he's alive," with an evil grimace, like he was going to wake up his little brother. He nudged the side of the sea lion with his surfboard.

Nothing happened.

Dave turned to me and in a low voice said, "No, actually, I think he's dead."

Before I could signal to Dave to run, the sea lion rose up, roared like a king bull walrus, and lunged at Dave's backside, pit viper style. It sank its teeth into the dangling beavertail of Dave's wetsuit jacket.

Dave yelled, "Oh shit! He's got me! I'm stuck!" He dropped his board and tried to run, nearly dragging the sea lion, until finally the beavertail snapped and set him free. Dave flew three feet forward into the sand.

The sea lion barked and moaned. It took full possession of Dave's surfboard by resting its head in the middle of it. As soon as I realized Dave was okay, I face planted into the sand and laughed my ass off. Dave, the football jock, was nearly in tears at the possible loss of his man gear. Up until then he'd only had a couple quick test drives, so he said. He bolted to the shore and got in the water and checked to make sure the nuggets were intact.

My theory, though not proven, was that he had to clean out the unwelcome contents from the lower part of his wetsuit, brought on by the surprise of the sea lion. Simple cause and effect.

Dave reported the nuggets were good, not even a scratch.

"You are a lucky son of a bitch, Dave."

"Now let's get my board," he said, walking back toward me, still visibly shaken.

"Let's? Pal, you're dreaming."

Dave's board was a new Infinity Winged Swallow Tail that had taken him all summer to earn. As his best friend, I had to go along with him and try to get it back.

We tried to distract the sea lion with a baitfish given to us by a nearby shore fisherman, who laughed his ass off at our demise, but was willing to help. After three hours, it was pretty obvious that we might finally be able to out-maneuver this dying friend of the sea, when he put his head back down and stopped moving. We were starved way beyond the munchies, cold, and in a state of total dismay as the sun went down. Dave moved serpent-like in the sand, slowly, slithering, to retrieve his board. The sea lion picked up his head as if to say, "Just take it asshole," and then took what sounded like his final breath. His eyes became still as the black wet sand. The moral compass of my soul began to spin. In our naiveté, we had disturbed the final hours of that innocent creature's life. In my new confidence, had I become like the assholes that would knock the books out of my hands and shove me into the lockers in freshman year? How could I allow this to happen? What was I thinking? The walk back up the steep cliffs was solemn, to say the least.

The fog was rolling in and I wondered if anyone else in the universe shed a tear for the old sea lion or witnessed how callous Dave and I had been. It was like the strings of my heart had unraveled, and splintered off. The van door shut; the music remained off, our hunger was lost in the haze. Dave and I said nothing as he dropped me off at my house on Palomar Street.

⁂

THE NEXT MORNING, I CALLED DAVE. HE PICKED ME UP. We both sounded better than the night before and felt pretty stupid. On the way to school, Dave and I decided to go back to the cliffs and check if the sea lion was there. He deserved a better send off than us two idiots. I was going to call the sea lion rescue if the old fellow was still there and possibly alive.

"I'm pretty sure he's dead," Dave said, as we pulled up on the edge of the cliffs. We jumped out of the van and ran down to the beach. We could see the empty impressions in the sand and the black remains of Dave's beaver tail. The sea lion was gone, like innocence in the back of Dave's van at the Hi-Way 39 drive-in theatre. We could follow his belly track to the outgoing tide.

"Oh my God, he was still alive. We didn't kill him!" I said.

"Hopefully, he was off getting a little lioness action," Dave said. "He was probably playing possum with us."

"Dave, have you ever seen a possum?"

"No."

"That's my point; you're always talking out your ass, man."

"Have you ever seen one, Mikey?"

"No."

We both looked at each other and dropped to our knees in the sand, and geyser-laughed our asses off. We didn't realize in that moment, we were having the time of our lives.

Chapter 5

SCHOOL'S OUT

The phone buzzed with static, voices blared in the background. Dana paused to clear his throat.

"He went over the side and then what?" I said. "Is he going to be okay?"

Dana's voice was erratic, revealing the need to lose it. "Sorry, Michael. Uh, he was riding along his usual bike trail at the River Jetty, a skater was sharing the same path as Dave. When he was passing the skater, the skater hit a rock and lost control of his board and fell into him. He hit him hard enough to push him over the side, Dave's in a coma. It's not lookin' good."

"Jesus, God!" My heart knocked against my rib cage. I imagined nothing but horror, a cracked skull, Dave's blood and brains spilled everywhere.

"He went over head first down the concrete wall and stopped just before hitting the water." Dana's voice cracked as he tried hard to hold back the tears. I could almost feel his trembling through the phone.

I squeezed my forehead. It became more difficult to believe that I was actually having this conversation. I was dumbfounded, numb.

"When help finally got there, the paramedics…Jesus…

they had to, they had to pry Dave's hands from his bike, man. I picked up the phone while I was at my mom's when the hospital called and…" Dana was sobbing. He could no longer stop the pain.

I fell to my knees.

"Look, Michael, you may want to come say goodbye to him at the hospital."

"You don't think he is going to make it?" I could barely breathe. "Fuck!"

This couldn't be happening. I staggered up and started pacing back and forth. I heard nothing but the sound of breathing and background noise on the phone.

"Dana, where you at? What hospital?"

"At Huntington Beach Medical Center, on Beach Boulevard."

"Okay, I'm leaving now. I'll meet you there, man."

I hung up the phone. In seconds, tears broke through a dam inside my eyes and rivered uncontrollably down my face. I was blind for a second. I wiped my eyes and bolted to my closet, grabbing my clothes and shoes. I threw on a pair of jeans, snatched my keys and wallet off the dresser, and ran out of my room, shoes and a shirt in hand.

I nearly ran over Trophy Wife because she was standing outside my door, clearly eavesdropping. "Where are you going?"

"Dave's in the hospital, he's had an accident…it's bad. I gotta go."

Trophy Wife stood there with her mouth open, head cocked to the side, and didn't have a response, just glared.

I raced to my truck. Tears streamed down my face. I stepped in, fumbled with my keys, struggled with the ignition, put my foot on the clutch and brake, and slammed the door. On the way to the hospital, my mind played snapshots of Dave and me, like an old silent movie projector, stuttering and spitting the frames of unforgettable moments. All our crazy antics, the laughs we shared, sneaking beers, and getting high.

He was always trying to set me up with chicks and wanted me to get laid this year. I had told him I didn't need his help. He would get this serious look on his face like a concerned parent, and say something like, "I know what's best for you, Mikey," and then we would laugh. He killed me when he did that. All our conversations ended up in laughter.

Right in the middle of the drive, I had a glimpse of our future beyond graduation. It flashed through my mind like a Polaroid camera. The image left behind was strong and clear, a fragment of truth that meant this wasn't the end. I felt it deep in my bones. The vision slowed my panic, comforted me. I found myself going sixty miles per hour down Beach Boulevard passing cars as if on autopilot. The buildings spilled by like thrown paint. I really needed to slow down.

The enormous hospital sign appeared from behind a billboard. It reflected the morning California sun; blinding white light shot out for miles. My stomach turned over like an old motor as I drove through the hospital entry and into the parking lot of the ER.

I parked the truck, and walked across the parking lot. The landscape was tropical and lush. The tall date palms shot upward through the yuccas, and the aloe plants stood still and proud. The fresh mulch smelled organic, familiar, like fertile soil or turned earth. It intensified as the sprinklers soaked the grounds. An olfactory portal opened in my mind, and led back to my mother's gravesite on the day of her burial. It smelled like that. A freshly dug grave was the last image I wanted. It was an unintentional morbid thought that disappeared as soon I walked through the automatic doors that led me to the ER.

⸎

THE HOSPITAL STAFF MOVED ABOUT WITH THEIR GAME faces on. This place was like a train station. Wheelchairs and gurneys were pushed through corridors, elevators opened and closed with their bells dinging, lights blinking, people coming, people going with faces of joy, sorrow, disbelief, moving carefully and systematically along an invisible highway.

I saw a sign that said "ER" with a big red arrow and a double door. I followed it, down another corridor that ran past X-ray and vending machines. I could smell janitorial chemicals, isopropyl alcohol, and coffee. I must be getting close. My path inside the maze finally stopped in the ER waiting area. It was huge, victims and families were lined up, some sitting, some standing. People were handled in the order of their severity. There were paramedics, police and police dogs, screaming kids and couples yelling at each other. It was a busy day, the lines were long. I spotted Dana across the room, standing under a sign that said "Admitting." He was tough looking; six foot three, broad shoulders, long brown hair, and a trimmed mustache. Throw in his swagger, and he's what you would expect a member of the Three Musketeers to look like. His eyes were red, his body, sunken, inward—a comma that was punched in the gut.

"Hey, man," he said when I reached him.

"Hey," I said.

The circumstances made everything feel intense and awkward. I didn't know how to act. I hardly knew Dana. I hugged him and tried to keep from breaking down. I could feel him cave further, and then he straightened up, shook his head a little. He wiped a rogue tear from his eye.

"You only have a few minutes with him. My mom is praying with the rest of the family in the chapel down there," he said, pointing down the sterile fluorescent corridor.

I nodded, too choked up to talk.

"Dave is down this way in the ICU."

Dana pointed with his head toward the opposite direction of the chapel. Like Real Mom, Dave's mom was a devout Catholic. I remembered a conversation from a long time ago that my parents had when we were driving home after my grandmother's viewing. Real Mom had been praying at the funeral home, which had no religious personality whatsoever. She told my dad that even in deep prayer, she felt like she had to pray harder as if by long distance, since there were no candles and no crucifix in the funeral home's generic chapel. I hoped that Dave's mom at least had a crucifix and candles to give her comfort.

Dana escorted me to the ICU where Dave was. I walked into his dimly lit room. He was bandaged from head to toe and kept alive by machines that were either bringing life to him or sucking the life out of him. It could have gone either way; I was no expert and no help either. There was an eerie quiet in the room with the exception of the hums and blips of the machines. It felt non-human. With all the bandages, his swollen face and head: I could hardly tell it was him.

Something inside of me was about to crack, seeing my friend, my brother, like this. I could have bawled my head off, seriously. Hope was wrestling with despair in some perverse boxing arena in my mind, as I watched the waves and pulsing lights of the monitors. It appeared his respiratory and heart systems were all machine as he reclined there in his own private universe. It was just like Dave to sleep while the rest of us were running around worrying and sobbing. Except he wasn't sleeping, he was fighting for his life.

After a short time, a nurse with kind eyes, wearing blue scrubs, came in quietly. Her nametag said, "Carol."

She checked some of the machines and gave us a soft smile. "Time's up. You can come back tomorrow, hon." Her voice was low, but sweet. She touched me on the arm with her left hand. An engagement ring with a huge diamond shone in the gloom, she left the room. I moved to the bed and put my hand on Dave's leg.

"I'm probably talking out my ass, but I swear you're playing possum, Dave. I'm pissed we didn't surf this morning, I should have called or something. I'm not saying good-bye, either. I'll be here tomorrow, bro, and I'm bringing donuts."

I patted the blanketed mound where his legs were. It was hard to tell if I was making contact or not, with the lights down, and all the layers of tubes and wires strewn across the bed. He was wrapped up like a mummy; it creeped me out, to be honest. I turned away and heard nothing but the haunting industrial sounds of the machines with their pumps and blips as I left.

I don't know what I expected, but I felt weirdly disappointed that Dave hadn't snapped out of it because I was there. He always acknowledged me. We had an understanding and knew each other's secrets. It was our friendship that made me feel that I existed and mattered. I was grateful for that, and hoped he had felt the same.

 JAMES M. FISHER

Dana had his back propped up against the glass door of Dave's room, arms folded. He looked like he was standing at the corner of Angry and Lost. I'd seen that look before, on dogs at the pound.

I moved through the doorway, squeezed his shoulder and said, "It's going to be all right, man. I'll see you tomorrow." Hope and despair walked back to their corners.

"Later, Michael," Dana said.

Thirty-five days passed, and though life went on for the rest of the world, I had a spike of despair through my heart. Though the light of my faith was dimming, I never believed the worst would happen. Every day, during homeroom at school, there was a reminder to pray for Dave over the intercom system just before we all mouthed the prayer of Saint Francis. Students stopped hearing it, I think. To pray for Dave, I mean. After a month, it was growing stale like the prayer of Saint Francis, every single day. Nobody was feeling it. The same monotone voice from the intercom was dull, faded, like the school's prison paint job. The difference was Saint Francis was dead, and Dave was not. Apathy, with its big ass, moved in.

The old days were back for me, before Dave and I knew each other. I became invisible, again. Lunch sucked, because Dave and I had hung out every day, just us.

Without Dave, I ducked into the library to avoid the ongoing questions about him from both students and faculty. I became the mouthpiece of Dave's progress or non-progress. They were all such phony bastards. The girls who flirted with me in my senior year had treated me like pariah during my first year as a freshman. Even Father Michael, who called me "Star" for whatever reason, only asked about Dave. I found out later Father Michael had molested some boys at Our Mother of God. I couldn't help be grateful I'd never taken him up on his awkward offers of 'special' tutoring. At the time I just thought he was a weird dude.

The friends I thought I had made when Dave was around remained his. They gave me the cold shoulder, not that I gave a shit, but no one ever asked me how I was doing. I was a natural loner, and the fact that Dave wasn't around took its toll on my fledgling social life.

I was at home, lying on my bed, like the previous thirty-five days, staring at the ceiling in my bedroom. I stare at the ceiling when confusion occurs and friends go into comas. The same ghoulish faces that swirled and turned in the textured plaster appeared just like they always had. One of the faces was an evil clown with jagged-pointed-teeth and Bozo hair. He had a claw, too. Nearly every ceiling I've stared into has an evil clown. I hate fucking clowns. Really, I hate them.

The house was quiet, dead quiet. I could hear the refrigerator kick on in the kitchen; a passing car sputtered outside. I had a hard time listening to music because Dave and I would sing all my favorite songs at the top of our lungs, embellish the lyrics, and make them our own. Songs paled in the void of Dave's coma.

The phone rang.

I jolted across my bed and picked up on the first ring.

"Hey, Michael, it's Dana." Dana's voice seemed clear, sanguine almost.

When I heard his voice I felt sick, anticipating how this call might end. I prayed for a happy ending, but how lucky had I ever been?

     James M. Fisher

There never seemed to be a happy ending in a John Wayne war movie. The hero always died in some glorious way or another. You knew that it was going to happen, and kept watching anyway. In the end, at the *ultima pugna*, the fighting is reduced to a trickle. The sound of the last bullet had been fired, and the hero, unbeknownst to the audience, was fighting with a fresh bullet wound. He took one for the team, won the war, had ten seconds of glory, and then the bastard kicked the bucket. I always felt cheated; I wanted the happy ending, but I never cried over it either.

It was one of those "Go out and die for your country, ain't it great?" war propaganda films. I call stuff like that Felonious Balonious. Okay, I'm a sap. What good is it, if you save the day and become the dead hero? If you can't come home and get the girl and the glory, then what's the point? Not my idea of victory. A newspaper headline popped through my head: "High school senior fighting for his life dies in a coma after thirty-five days."

"I'm not ready for bad news, man. I'm sorry."

All of us who knew Dave had high hopes for his recovery. After over a month of visiting and talking to him, with no response, it was becoming hard to keep up a Pollyanna attitude, but Dave kept on breathing, so we kept visiting.

I was not going to give up the fight, either. I believed that cosmic moment that had told me that Dave was going to be all right. It had certainly seemed real at the time. Maybe my brain had taken over that day, when Dana first called, and concocted a placebo. Had it been an illusion or a phantasmagorical moment that kept me from wrecking the car on the way to the hospital? My mind was all over the place, for sure.

The truth was Dave had been in a coma for over a month. If he did wake up, would he recognize me? Would he be paralyzed or be unable to communicate? He wouldn't want to live like that: neither would I.

"I can't do bad news right now. I gotta go," I said.

"Wait!"

"I can't hear it. I haven't paddled out since we surfed last. I've dropped weight, lost interest in everything," I rambled, "I'm not giving up though…"

"Michael, shut the fuck up and listen! Dave's come out of his coma. He's dazed and moaning a lot. Get your ass down here. Now!"

"What? No shit! I knew it. Fuckin'A! He's going to pull through; he's really going to pull through!"

Dana busted out laughing. It was a Three Musketeer laugh for sure, possibly d'Artagnan's.

"Thanks for the call man. See you in a bit." A surge of energy lifted me out of the mental bog that I'd been trapped in. It had been a thick, muddy crawl. I was a bigger mess than I'd thought.

⚬⚬⚬

Dave was upright, supported by the elevated bed. The wires to the machines and IVs were still in. The white tube was out of his mouth, which meant he was breathing on his own. He moaned like an animal in pain. It didn't sound like him. The moans progressed to creepy, reminded me of the black and white Frankenstein's monster coming-to-life, a Boris Karloff grumble. Dave's eyes were covered. The blinds on the windows were down, the room was dimmed down. A doctor and Nurse Carol hovered nearby. Dana and I stood in the doorway thinking we were going to strike up a conversation at any moment with Dave. We were denied. Instead, we got agony, and it got louder while the doctor tried to ask Dave questions. Dana and I waited intently for a sign that he was okay and could communicate.

The doctor asked, "Dave, how are you feeling? Do you know where you are?"

Agony answered in a series of moans and grunts. I could see panic on Dana's face.

Carol came over to us. "I know it looks bad, guys, but this was normal. Why don't you come back later? He needs to rest." She motioned for us to step out of the doorway.

Dana and I looked at each other in grave disappointment. We went to the hospital cafeteria. After staring at our food for too long and not saying more than a few words to each other, we returned.

Dave was still propped up, supported by Carol. The bed rails were up. I had hoped Dave's bandages would be off and he would be able see Dana and me. Dave was trying to say something between the moans and grunts, really trying to come out of his fog, I thought. The doctor and Carol tried to keep him calm, but his shoulders and spine started to contort uncontrollably. Quickly Carol pulled out a syringe from her pocket and injected something into his IV. Dave calmed, muscles relaxed and he returned to sleep.

Carol shoed us out again. "Tomorrow, guys."

We left without a word to each other.

The whole process went on like that for days. Dave kept his eyes closed and didn't respond to our voices. As far as the doctor knew, he wasn't seeing yet either. Dave's parents were in and out. His brothers and sisters visited every day, but Dave didn't respond. It seemed like he was still lost somewhere, with one foot here and one in the nether world.

A COUPLE OF WEEKS PASSED. MY VISITS PETERED OFF until I was only coming once or twice a week. I wasn't sure if Dave would have liked me to see him in the condition he was in. The drooling, the shaking, the horrific moans and screams of his rebirth seemed private and personal. His eyes remained closed and he didn't respond to touch. He was losing weight; they continued to feed him through a tube. I wanted him to know that I was still in his corner.

IT WAS NEARLY CHRISTMAS WHEN DANA CALLED TO TELL me that Dave finally opened his eyes. It was in a message on the answering machine. He said Dave recognized their mom.

I wasted no time getting to the hospital after hearing the message. I was so exhausted by then, with all the up and down drama. Would he know me? Would he remember our times together? I obsessed about it. Asked the clown in the ceiling. Would this all be for nothing? Selfish, I know. Going to the hospital was becoming a lifestyle. It was tiring. Being honest, I was starting to resent it.

After many weeks, a lot of the staff knew my name and I knew theirs. They were very friendly and wonderful. I navigated the corridors without hesitating, knew which elevators were the fastest and where the Coke machines were, the fact that candy stripers showed up every day at three o'clock. I didn't want to know that stuff.

My heart was beating fast as I approached Dave's room. I knocked. Dana opened the door. "Hey man," he said.

"Hey," I said. Dana gave me a hug and a slap on the back, reassuring, confident.

Dave was awake and elevated. The bars on the bed were up.

"Hi, Mikey," he said, with a voice crumbly, broken.

I approached the bed and said, "Hey Dave, welcome back." I bent over the bars on his bed and hugged him. His arms, fragile and weak as bird wings, reached around my back and tightened. I lost it, and cried on his shoulder.

He patted me on the back and said, "Is okay. Is okay, Mikey," in a growly voice, like a monster coming to life.

I believe something incredible, God, quantum events in the universe, prayer or whatever (all connected, all the same to me, really) saved Dave the day he woke up. I believed deep within myself that it was all going to work out. But seriously, who comes out of such an ordeal normal? That lucky son of a bitch Dave, that's who.

The guy was a walking miracle. He had no concept of time when he came to. His world had stopped or was held suspended in some cosmic net; ours, on the other hand, forged ahead like a tornado of ball peen hammers. The whole ordeal was a nap to him. Dave didn't remember the accident at all, or the amount of worry and shit we all went through. Haha, so like him. After only four months of extensive therapies, he made an amazing recovery.

GRADUATION WAS ONLY MONTHS AWAY, AND IT SEEMED everyone had paired off. Dave had had two or three girls by then. Everyone was focused on getting laid. It's not like we were all off to war or being invaded. It seemed to be a nervous priority for many. As we got closer to graduation and campus life as we knew it was ending, the vibe was frantic, as if life was about to end and drain, like the last chug off a beer bong.

I was still looking for *her*, the girl I imagined over and over in my head. I would not settle for less, even though I would be the only one to graduate without getting the girl, a girl, any girl. So what! I had the ocean, and the mystery door of adventure with its shiny knob, just waiting for a turn. I was free of the fear of getting someone pregnant; though making it to first base would have been nice, but only with *her*.

I was done with high school and ached for something new. Dave and I had packed a lot of events in our four years at Our Mother of God; surfed a ton, gotten jobs, partied like sailors on leave, bought our first cars, grew up some, filled out a lot and laughed way more. We were humans becoming, on the uneven road to nowhere.

These were the best of years for some of my classmates, who would remain stuck there, living off the fading glimpses of those memories as their lives trudged on for decades in nine to five office purgatory.

For me, much of high school was about survival. Certainly, I'd had some fun times and great moments with Dave. But I hadn't wanted to attend school there. Trophy Wife and Jock Dad had never asked me, never cared about what I thought. They just sent me there. It felt like detention the whole time. Partly, because I literally spent the last two years of high school on indefinite detention. It was due to surfing early in the morning at my home break, which led to being late for homeroom. In my defense, I didn't see the need to be in homeroom. I could have cared less about all the announcements and when the next lame dance was scheduled. I thought being on time for first class was sufficient.

Dean Dumar had disagreed. "Mr. Price, you need to do something with your attitude."

So I refused to sell chocolate bars for fund-raising. Nail me to a cross for that one, Dean Dumar! The funds went to the various school clubs and sports teams, which I didn't care about. They didn't care about me either, let me add.

I had numerous uniform violations, and got dinged for forging hall passes too. I felt like I'd been held against my will and the leash around my neck was about to snap. I would soon be free to charge, like the hungry dog that I was, down the open road to distant places that awaited me beyond the fringe of Seal Beach.

I wrote a graduation speech. I was never asked to give one, but I wrote one anyway.

Three hundred and twenty-three red mortarboards
are about to be launched like middle fingers to
the palm-tree-and-blue-sky-puzzle-piece of the
universe that is Seal Beach. We claim this moment
as our own. It is borrowed, like the words and
promises of many speeches that seek to bring
hope and prosperity, which only die hard like rose
petals on the bottom of a soldier's boot. The door
of tomorrow opens up to a road that is divided in
two, like a serpent's tongue. One path is the most

popular and well-travelled, with hotels and Vegas lights, and the all you can eat buffet, vibrating beds, free TV, free soda, and mega malls: A road where the sheep can go to graze, and every comfort imaginable is warmly provided. There are banks and jobs and a dream provided. Into the sensual mouth of the machine, most of us will go, riding atop couches on a wave of light, produced by our own ion-trap screens. The TV will be forever centered proudly, sitting amongst our family pictures, religious objects, and impulsively purchased knickknacks, staged perfectly for all to see, in the living rooms or dying rooms, depending on the degree to which the life is sucked out of us all, only to be replaced by someone else's thoughts and philosophies. Like a great family of whales inhaling plankton, we feast, tantalized by the moist wet lips of the American dream, with breath like napalm and eyes so blue. Confirmed, conformed, and complacent, apathetic like old chewing gum, churned cud-like, choking the fire in the belly of our adolescence.

The other path can only be seen if the door is pushed beyond its hinges and tugged from the jam. There is no safety net and no money back guarantees. This path is only limited to an endless sky, where the universe listens in to your thoughts, and the ocean runs up to you, like your pet dog. To be moved by beauty is like finding your own truth and self worth. Spinning a web of awareness is the most powerful thing, unless you are one of those who cling to the conveyor belt life, stuck inside the machine.

JAMES M. FISHER

In my mind, Dave and I would strike out, glorious and free on the path of endless sky. But, six months after graduation, Dave and I had chosen our paths, and we would be attending different schools. Dave would enter the machine; I would run from it.

⸎

AFTER THE GRADUATION CEREMONY, DROVES OF FAMIlies and friends emptied out the convention center. To our surprise, Nurse Carol was in the audience. I made eye contact with her and pointed toward the doorway. She nodded back. I hurried to catch up with Dave. We met up on the steps just beyond the exit doors.

"Nurse Carol," I yelled.

"Over here," yelled Dave. Carol turned and walked toward us.

"Hi, boys, I just wanted to stop by and wish you good luck," Carol said.

"This means a lot—you came," Dave said. His lip quivered and a tear welled in his eye. I choked up. It was almost too much.

"You both are very special, and it was a lot you went through. I love happy endings and had to see you both graduate. Good luck boys," She hugged us both and flowed away like a goddess.

"That was the coolest thing. She's the best," Dave said, wiping his eye and shaking his head trying to break the emotion.

"The Nurse of the Year Award goes to Carol," I said, in my announcer's voice, clearly trying to break from tearing up. We chuckled.

Dave and I looked at each other and stood there speech-less; the silence between us said everything. It was crowded and chaotic as the proud parents and joyful graduates poured into the courtyard. Emotions ran through the crowd like drunken fire. Cameras flashed, and mothers yelled, "Hold still for the picture!" Everyone crying and smiling in all directions. The faculty members were moving as quickly as they could to their cars.

"Quite the journey so far, huh?" I said.

"Yeah, it's been great, Mikey," Dave said.

"It's not good-bye man, it's only graduation." I slapped him on the arm. It felt like a crossroads in that moment. For the first time, we didn't know what to say to each other. Dave had liked high school more than I had. He looked like he was sad it was over. I was ready to move the hell on.

"We'll always be brothers, right?" Dave asked.

"Always, man, always."

Fear crept into his face. More of that awkward silence moved in like fog with a bad leg.

"Where are your folks?"

"I'm meeting them at Delmonico's. They took off early."

"Ha-ha, some things never change, because…"

"Trophy Wife waits for no one!" Dave and I said in chorus.

"That's always funny, bro." I said. We both chuckled.

Dave's family was across the lot waving him over.

"I gotta go, man."

"I know, me too."

After a quick hug, we walked off in different directions to join our families to celebrate.

I looked back for Dave, but he'd disappeared into the crowd.

Chapter 6

PACK IT UP

I finally made it out of the bottleneck in the parking lot and onto the highway. It was really weird to think that high school was really over and I would not be returning back to Mother of God. It was finally over. My post-graduation plan was to meet up with Jock Dad and Trophy Wife at Delmonico's, an Italian restaurant that Real Mom, Jock Dad and I used to go to when Real Mom was alive. I have to believe Jock Dad knew this would mean something special to me even though Trophy Wife would have rather dined at the Bouzy Rouge or the Monarch Bay Beach Club where her daddy was a member. I'm not sure how he persuaded her to lower her standards but it was a cool move on his part to think of it.

Trophy Wife hated being stuck in traffic, especially in a parking lot, so they left just after I received my diploma. I had seen their empty chairs after I had returned to my seat. I didn't want to sit through the rest of the ceremony, either. The haze of empty platitudes and speeches cobbled together out of clichés and quotes by saints and the successful made me nauseous. *This is the last time I'm held against my will.* One more detention for the road, I guess.

Delmonico's was one of my favorite restaurants. You could smell the roasted garlic for miles, and after you entered the bistro doors, you slipped it on like a coat. The garlic bread was legendary. Gina Delmonico, the founder, fell into some type of dementia after she reached her seventies. She peeled garlic for the last five years of her life at a special table set up for her in the restaurant. I used to say, 'hi,' to her when we would get pizza to go. Real Mom would bring a small bouquet of her gardenias and place them next to Gina on the table. She could make Gina smile. Real Mom said that Gina liked the gardenias and knew we were there. Gina just sat there peeling the garlic like a machine, and stared off into some other room that only she could see. After her death, her sons kept the business going, along with a small memorial in the restaurant dedicated to her. A photo, a vase of fresh flowers, a lit candle, and a table setting for one kept watch on the table where she used to sit. The photo showed a young Gina, stirring her sauce in the kitchen, with the smile only successful immigrants have.

After slipping through the front doors and the jammed up crowd in the foyer, I took a deep breath just before the turn in the restaurant near the nook where my parents were sitting. The restaurant was full and it was hard to tell which was louder, the forks hitting the plates, or the many voices that competed between sips of wine. Trophy Wife had to be on her second, maybe third, Cosmo by the time I arrived. I could see the tops of their heads as I neared the table. Trophy Wife's voice thickened and carried through the dining room the more she drank. I heard her nasally pitch, completely devoid of sonority, find its place in the symphony of broken dishes, dropped pots, pans, and bain maries of the kitchen. It was easier to decipher what the broken dishes were trying to say than what she was saying. I noticed Jock Dad's hair was thinning in the back, a small moon peeking through a woven blind.

"Hi, guys." I reached across the table and grabbed the plate of fresh garlic bread with one hand, sliding it with me to my side of the booth, carefully guiding the long white tablecloth with the other, to avoid spilling the water goblets and wine glasses everywhere.

"And the glasses are still standing!" I said in my presto-change-o magician's voice as I settled into the slippery booth cushion. Jock Dad laughed like he did back in the day. It was an inside joke between us. My first attempt to slide into a booth like that was when I was eight. I spilled our ice waters all over everything. Real Mom had laughed, covering her mouth, but she couldn't hold back as all the water channeled down a fold into Real Dad's lap. Real Dad yelped with a falsetto like a twelve-year-old girl as the ice cold water poured onto his crotch.

"You need to work on your landing, Michael," Real Mom had said. She laughed so hard tears readied to swan dive. She had patted Real Dad's lap with her linen dinner napkin in a failed attempt to be discreet. She glanced up at me from across the table with a reassuring smile, and one of her tears landed perfectly on a teaspoon. I never forgot that.

"Yeah, please leave the glasses standing next time, buddy," Real Dad had said, his face red, but he smiled as soon as Real Mom kissed his cheek and told him she would make it all better, later. He had reacted by pulling up the tablecloth to damn the flow, but was too late.

It is fair to say that I perfected the landing over time.

"Hey, Michael," said Jock Dad. He sipped his drink. His tie was gone, a slight smear of pink lipstick rested on his collar like a flamingo feather. He had a couple more buttons undone than usual too. The images that crept in my head were not pleasant. Reason number two for leaving the graduation early, I presumed. Jock Dad looked pretty dapper in his black sports coat. Trophy Wife seemed to be swooning. I felt like a third wheel on date night.

"What did you think of the graduation, Michael?" Trophy Wife asked, her demeanor pleasant. Yeah, she'd been drinking. She had on a sleeveless red dress that revealed her tanned, thin shoulders and most of her well-defined tennis arms. The dress was cut tightly around her frame, exposing her cleavage that modestly bordered a tan line. She delicately placed her left hand on the stem of her martini glass and the other under the table. Though she was being very subtle, the muscles in her shoulder suggested she was carefully rubbing Jock Dad's leg, slowly, back and forth.

I tried not to look at her, but I had to give an answer. I held her gaze. "It was pretty generic, programmed, and impersonal."

They were both half listening, not making eye contact with me. I paused until Jock Dad set his drink down and looked in my direction.

"I am glad it's over, so I can get on with the rest of my life," I said as politely as I could. I reached for my water goblet and clung to the stem.

Jock Dad smirked, taking in a breath and raising an eyebrow, about to say something. His head moved slightly like what I had just said was going to require enormous thought. He held it in and looked away. Jock Dad had a couple drinks in him too. The collection of empty rocks glasses told the

     James M. Fisher

story. Trophy Wife's hand remained under the tablecloth. The shoulder muscles again…oh god please, not the shoulder muscles, not the shoulder muscles. I grabbed a menu and put it in front of my face.

"Michael, since when do you need a menu? Besides I already ordered for everyone," Jock Dad said. He was the master at changing the subject. Whatever.

"Right, I don't need a menu. I'm good." I put the menu at the end of the table. Were they for real? I caught myself staring at Trophy Wife. I couldn't help it. She wasn't paying attention anyway. It came to me: she was a dead ringer for Maleficent in Sleeping Beauty. She looked even more convincing with her lipstick slightly smeared. I looked away as soon as she made eye contact with me. A very uncomfortable few minutes followed. I couldn't think of a thing to say. Trophy Wife's hand resurfaced, and I was grateful.

She signaled the waiter for another round. "Would you like another one, honey?" she said, looking at Jock Dad.

Another what? I was so outta sync here. This night was a bust. I thought she'd had enough. I wasn't usually around when the two of them were drinking together.

"No, I'm still sippin this one, baby." Jock Dad cleared his throat. "Now that graduation is over, do you have any career choices in mind?"

It was a sorry attempt to keep this mediocre conversation going. We had never discussed that question in depth before. It was more like, what do you want to be when you grow up? I started to feel boxed in.

"Nothing concrete. I thought if I go to college, I would try to get my associate's out of the way and maybe intern at some places, once I get a clearer picture of what I want to do." I was completely lying. I had overheard someone give this answer outside after graduation, and it was all I could come up with.

I lie with the same quickness as telling the truth some-times. The guilt, I don't feel for days and sometimes not at all. I get crazy when my cage gets rattled.

It was clear from the look in Jock Dad's eyes, he was dis-appointed with my response. None of this seemed sincere to me either. He picked up on it. It had been years since we had a real conversation about anything. Why today? They hadn't even stayed for the entire ceremony. Real Mom wouldn't have left my graduation early. She would have endured it, and probably would have embarrassed me by taking a hundred pictures. Not that I gave a shit now.

Trophy Wife chimed in with that poker smile of hers; a bellwether for bad news. "So, Michael—" she started to say.

"Here's your Cosmopolitan," the waiter said, as he cleared a few glasses from the table. This guy had just appeared out of nowhere. He was a tall preppie type, probably into disco with that perfect hairstyle of his. He winked at Trophy Wife as she delicately gripped her drink. He probably went for older women at the discos, strutting his polyester pants and thick-heeled shoes. Trophy Wife smiled back like a flirt. Jock Dad missed it; he had become mesmerized in his swirled cauldron of ice and scotch. I looked at Trophy Wife as she carefully brought the glass to her lips and sipped her Cosmo. Her hands were quite beautiful, delicate, feminine, nails polished and manicured. The thin-walled martini glass was filled to the brim, but she didn't spill a drop. She left a lipstick mark behind on the glass. The traffic in the restaurant was building. Servers were moving quickly, dodging one another in the aisles. A plate hit the floor and smashed behind us. She looked across in the direction of the clatter. She went back to her glass and fumbled with the slivered lemon peel garnish.

"You were saying?" I said.

Trophy Wife's face looked as if someone changed her channel by remote. "What?"

"Honey, you were about to tell Michael something." Jock Dad said. He sipped his drink and glanced over at me.

"Tell me what?

"Oh, I was just going to talk about…your hair, that was it, Michael, your hair."

Jock Dad gulped his drink and signaled for another as the waiter zoomed by.

"Are you kidding, my hair?" *What the fuck?*

"Girls are turned off by that…punk thing. They might think you're dangerous or something."

The disco boy with the feathered hair came around the corner, gliding in with a large tray with our food and another drink for Jock Dad in his hand.

"Here you are sir, Dewar's rocks, and linguine with clam sauce, osso buco with penne, rigatoni with meatballs, tossed Caesar and another round of garlic bread," he said with a fake Italian accent, looking again at Trophy Wife. Jock Dad had ordered family style, the way we used to get it with Real Mom.

"Fresh Parmesan cheese, anyone?"

"Slur, I'd love some," said Trophy Wife, totally unaware she had just strangled the neck of articulation, and provided me the only thing I would probably remember about this day in the years to come. She sure slurred. Haha. That killed me. Jock Dad and I chuckled and made eye contact. Jock Dad covered his mouth and leaned back to suppress his need to belly laugh. It was so hilarious, my eyes teared up.

Trophy Wife picked up her cutlery like a dentist about to drill. "What's so funny?" she said, totally poker faced; her flush never made it to her cheeks.

"We might have to cut you off, darlin," Jock Dad said softly, then laughed uncontrollably in her ear.

"Oh, you guys. Now Michael, your hair, the spikes."

C'mon, really?

"Can't we just eat? Is this what you wanted to tell me?" I stabbed the linguine like it was her heart and twisted it onto my fork.

"Let's just enjoy the meal," Jock Dad said.

I don't think it's healthy, to go from laughing hysterically to rage in the same breath. I would have assumed it to be impossible if I hadn't just done it. Maybe that's how people spontaneously combust.

"I just don't think you will meet a nice girl like that, that's all."

For God's sake, my head was about to explode. I clamped my jaw and tipped my head forward. I went inward and took a deep breath. I looked across the restaurant where Gina used to sit. I looked for Real Mom, the smell of her gardenias, evidence of her somewhere—even her wraith would do. The candle flickered on Gina's table.

We ate quietly. I was starving and horsed down the meal, thinking of better times. The waiter whisked by like a phantom.

"Save room for tiramisu and coffee," he called as he picked up the empty plate where the linguine used to be. His perfect hair danced on its own. This guy was too giddy to be real.

"We'll think about it," Jock Dad called back.

"Michael, you got quiet, you must have been starving," Jock Dad said. I nodded, still chewing an oversized bite of the linguini. I grabbed another slice of garlic bread. Trophy Wife was cutting into her osso bucco like a surgeon. After making her first incision, she set her knife down, placed the cube of meat into her mouth, and pulled her fork out from between her lips. After resting her fork on the rim of her plate, she dabbed the corner of her mouth with her dinner napkin, like a queen.

"I know a career choice for you is way off in the future, but what are your interests or something you are passionate about?" Jock Dad took a bite of pasta and a sliver of osso bucco. I sat in silence and watched his face while he talked and chewed at the same time.

"Besides college, have you thought about a trade or tech school? That might be something to consider." He was not giving this a rest at all. His face was serious and caring. I believed in the moment that he was sincere.

"It's not really the time or place for this, Dad. Can we talk about it later?"

"All he seems to want to do is play that guitar and sing in his bedroom all day and night, unless he's off to the beach to surf," said Trophy Wife.

"I do other things, too, like work, by the way," I said.

"I agree, you are in your room a lot, Michael. I'm sure it's normal, sweetheart. Besides those are healthy interests," Jock Dad said.

Hell yeah, it's normal, how did we end up here? I needed off this bus.

"You just can't make a good living doing that, that's all." Trophy Wife said as she chewed slowly, as if counting each bite. "Those interests are hobbies, not career choices. You need to be thinking about getting a real job and get motivated." She sipped her drink, as she mounted her high horse.

"Who said I was doing that in the first place? Besides it's

my choice to do whatever I want with my life. Not motivated, are you serious?"

Trophy Wife's face tensed up as if chagrined by my tone.

I wasn't done.

"Look, I'm not interested in what you think, as far as I'm concerned, you can take your opinions of me, and what you think I can or can't do with my life and—"

"Michael! For God's sake let's drop it and finish dinner. We'll talk about it later. Let's calm down." Jock Dad sounded like a school crossing guard directing second graders.

"Shove it up your ass, Maleficent," my eyes said. I tried to move on from talking about myself. That always happened. We'd start having a conversation, and she'd interrupt. I couldn't ever seem to get my dad to myself for one minute before she butted in. My dad, who had sounded really interested in my life, chose the wrong time. That moment, like so many others, was now snuffed out forever. She had murdered it. All I could do was stare her down. They seemed to forget I was no longer that kid at the poolside barbeque.

"I was just trying to help, just some friendly advice, I don't know why everybody's getting so upset at me," Trophy Wife said. Next would come the whimper and the drama.

"I know you were, hon," Jock Dad said as he panned in my direction. His face was one part apology and two parts exasperation.

Silence and awkwardness pulled up chairs and joined us from time to time. That moment was no exception. They would show up again and again, uninvited, and proceed to dig into the leftovers of our life. We didn't have meals together that often for a reason. Over the years, Jock Dad had become passive and allowed this woman to infiltrate a space where she didn't belong—at least with me.

I continued to poke at my food. The restaurant was filling up and a line had formed up at the front entry.

"Anybody want anything else?" said Jock Dad.

"I'm stuffed." I was done with everything. Trophy Wife was buzzed and obnoxious.

"You, dear?" Jock Dad said. He looked at her. She was adjusting her dress, and trying to sit up straight.

"I'm good, but before we leave, I would like to make a toast." Trophy Wife's head looked like it was getting little heavy for her shoulders; she looked up into Jock Dad's eyes. I sensed a big production coming on. She turned to my dad.

"We need to acknowledge your achievements and accomplishments this year, sweetheart. Congratulations on your hard work and your promotion. I'm so proud of you, honey," Trophy Wife said, her lips quivering because she was too drunk.

"Here's to you, my husband, who I love so much. Cheers honey." She raised her glass toward Jock Dad. I was paralyzed, held against my will, trapped inside a really bad scene from an old Hollywood film.

"Cheers, honey," Jock Dad said. The glasses clinking together made a sound like rusty chimes. Their eyes froze in adoration. I was being prepared for crucifixion, (no really, one more nail to go). Jock Dad broke away and looked at me.

"Yeah. Cheers, Dad," I said instantly, ready to throw up. I thought some part of this was going to be about my graduation. I thought they would have already celebrated his promotion; instead I was a third wheel on one of their dates. Even the toast was ruined, I raised my glass of diluted ice water to meet his and had to quickly place it on the table because Trophy Wife's octopus arms tied up Jock Dad, which made it impossible for our glasses to meet.

"Congratulations to you too, Michael," Jock Dad said, with a head nod. Awkward. It was the worst attempt to acknowledge that we were actually celebrating my graduation.

Trophy Wife had conveniently forgotten, so clueless. Jock Dad was getting more uncomfortable the more she talked. The vein in his right temple was showing. It resembled a small lightning bolt.

"Thanks, Dad,"

He looked at me with pity, like I came in last or something.

All I had was bile. Trophy Wife's infant head bobbed toward me, her eyes glazed over like donut holes, and her shoulder muscles began to move again.

"Can I get you folks dessert or coffee, anything else?" asked the waiter. I was never so happy to see this guy. He read my mind.

"I think we're all good," Jock Dad said. He quickly reached into his wallet and handed the waiter his credit card without receiving the check first.

"I will be right back with this, sir."

"Well, Michael, we have another announcement. Now that your dad has graduated and earned his degree, and has been promoted…" Trophy Wife was unceasing, her arm on Jock Dad's leg had begun to move like she was sanding something. I looked at Jock Dad dead in the eye.

"Here you are, sir. It was a pleasure serving you all this evening," said the waiter appearing in thin air again like the great Houdini. I really didn't know how he kept doing that.

"Thank you," Jock Dad said. "Honey, let's go home. We can talk about this later." Jock Dad grabbed the check and signed it. He tapped Trophy Wife on the arm motioning to her that it was time to leave.

"Wait, wait a minute, what's the announcement? You can't just make a statement like that and leave it for later," I said. Jock Dad gave me the what-the-hell-look. He was clearly finished with the evening.

"In the best interest of everyone, and for the future of the family," Trophy Wife said.

"What?" I said.

Jock Dad stopped in the middle of his departure and raised both eyebrows to the heavens.

"Let's table this and talk about it when we get home, honey. C'mon Michael, we can talk about this at the house."

"Dad, stop, just spill it, I don't want to wait until we get home."

Jock Dad slumped back into his seat, took in a half breath and exhaled.

"Okay, Michael, we're moving. The 'For Sale' sign goes up on Monday."

Trophy Wife's hand appeared and snatched her martini glass. She cocked her head back and drank the remaining drops. The lemon peel garnish hung on the edge of the glass like a yellow crescent moon. She dropped her hand underneath the tablecloth, and put her head on Jock Dad's shoulder. I sat there like a deer into the headlights, becoming one with the grill of a speeding truck.

Jock Dad dropped his shoulders, took a sip of what was left of his scotch rocks, and said, "That's right. I was offered a new position, a good promotion, and…well, we have to move." He set the glass down. The ice crackled and turned as it rested in the bottom, finished. The restaurant was packed with a line leading to the outside of the restaurant.

"Okay, I get it. Where to, Dad? LA or somewhere in Orange County, Northern Cali?"

"No, Ogden actually."

"I've never heard of it. Is that in the Valley?" I glanced across the dining room. The manager looked over and pointed at us with concern while talking to our waiter. The waiter's hair gestured 'Yes', as in 'Yes, they've paid already. I can't make them leave."

"No, it's in Utah," Jock Dad and Trophy Wife said in stereo.

"Excuse me, did you say Utah?"

"I'm afraid so, son." Jock Dad's face was serious. Trophy Wife gave a condescending nod of approval.

Presto-change-o, Houdini appeared again.

"Have you folks changed your mind on the coffee and tiramisu?"

Chapter 7

1945

Jock Dad was an aerospace engineer and, in a prior life, a boxer in the Navy. Like my grandfather who also boxed in the Navy, nicknamed "Jimmy the Jabber", my dad had also lied about his age to enlist at seventeen. Instead of going to the senior prom and dancing to a slow song with his girl, my dad found himself in a boiler room on a battleship headed for Korea. His graduation a couple years later consisted of receiving his GED, a new stripe on his uniform, a twelve pack of Miller, and a tattoo. He never elaborated on the details of that day, but I hoped he would let me in someday.

At six-foot-three and two-hundred-twenty pounds, the man was a presence, indeed. His confidence and stride were like an ocean wave bearing down on a rock reef. Old bodysurfing buddies said he was fearless on those big days at the Wedge. They would get out of the water just to watch him cut through the big waves. He would come home later, smelling like salt, sand, and suntan lotion. His face would be relaxed, sporting a Zen smile, especially when Real Mom walked into the room. When their eyes met, it was over. Instantly, they would launch into their own dimension, leaving me to ride in the backseat.

"No thanks, I am outta here," I would yell, drawing attention to myself with the assumption that I was the mature one in the room. Real Mom would blush and laugh like a schoolgirl.

"Oh, Michael," she would say.

Real Dad would stand there, trying to be cool. "What, what?" he'd say.

Awkward. Little did they know that I actually read the volumes of material in the "Encyclopedia Britannica" and "Lands and Peoples" books for fun. I had a basic idea of mating rituals and figured out what was going on. The truth is, I didn't enjoy thinking about such things at that age. However, I had control over my own space and time, at least in my room, a kind of portal to a world that I created and where I was king.

They used to make me want to throw up, really. As soon as I closed my door their bedroom door would close. I could hear Real Mom giggle again. I hid in my books and I had lots of them: comic books, Mad Magazine, mysteries, the works of Edgar Allen Poe, science fiction stories by Harlan Ellison and H.P. Lovecraft, Homer, Plato, Shakespeare, Grandpa's geology books. The volumes of encyclopedias were purchased in a weak moment. Real Dad had been suckered into them by a door-to-door salesman, after they offered to throw in a set of "Lands and Peoples" for free if Dad "acted now". Real Mom often brought me books from the used bookstore, too. I loved books. I inherited all the books from when Real Mom was in school. My library spilled over into my closet, eventually. When those two would get busy, I'd turn up my record player to help undo the images in my head of what they might be doing and spare myself the chance of hearing any of it. The Beatles'

"Sgt. Pepper" album did the trick. My favorite song was "Lucy In The Sky With Diamonds" I was gone and nobody could touch me.

EVERYONE RESPECTED REAL DAD. HE WAS HANDSOME, but never played on his good looks. He wasn't an asshole. In an innocent time, we played catch and hit baseballs. He was so big to me back then that he eclipsed the sun during moments of throwing grounders to me. Real Mom was quite the athlete herself. She would help me warm up before each Little League game, her pigtails flipping about as she threw the ball back to me. I was a starting pitcher at only eight years old and I had some talent and showed promise on the mound.

"Show me that slider, Mikey," she would say. "Don't lighten up 'cause I'm your mother, throw it like you mean it." Real Dad had eyes for only one woman and he married her. Real Mom was gaga for him too, and she gave him her heart. I witnessed an ongoing fairytale between them. I took it for granted in later years and thought that was just the way it was for everyone. That's why you marry and that's what love looks like. When the darkest day of my life arrived and she passed, Real Dad moved on and became someone else.

JOCK DAD HAD MADE HIS PEACE WITH MISSILES BACK IN the 60's. Not the puny conventional guided or basic tactical missiles, but the big ones, the nukes, like Little Boy, only deadlier, and more efficient, capable of bringing Armageddon to a neighborhood near you, roasting us all in one big nuclear sneeze. "Gesundheit!"

Besides the ability to produce generations of fodder for great science fiction stories, Jock Dad believed the missiles were a necessary war deterrent. He felt he was a peacemaker and his job was of great importance. Jock Dad taught the Air Force how to aim and fire nukes with great accuracy.

"Better for us to have them than anyone else," he would say.

He understood their mechanisms, the heart of the gyro and what guided them to their targets. It was the Minuteman and the Peacekeeper missile programs that he knew.

"I pray we never use them," he would also say.

Jock Dad received his college degree a few months prior to my high school graduation. The aerospace company he worked for gave him a raise shortly thereafter. An opening for a position that needed a missile guidance expert also became available, meaning another pay increase and a huge promotion for him. His new work location would take us eight hundred miles inland from our home in California to Ogden in the heart of Utah. I ran my fingers through my encyclopedias to find out a few things about Utah.

"Is it safe?" I asked Jock Dad. I read about the radiation levels from the nuclear testing in Nevada and how it drifted into southern Utah, killing sheep and how people died from leukemia and cancer. There was evidence of a huge cover up by the government and the military. What about the polygamist families that lived in Utah? Inbreeding too? Nothing but silence from Jock Dad, like a verbal air ball. I could depend on the disapproving eyebrows from Trophy Wife, however, as she sat next to him clinging to his arm. Thanks, Trophy Wife. This move seemed to be a huge gamble. I had just turned eighteen and had a part time job, but there was no way I could afford rent somewhere in Cali.

It was too soon, too sudden without any time to plan. Deep down, I thought there was still hope for Jock Dad and me to work things out.

The day of dread was here—like—here. Dave and I met at the Huntington Cliffs which bordered Bolsa Chica at some point. It was our home break for most of our lives and today was going to be our last supper, or last session for a while. The overcast grays of the sky matched the dull obituary page I had dreamt about the night before, about a life I used to know. The nightmares of war and death that used to plague my sleep were being slowly replaced by the important faces and moments that I had to say goodbye to. My own war surfaced, a reckoning of sorts. With it came a new voice in the distance, pulsing, demanding to be known. The goodbyes, Real Mom, Grandpa, the Dad I used to know, Charlene, and now Dave. I wasn't dreaming: the day had really come.

"Hey, bro," I said.

"Hey, Mikey," Dave said, nudging my shoulder.

"Wow, check it out. It's going off," I said. Dave and I did a double take at each other like we were trying to take a photo of the moment. My upper lip twitched, then Dave looked the other way. His hand swiped the corner of his eye.

"Yeah, buddy. Ma Ocean is giving you a proper send off. It's so glassy! Let's go!"

"Fuck yeah, let's do this!" I said. We took off running, down the traverses of the cliffs and onto the beach. We ran into the water, the cold Pacific rushed into my wetsuit as we hopped on our boards and paddled hard toward the oncoming set. We duck dove under the closed out sections and came up on the other side to blue-green translucent peaks. This was Heaven and limited to a few surfers in the water.

"Big wave outside. I'm going," I yelled.

"I'm feeling pretty good today, I'm going to pull off some insane off-the-lips," Dave said, paddling in for position.

"I want to see it, brudda!"

"I'm going left." I dropped into the wave.

"I'm going right." Dave took apart his half of the A-framed shaped wave. I could hear Dave hooting and shouting behind me. I smiled so much that day my face hurt.

"That was insane," Dave yelled as I approached him in the line up.

"For sure. It looks like it's going to fire like this all day," I said.

Dave nodded, and went quiet, staring out into the next set. We floated on our boards as the next set passed under us. Dave was stone faced, trying not to look at me. I could see something was on his mind. I paused and looked over at him, distant, spinning on something.

"Hey, Dave," I said, not yelling but intense.

"Yeah?"

"I'm going to miss you, man," I said, looking at all the beauty around us, and that face of Dave's, like a big dumb dog. Probably the best person I've ever known.

"I'm gonna miss you, too," Dave said, avoiding eye contact.

"It's only temporary, I can't imagine being away from here and you, my brother. I'm going to come up with a plan to come back. Maybe we can get our own place."

"I hope so. I really do."

Our eyes fixed on the next set. We charged and both of us hit the lip of the wave a couple times and rode the foam.

"Let's take this the rest of the way. I'll buy breakfast," I yelled.

"I'm pretty hungry. Are you sure you can afford it?" Dave said.

We took it in and laughed all the way to shore, like we always did.

That day was something to celebrate, not just because it was our last surf session for a while, but because the surf had been flat for nearly a month prior. Dave and I had surfed those days anyway. We didn't care about the wind chop, size or shape of the waves, just the remaining time. We surfed one-foot slop and it was awesome. The antics with Dave in the water were like being a kid for the day. The years of pure stoke I'd enjoyed were taken for granted. I thought it was going to last forever, an endless summer. I never imagined being forced to leave my home. This was really fucked up. Everything I knew and loved was going to disappear.

After a late breakfast, it came time to say goodbye to Dave. Not really a goodbye, but more like a pledge this was going to be for a limited time only.

"I love you, man. You'll always be my brother," I said, giving Dave a hug.

"I love you, Mikey," Dave said, pulling me in. At that moment neither one of us cared about the duration of the hug, though I'm sure we both thought about how it might look. We didn't care.

Dave followed me to my truck as I got in. "Good luck in Utah."

"Thanks, bro," I said, and drove away wanting another ending to this story.

Leaving Dave standing in that parking lot, doing the brave wave as he tried to smile and wish me well, was too much. Two blocks away, I pulled over, and in anger and heartbreak, I bawled. A rocket hit my chest. It was almost as bad as saying goodbye to Real Mom. The good-byes in my life were stacking.

The last year of high school had been tough with Dave's rehab. We had finally gotten our lives back to normal. Now, I just felt fucked over. Don't get me wrong, I liked adventure, but I liked it on my own terms. Utah was not part of my plan. It was all too soon, and too fast.

The sign on the front lawn had changed from "For Sale" to "Sold." The oversized United Van Lines truck with a team of packers and loaders arrived and emptied the house in two days. I heard a couple of the loaders bitch about all my books and how awkward my boards were to pack and stow. Excuse me for living, assholes. They had no clue.

We found ourselves on the road away from the only place I knew. Dave, my memories, and the ocean defined me. Who was going to visit Real Mom and bring her flowers on her birthday and keep her gravesite weeded and cleaned? It was confusing and complicated. In a short time, I would realize how much I really loved ocean sunsets, Dave's big, dumb, dog face, the brotherhood in the water at my home break, sun on my skin, flip flops and surf trunks everyday, palm trees, and the smell of Dr. Zog's Sex Wax on my board.

A few scenes from the movie "The Hills Have Eyes" crept into my mind during our exodus from my home in Seal Beach. The signs of civilization began to disappear the further we drove. I remembered the movie like I had just walked out of the theater. A typical American family goes on the road for a typical American vacation when they break down…

I was grateful that I could follow Jock Dad out in my own car without sitting in the back seat while Trophy Wife blah-blah-blahed on about nothing the entire way. It gave me an opportunity to see the road through my own eyes, and to contemplate and scheme my return to California.

I imagined myself driving in the opposite lane back to Orange County as we headed east toward Nevada.

The barren landscape of Barstow and the emptiness of the Mojave offered refuge for the tumbleweeds that spun like chaotic pinwheels in my soul. It was an emptiness that only God could provide. The idea of breaking down here at midday at one hundred and ten degrees was bait to attract my scariest thoughts. "The Hills Have Eyes" had given me nightmares and seemed plausible in this environment. The San Bernardino Mountains were at our backs, hot desert winds were blowing pretty hard. I wondered if I should have brought a Geiger counter. This was certainly the type of place where nuclear fallout might have collected, especially with those winds.

Further along in our journey, after driving a couple hundred miles straight, the landscape had melted into the same shape, color and texture. The heat waves quivered above the approaching road. My imagination spilled out of its own delirium and into some sort of cerebral blender. I felt my eyes becoming heavy and just before I fell into a hypnotic trance, something red and triangular appeared in the distance. A new ingredient dropped into the blender.

I snapped out of the trance, straightened up in my seat, and fixated on the object. In minutes we were close enough to see that it was a sign on the highway that said, "Last Chance For Gas." It forced us to get off at the next exit. As we left the safety of the highway and drove another two miles of windy roads, we followed large arrow-shaped signs that read, "Gas this Way," "One More Mile For Gas." The road led us to the only gas station in what I would call a 'microtown', since the town was no more than a block long and we could see its entirety. I have heard people say that they have travelled to towns so small that they could throw a rock from one end to the other. This was my first. As we turned the corner and neared the station, I saw a tall bald guy leaning against one of the pumps. There were no other cars in sight. It was weird.

A large metal sign, "GAS," hung from rusty chains; it swung in the desert wind and creaked like it was in pain. The small garage was concrete block, painted mostly white with a blue stripe that wrapped around it. The gas pumps were old and dated, the hoses, cracked and peeling. The entire building, and what I could see of the town through my windshield, appeared sandblasted and pitted. I rolled down my window to get a better look, and gasped when the hot-dusty air hit my lungs. It felt like we had entered a 1950's scrap yard of a place.

The gas station attendant could easily have been Pluto, the scary guy from the movie I had been thinking about. It seemed possible the closer we got to the station. Maybe he was a descendant of the Bean Clan from the Middle Ages, or the son of the son of Pluto.

"Oh my God," I gasped when Jock Dad drove right in. Pluto was waiting for us. He shrugged off the gas pump and guided Jock Dad to the outer pump to make room for me as I followed behind. Jock Dad approached carefully as he lined the car up to the pump nozzle.

"Fill up sir?" the guy said. His voice was coarse and dry, sandpaper and old rope. His bug eyes looked over at Trophy Wife sitting in the car, looking the other way. His left eye twitched as a gust of wind and sand came through.

"Yes, please, unleaded," Jock Dad said.

"Yes sir," Pluto said as he twisted the cap and inserted the tip of the nozzle. His r's stretched like a growling dog when he spoke. Okay, I should stop calling him Pluto. He was clearly not the Pluto from the movie. His sinister eyes, elongated forehead, pointed scalp made for a truly remarkable resemblance, though. He had ripped jeans, old cowboy boots, a black wrinkled button up shirt, where he had inadvertently skipped a button. It made his bony posture worse. His half-smoked cigarette was gnarled and it dangled on his lower lip like it was part of his anatomy. It remained there, unlit and stuck, cemented perhaps by saliva, dirt, and desert heat. It was a fixture, a vile appendage that moved like something suffering when he talked. He moved slowly. He didn't smile either. This made him much scarier than the guy in the movie. No Hollywood wardrobe or makeup here. This was raw, real life, and we were on his turf.

He finished filling up Jock Dad's car, and it was my turn. "Fill up?"

"Yeah, man, unleaded, thanks."

I tried not to stare, but it was hard not to look. I couldn't imagine living out here in the middle of nowhere, pumping gas in that dilapidated dustbowl of a town. How could anyone do it? Maybe he felt the same way about us city dwellers. They probably didn't even use that term. I got that from some old Western movie. Why didn't someone throw a little paint on this town? The buildings and shops were slowly fading into the color of sand. Without the signs, you would miss it altogether. Maybe, that was the point. I was starting to spin on that. It could be a front, a way to size up the travelers and then rob, rape, and kill them down the road. The number wheel inside the pump seemed to stick every dollar or so, the gears sounded strained, metal on metal. The pump stopped at 15.83. Pluto squeezed the handle several times to make it reach exactly sixteen dollars.

"That'll be sixteen even," he said with his face almost inside my car. I got a whiff of his sour cigarette breath, and his body odor was sharp like old cheese.

Jock Dad got out of his car and said, "I told you I would take care of his, my friend."

"Yes sir, forgot," son of Pluto said churning his r's. He walked slowly away from my car. I turned my key and started the engine, rolled my window up and waited for Jock Dad to finish the transaction. Pluto's head followed us as we drove out of the station, watching us with his peephole eyes. I didn't mean to look back, but I did anyway, pretending to adjust my rear view mirror. I expected to see him walking into the garage, but there he stood with one hand in his pocket, eyes fixed on our exit with a mortician's smile on his face.

That was tense, I thought, shaking my head. I expected at any moment to see members of his clan blocking the road or forcing us off before we could make it back to safety. Only another mile to go. Almost there. Finally, the sign of the on ramp was in sight. I was never so glad to be back on a highway in all my life. We didn't stop for a hundred miles after that. That micro-town gave me the creeps. It might be a cool story later, if we survived the trip, and at that point I might stop referring to the totally scary guy at the pump as Pluto.

I remember the adrenaline rush Dave and I had when we snuck in to see "The Hills Have Eyes." We were under-age. It was rated "R." That movie might have kept me from traveling inland in California when I first got my license. Okay, a slight exaggeration, but breaking down anywhere but the beach cities might result in getting tortured by freaks, while they masticated the bones of your family right in front of you. Images like this blew in and out of my head as we made our way toward Utah. I was able to keep myself from falling asleep with my ongoing cerebral horror movie. At the Utah and Nevada border, there was a sign that said, "Welcome to Utah," and below it, sprayed in black graffiti, "Now turn your watch back 50 Years."

The road trip finally ended. We arrived in the southern part of Ogden at 11 pm and stayed in a Ramada Inn. We were three days ahead of the United Van Lines truck with our furniture and I was ready to crash. The air was clean but harder to breathe because of the altitude. It smelled like pine and fresh wood, similar to my cousin Frank's cabin at Big Bear Lake. We used to visit there every summer when Real Mom was alive.

Our new house was close to Hill Air Force Base, where Jock Dad would work and teach. With the help of Trophy Wife, they had purchased a little land along the bench of the Wasatch front. There we were, like an obscure patch on a Mormon quilt.

The house was huge. Two more bedrooms than our home in Cali. It had two floors. All the western windows had a view of the Great Salt Lake and the house, half-timbered architecture, looked like it was designed in Germany. It was very similar to a picture of a house in Idstein in one of my Grandpa's photo journals from his time in the military. It sat high on the bench in south Ogden at the middle of Jefferson Street. It wasn't the biggest house on the street, but it was close.

Jock Dad's California salary went a lot further in Utah and the house was huge. I liked it for the separation and privacy of the basement and second floor. The basement was finished and seemed like just the downstairs to me, but here they called it a basement. The parents were moving up in the world. Trophy Wife was getting what she wanted, a big house on the hill.

As the days progressed, I found myself trapped, longing to get back home where my friends were. My wish list had begun: the surf, the sun, and meeting a girl. Not just any girl, but somebody special. I'm talking about a partner in crime, so to speak; perhaps someone like me who was fresh out of the mold, not tainted by the brokenness and cynicism of life inside the machine. Maybe I could have a fairytale of my own. I was eighteen and overdue. Dammit, it was my time.

One drawback: I feared that the girls in Utah would all be "mountain grown"—raised to be big eaters with big hips, pale skinned and ignorant. I knew the guys here would hate my guts. Even in Cali I got in fights when I travelled inland for the way I looked and had to learn to stand up for myself. Punks were misunderstood everywhere. I prayed I was wrong about the girls.

With the not-so-subtle pressure from home, I enrolled at Weber State College to please Trophy Wife and attempt to bridge the enormous gap between Jock Dad and me. We had missed the bonding years many fathers have with their sons. Since Jock Dad was in college while I was in junior high and high school, we had graduated the same year and coexisted like rivals. Unknowingly, I was competing with his endeavors to provide better for his family. I was frustrated and naive about that, and yet I thought I knew everything. I just wanted to try to get to know him better and get some sort of approval or something. Instead, we spiraled into our own oblivion like some of the missiles he tested.

 JAMES M. FISHER

Chapter 8

SMOKIN' IN THE BOYS' ROOM

Summer was passed out and badly beaten in the corner. Fall crept in like it just left a crime scene. The air was crisp; winter yawned and turned in its sleep. The live coverage from the local news sky copter that hovered above filmed what must have looked like mayhem and panic, but was simply the first day of school. It was double the record enrollment for that term, according to local news a few days later.

The overcrowding forced me to park all the way across the campus in a grated field of turned dirt and weeds. *What the hell?* The mandatory parking pass cost a fortune, and should have included a paved parking spot. In a huff, I grabbed my skateboard from my truck, found some pavement and skated to class. It had been months since the last time I had picked up my board, and it felt good. No, it felt great.

Before skateboard parks, Dave and I used to hit the homemade ramps in our neighborhoods. Our favorite ramp was in Huntington, near his house. It was popular; the best skaters flocked there. It was called, "The Scab."

The cool air made my eyes water as I picked up speed, visions of glassy waves peeled through my mind as I carved toward the main entry of the campus. The clock tower, the red brick walls leading into an open quad, the disheartened looks on freshmen faces as they navigated the badly-copied campus map, reminded me of high school, only bigger, and just as lame. College felt like a bad idea.

On that cool autumn day in the heart of Mormonia, skateboarding was yet to be thought of as a crime, and snowboarding was but an embryo. A couple of other guys were skating to class, too. An especially nimble campus security guard was able to block and stop one skater, and tell him to slow down. In the same flow, another guard, not so nimble, attempted to catch the other skater with his bare hands. The guard was red faced and determined; the skater had a lit cigarette in his mouth and was flying through the quad. Unfortunately for the out-of-shape guard, he was out-maneuvered by the skater who had increased his speed then guffawed at the attempt. The guard ran as far as he could before giving up. The skater had spiked dark hair, an unbuttoned flannel shirt that waved like a battle flag, and sunglasses. Underneath the flannel, he wore a white T-shirt that bore a large anarchist "A" in the center of the chest. By the time the guard was able to catch his breath, the skater was long gone, leaving nothing but the smoke trail from his cigarette. The out-of-shape guard decided not to call it in on the shoulder-mounted walkie-talkie he held in his hand, probably in order to avoid ridicule by his peers of donut dunking crime fighting dreamers. He stood bent over, face flushed, until he could resume normal breathing.

Perhaps the skaters would be transplants like me, with a similar story of moving with the parents and feeling trapped behind enemy lines. Moments later, through some sort of cosmic intervention, I met up with the infamous smoking skater.

We were both forced to slow down and get in a line that funneled along with the rest of the mob, wobbling and bumping into each other like pachinko balls, to enter the small mouse hole of a doorway that led into the science building. I had a first period physics class to get to. I was early, since I had made great time skating across the campus once I hit the concrete ground.

"What a fiasco," I said. The skater and I made eye contact.

"No shit," he said.

I was wearing a black gas coat. I had coined the name since it was an old chemical warfare jacket I had picked up at an army surplus store and dyed it black, which looked good with my favorite pair of converse high tops. The coat hung on me and draped at the knees. I sported a fine rooster-style Mohawk.

The other skater had splintered, coffee black hair, a pair of shabby looking checkered Vans, a couple chains, several earrings, and a confident smirk that bled attitude at first sight. In the bustle and scuttle of the crowd nearing the door, the smells of freshly applied girly fragrances like flowers, musk, or rosy oils and cheap aftershave some of the guys had splashed on nearly overwhelmed my nose.

"Who are you guys supposed to be?" said some faceless jock that moved and shoved through the crowd like a… what? A dinosaur? No, a troglodyte. Yeah, that was it.

We could only make out the back of his massive head and his purple letterman's jacket as the crowd veered to the right in an attempt to align with the doorway and adjacent stairway.

"Whatever we want to be, what's your excuse?" I said.

The skater laughed and said, "What a dick, right?"

"Whatever," said the faceless jock in the crowd tromping up the flight of stairs, not like a dinosaur but like a two-year-old, a two-year-old troglodyte. The squeeze into the mouth of the double doors intensified. Could it be we were all being tasted and chewed to satisfy some unknown hunger? Figuratively and physically, yes. The machine I'd always feared entering was there, like there in the bottleneck. The smoking skater and I were caught in the undertow, and we both tried to avoid the same large, pimple-faced dude with Elvis hair, like old Elvis—big black sideburns, hair combed back into a pseudo duck ass. The front widow peak bobbled slightly over his forehead and touched down between his eyes. He was eating a Danish and spilled coffee on himself. He had an oversized backpack with a patch on it that read, "No Fat Chicks," that was pitching in all directions like a drunken wrecking ball. He needed an entire door to get through.

The skater and I went left and Big Boy went right. He forced the last third of the Danish into his mouth and birthed himself through the door, wrecking ball and all.

"What the fuck was that?" said the skater, as he looked down at his binder and textbook which he miraculously one-handed through the pinch, while holding his skateboard in the other. Big Boy was focused in the opposite direction, never made eye contact, and just preceded to stuff his face. He totally avoided us. The skater looked at me and we laughed as Big Boy collected himself and drained the last remnants of his coffee. He wiped his chin with his sleeve and moved on to the restroom. As the dam broke, a steady flow of students scooted by, attempting to pass without banging arms and shoulders into us.

We stopped mid-stream. The skater turned to me as we tried to find an eddy and slow down.

"Hey man, what's your name?"

I watched as he adjusted his load. "Michael. What's yours?"

"Tony. Good to meet you, man."

"Yeah, you too, brudda." The river of students trickled into upper floors and nearby classrooms. I call everyone I know brudda if they surf or skate. I stole it from Hawaii Five-O. The cops all called each other brudda, and I thought it was cool.

"This is nuts!" Tony said, as he stood straight up and balanced his load. He took off his flannel shirt and tossed it over his shoulder. We paused for a second to get a good look at one another. I towered over Tony by five inches. He was a good-looking guy, in shape. The anarchist T-shirt was untucked, tight around his chest and biceps, and his face was fearless like he was going to double-dog-dare you at any minute. He looked up at me with a grin that only predators have.

"You're a tall S.O.B," he said.

I smiled. "Yeah, I've heard that once or twice."

He laughed like only predators laugh.

"I'm not sure I even want to do this." I squinted hard down the corridor, trying to make out the hands of the clock that was mounted on a wall just above the flowing heads of students.

"Where are you from?" asked Tony.

"Seal Beach, California." I straightened up my own coat. "You?"

"Newport, Oregon."

"Cool. Surf by chance?"

"Yeah, and it's cold water all year round, 5 mil wetsuits, man." He paused for a second as if his home break had just flashed through his mind.

"We have to wear wetsuits most of the year in Cali, too. We should hang out sometime."

"Yeah, cool, what are you doing tonight?"

"Not much, I got nothing planned."

"Do you know where the Gimlet is?"

"That private club down on Washington?" I said.

"Yeah, next to China Nite. The place with the smiling Buddha out front with hunting arrows sticking in his belly."

"I know the place. I used to think it was a front for laundering money after I found out the arrows had been there for years. Seemed sketchy."

"Ever eat there?" Tony asked.

"Once, but I haven't been back. The door to the kitchen was propped open when I left the place. I glanced in and something about the cooks smoking and flipping Kung Pao Chicken at the same time made it unappetizing. The waitress was cute, though."

"Did you ask her out?"

"No, but she told me about the arrows."

"Okay, I gotta hear this," Tony said, looking at his watch.

"Quick version. The chick's name was Kimmi. Her parents were both from China and the restaurant was a dream they shared. She was raised here and speaks English, Spanish, and Chinese. Anyway, not long after she was born, her mother died, leaving her dad to run the business by himself."

"Man, she told you all that?"

"Yeah, it was actually a cool story."

"Okay, go on. I got a minute. I want to hear about the arrows."

     JAMES M. FISHER

"Her dad fell into a serious depression and almost lost the business. One morning he came to work and there were these three arrows protruding from the Buddha's belly. Instead of getting angry, he just put his head down and went to work. That day, as he was getting ready for lunch, a crowd gathered outside his front door. They were talking and pointing at the arrows. He ran up to the front door to see what was going on. The crowd was like amazed that there were actual arrows in the belly. Anyway, the number three is special in Chinese culture. Kimmi said three is lucky, but it also represents the three main stages of life: birth, marriage, and death."

Tony was beginning to put on the polite face so I sped up to get the story out. "It can mean heaven, too. Kimmi's dad believed all that, too. The cool thing was that the business blew up and became profitable. Everyday somebody comes in and mentions the arrows like it just happened. Like, 'Do you know that there are arrows in your Buddha's belly?' 'They've been there for years,' he'd say, and then they would sit down and eat a bowl of noodles. He said it was a miracle from his wife. The three arrows hit the Buddha in the belly and not in the heart. Kimmi's dad said his heart was still intact and full of love for his wife. He used that energy to keep the restaurant going ever since."

Tony was not as impressed by the story as I was. His eyebrows and the skin on his forehead formed a "V" which is never a good sign. "That's it? I thought you were going to tell me about some battle with the cops. Like cowboys and Indians, or gangsters. Not sure I needed all that info, bro." Tony laughed, then he smacked me on the arm. "Only a redneck could have pulled that drive by off, not some dead Chinese woman."

We both cracked up.

"Ogden's got a lot of stories and myths. There's definitely more here than the town lets on. Sorry that went long."

"No worries, man. How 'bout nine tonight at the Gimlet?" Tony said, still chuckling and shaking his head.

"Works for me," I said.

Tony looked at his watch again. Both of us needed to hustle and get to class.

"Okay, later, man," I said. I started walking toward my class.

"Be sure and bring your ID," he called as he turned in the opposite direction.

"Will do. See you tonight, Tony."

"Later, Mikey!"

I ran to my lab and stopped ten feet before the door. I sauntered in and sat down with minutes to spare. In those minutes it occurred to me, he'd called me 'Mikey'. Only Dave and Real Mom called me that. As dumb luck would have it, I found myself stuck between two nerdy students already engrossed in conversation and debate. From their quirky disregard of the moment and matching school logo sweatshirts, it was obvious they were freshmen. They were going back and forth about the Many Worlds theory of quantum physics, clearly caught up in their own universe.

A tall, gray-haired man dressed in beige pleated slacks with a brown belt, black loafers, and a white collared shirt wrinkled in the front approached the podium. He rolled up his sleeves and exposed a black-faced watch with a black band. My theory was he had turned the face of the watch to the inside of his wrist so that when he extended his hands forward as he lectured, he could see the time. The lines on his forehead ran in the same direction as his wrinkled shirt when he slid his glasses on and peered over his paperwork. There were 122 students in this lecture, according to the roster. Two of them did not take notice of the professor who was about to speak at the podium.

"Look, if the world splits in two every time there's a quantum event, the universe has to have infinite space and time to accommodate that, and if the universe is closed, there isn't any goddamn room," said the long haired nerd.

"But what if there's, like, a more probable timeline where events don't just keep splitting off on infinite branches, but come back together around the most probable reality. Or, realities. Anyway, then the Many Worlds theory works whether the universe is closed or open," said the nerd with black-framed glasses. His throat was turning red the longer he talked. He raised his hand to stop the other guy from interrupting him. No luck.

"That doesn't make any sense! You're saying there are favored realities, which is just like saying consciousness collapses the wave function into reality!" the long haired guy cried. "That defeats the exact problem Many Worlds is trying to fix!" Suddenly, at once, both became aware that there were 120 pairs of amused eyes on them.

The professor moved in close to the microphone and cleared his throat to get the attention of the two nerdy boys and said drily, "A little passion is good: disrespect, not so."

The boys hushed and found themselves trapped in a black hole of embarrassment without a portal, nowhere to go. They glared at one another and melted into the metal and wood of their chairs like liquid shame. The professor politely moved on. The faces of the two remained fixed and still. They both had red blotches that ran along their neck and cheekbones. The lecture went quickly. It didn't really qualify as a lecture. We just covered the syllabus for the semester, and what books were necessary and correct for the class. There were four exits in the lab, three of which the majority of the students used. I was closest to the door that was near the podium where the professor was standing. I headed in that direction. It seemed the class was in a hurry to leave to get to their next period, or smoke, or simply just run away.

My eyes met up with the professor's at the door. "Have a good day," I said.

"Yeah, have a good one yourself," said the professor, giving me a half wave out the door. When he extended his left arm, I noticed his watch was missing all the hands. Maybe the professor was really into quantum physics, and rode on the tail of its mysteries of time travel like an imaginative child. Maybe he needed an object, like the watch, to represent the emotion and great passion of his pursuits. Maybe at faculty dinner parties someone would notice the upside-down, handless watch strapped to his wrist, and strike up a conversation. It would enable him to share his own questions and theories, and talk about the unfinished equations that kept him up at night. Others would join in and give their insights. The wine would pour on; the brandy would swirl in snifters by hands that moved counter-clockwise. Or, maybe there was a ridiculous cliché that went along with the missing hands like: the time is now, now is the time, live in the moment.

I tended to stop paying attention during mindless conversations and start looking for an exit. I wanted to avoid the disappointment and embarrassment that often results from talking to people who had created their own personal philosophies, built on some simple cliché phrases of three

     James M. Fisher

or four words or a random bible verse. These informal philosophers would spit out their slogans over and over without cognition or synapse, repeating them for years until they became a part of their being. Kant would say their 'essence'. It would have detrimental consequences not only to the conversation at hand, but to the listener, as such phrases could be caught like a virus. In time, the life could be stomped out of the listener's own personal evolution.

I call this condition Parrot Head Syndrome, or PHS. "Altitude is determined by your attitude." Or my prior dean's favorites: "As ye sow, so shall ye reap", "Absence makes the heart grow fonder", and "An idle mind is the Devil's playground." When you hear these words or words like them come out of a Parrot Head, simply feed them a cracker or a peanut and walk away. Sometimes running is necessary. The emptiness that results from a conversation that begins or ends with such phrases tends to leave the soul of the receiver in a desert with a hole in the heart and their dick in the dirt.

See what I mean?

 little traffic. I entered the house. It was quiet. The breakfast smells were gone, replaced by the odor of Trophy Wife's daily cleaning habits. She had freshly wiped down the countertops with a concoction made with isopropyl alcohol, and the wood furniture reeked with lemon scented Pledge. I ran through my day as I walked downstairs to my room. I thought about the handless watch, the two physics geeks, the fact I actually had plans that night, thanks to meeting up with Tony. I tossed my books on the bed, happy to be home. Trophy Wife was probably trying to close a deal at the real estate office and Jock Dad was probably teaching the military about gyros. I had the house to myself. The finished basement had a den and my bedroom. The carpet was new and sandy brown, and in the center of the room was a cozy brick fireplace. The house burrowed into the mountainside so that a large window could face the front yard grass and azalea bushes with a view of the Great Salt Lake. In the distance, dark clouds were creeping in, sniper-like. The window in my bedroom had no view as that part of the house backed into the hilly landscape. You could see daylight if you tilted your head just right and looked straight up where the metal window well met the level ground of the backyard. Trophy Wife had custom shutters installed to cover up the eyesore of the dark shadowy tomb appearance of the window well.

I looked over my school and work schedules. Tonight was my only night off for the week. At least I had plans, real plans for the night. I was pumped up with the chance to meet new people. So far, I hadn't met anyone that shared my music tastes or outlook. Most people just stared at me. I got a few looks and smiles from the chicks.

Speaking of chicks, I had been wrong to assume the girls here would be mountain grown heifers. Instead, they were really attractive. They wear more makeup and perfume than the girls in Cali. I guess the Cali girls had tans all year long and didn't need as much. Either way, they were all beautiful.

I just had to work hard and make the best of Utah until I could go back home.

I went upstairs to the kitchen. On the counter was a note from Trophy Wife. *Michael, you are on your own. We have things to pick up for the company coming by tonight. We will be home later than usual.* The day just got better. I opened the fridge and pulled a gallon of milk and shot gunned several gulps. I welcomed the cold surge down my throat and reached for a tray of double chocolate icebox brownies. Trophy Wife had made them for her women's group that was coming over that night. She had them cut and stacked neatly on a fancy plate and underneath each one was a loose piece of wax paper. I grabbed one. I have to admit: the woman could bake.

I plunged into that wedge like a beast and repeated the shotgun process with the dwindling gallon of milk. I was taken prisoner by the complex chemistry of chocolate, sugar, and ice cold dairy exuberance that freight-trained my entire being. I was somewhere else. In those gulps and swallows, I managed to lose all sense of place and time inside an illuminated cold air portal that provided a momentary escape from life, and delicious food. Or, was it the perfect crime with the vault doors wide open. Either way, I stood there like nobody's business with full reign over everything in the vault. When it came time to leave the scene, like a thief I carefully wiped down the chocolate lip marks around the spout of the milk bottle, and then wiped the crumbs from the floor. I placed the wax paper back over the remaining plate of chocolate madness and returned the milk to its previous spot with the label facing out and the handle pointing right. Trophy Wife had an exact place, and order for everything. I broke her code, I deciphered her language. I devised a plan to hit the vault again later, for the leftover lasagna that was also individually cut and wrapped and placed neatly in the right corner of the fridge. I walked away from the crime scene, and by the time I was back in my room to change clothes, I had forgotten the whole thing.

The end of the day closed hauntingly with deathbed eyes. The blackened clouds that crept along the horizon earlier were joined by another dark front. It had a mysterious and chaotic smoke-like pattern that moved quickly and purposeful, like it knew where it was heading. It rumbled with thunder, rolled its plumes of clenched fists. Winds gusted upward to forty miles per hour. The wind blew so hard that the trees wore their skirts over their heads. In shock and awe formation, the hellish curtain of black clouds snuffed the last flicker of sunlight and unloaded. Trophy Wife and Jock Dad were back. The festivities began despite the mood of the weather. The heels of the guests pounded above my ceiling. Laughter and raillery ensued. The time neared eight-thirty. I slipped out unnoticed and jumped into my truck.

The rain had started in small change with nickel-and-dime-sized drops. By the time I was down the hill it was raining Eisenhower's from a one armed bandit in the sky that hit Jackpot. The wipers on my truck couldn't keep up with the battery of watery coins that thudded against my windshield. With limited visibility, I managed to eke out of my neighborhood that appeared to be transforming into a 3D painting by Van Gogh.

I rounded the hill of Jefferson Street with the rush of flooding rain at four inches on the road and made my way onto Washington. The sky erupted with more thunder and relentless rain. Lightning splintered through the blackness of the sky. Images of Dr. Frankenstein and his lab went through my mind. Just like the night in the book by Shelley. This was the night of *elan vital.* This was the perfect night to awaken the monster. Haha! I laughed like an evil genius, and pushed in a cassette of the Misfits. "Die Die My Darling" began to play.

The traffic was backed up from 36th to 12th. A few of the neighborhoods and businesses were blacked out. A few cars were stalled, up to their bumpers in water along the curb. The lift kit on my truck made cruising through the flooded streets a breeze. I was getting a little impatient with the congestion on the main roads. I was trying to keep positive because the idea of being out was either going to be fun, or a real bust with this evil weather. The lightning was relentless, it scattered like electric veins. The thunder cracked like the Monster trying to pronounce its first word. The only reason I didn't turn around was because I could clearly make out the neon martini glasses of the Gimlet marquis, and the partially lit neon of China Nite. They still had power. The dying neon sign in front of CHINA NITE spelled IN__IT and the pulse of the neon was slow like a clogged artery. It flickered, barely pulsing, a dim throb, like it might be its last. The happy Buddha above the sign was still smiling, like he was enjoying his shower. Not bad, for having three hunting arrows in his belly. Very Zen, I thought. Or, it might be construed as a warning. You don't pay for food, we shoot you with arrows. Have a nice day. I cracked myself up.

After countless stops and gos, and watching the brake lights and turn signals of countless cars, I finally reached my destination, and pulled into the parking lot of the Gimlet. It was surprisingly busy and finding a place to park my truck was a challenge. I lucked out and tucked into the last available space in the lot. It was still raining. There was no light in the parking lot. Just shadows and the sound of the rain *tink-tinking* off the cars and exposed pipes of the neighboring buildings.

Walking across to the Gimlet, I smelled the odor of new paint and deep fat fryers that pervaded the air. Music rumbled through the concrete block walls. There were no windows, just a back service entrance and a front door. I approached with caution. It was well lit, almost sterile with the buzzing fluorescent lighting above. The doorway was protected by a concrete wall that hid the view from the street. I stood in front of the door and fought down a rising apprehension.

The door was oversized, metal—iron possibly—and painted white like the rest of the building. It had an orbiting peephole. *Strange. For what purpose?*

I could hear laughter and music, glassware clanking inside. I hesitated. My fake ID was from California. It looked good and dates were believable, but this was Utah. Laws are different and bars here required a membership. This was nothing like sneaking in with the crowd at the Beach Ball bar in Newport Beach on a Friday night. Dave was the master. We made a good team back in the day rolling into a packed house. It seemed unnatural doing this without him. He would say, "Just do it. Go in. Don't be a wuss."

I took another step. I extended my hand to open the door. The door swung open before I could tighten my palm around the handle. A very large bouncer in a black sportscoat with a white shirt, black slacks, massive shoulders, and a freshly shaved bald head came through. He moved like a territorial gorilla, the type of guy you wanted on your side.

I anticipated his tone, something between a base rumble and a grunt. He'd say, "What the fuck do you want?"

What I got was a deep, but not hostile, "Hi, welcome to the Gimlet."

When I didn't respond right away, he followed with the same intensity. "Are you on the list?"

"Excuse me? List?

"Yeah, the list. This is a private party." Both rows of the bouncer's front teeth lined up perfectly, horse-like. He bit down and looked at me with disapproval. I was feeling his alpha energy starting to buzz. I was feeling mine. I thought, "Go for it. Double or nothing. Don't hesitate. You don't do it when the waves are big and definitely not now."

"Yeah, I'm on the list. The name's Price, Michael Price."

"I don't have a Michael. I have a Mikey. Is that you?" He gritted his teeth again, and then side to side, made a clicking sound like a couple of coconut shells.

"Yeah, that's me."

I thought, "dammit, Tony. Only Real Mom and Dave called me that."

"ID?" he said. I handed him my fake license. He looked at me up and down, gritted his teeth side to side making that clicking sound again.

"Seal Beach, California, huh?"

"Yeah." I said.

"Ever been to the Irisher bar on Main?" His face relaxed and softened. "I used to go there when I worked the oil rigs. You know the platforms offshore?"

"Yeah I do. The Irisher, next to Clancy's. Small world. That's intense," I said.

He smiled and gritted his teeth again. "Yeah. Name's Sarge."

"Good to meet you, Sarge." My shoulders could have hit the pavement as they relaxed. I had been so tense.

"Have a good night, Mikey," Sarge said. He handed me back my ID. I was in.

"Thanks, man."

I've never had so many people call me Mikey in one day. Sarge was cool. The only time I saw anyone gritting their teeth side to side like that was Dana. It was the last time I saw him. He was coked up at a party in Huntington. It was when Dave finished his last day of therapy. We didn't stay long, maybe for one beer. Dana could party for days. Our idea of celebrating was seeing Black Flag and the Circle Jerks perform in L.A. Dave and I had a great time seeing those bands. Henry Rollins from Black Flag slammed into me as he jumped off the stage. The guy was a beast. It was an awesome night. It was cool how an unrelated experience like Sarge gritting his teeth could transport me back in time to relive an experience all over again.

Dave and I would argue whether or not things like that were completely true. I also argued we have one hundred trillion neural connections in our brains, a thousand times more than the stars in our galaxy, so the potential for us to tap into our own past through a random event, or a common scent for that matter, was as easy as breathing. It's so much more than just a memory file being pulled up.

This type of conversation would often result from smoking a bowl or two after a surf session. Dave would argue just to argue no matter how right I was and then we'd laugh our asses off. I missed him a lot.

That night at the Gimlet, I didn't care where the memory came from, I was just glad I had it.

I made it to the inside of the Gimlet and it was time to party. I made my way around the nook of the entry. It was crowded and dark. My eyes were still adjusting after standing under the white fluorescent light with Sarge. There was a small satellite bar with a young, good-looking bartender pouring drinks. The entire interior was in full view. A smoke layer hovered over the main bar, which was horseshoe shaped. I could smell clove cigarettes mixed with the regular smoke. The beer neons and stage spots reflected off the mirrors behind the bar, exposing the faces of the people sitting and standing along the bar rail. The bar had four drink pouring stations, with two cocktail waitresses per station. To the left was a sunken wooden dance floor, above it, a mirror ball and an assortment of light wheels, strobes, and more spots. The darkness made the black light effects more noticeable. Mirrors lined the outer walls so the clientele could watch themselves drink, dance, converse, and everything in between.

The black lights picked up messages painted on the mirrors, a couple of them were drink specials. Others announced coming events: "Catch Oil Wrestling on Wednesdays," and "Bikini Night on Thursdays," "All Male Review next Friday at 8 pm, Women Only until 10 pm."

This place rocked the only nightlife Ogden had to offer. The mystery was 'The List'. What was going on tonight? It was a Wednesday and the place was packed out. The music was lame because the DJ was playing crap-pop-dance vinyl. Only chicks were dancing at the time. The further I went in the stronger the smell of clove cigarettes. I entered the cloud; breathing was optional.

"Hey, Mikey! Mikey!"

I turned to see Tony walking through the crowd. He had lots charisma, even his white perfect teeth sparkled in the shadows of the bar. He came up to me with a woman on each arm. They were bad-girl cute, thick red lipstick, heavy eyeliner, their hands traveling up and down Tony's body like they were polishing a trophy. He was the center of attention; he must have majored in charm, wit, and rebellion. He was like a new wave pirate, who discovered how to navigate through the most unfamiliar waters of Zion. The music was blasting and the kegs in the bar were emptying faster than the bladders of freshmen rushes open-throating a beer bong.

"So cool you made it, man," Tony said. "What'd you think?"

"Pretty cool place, but the music is kind of lame, no offense."

"Gary, the DJ is a friend of mine. If we get him a drink and a tip, we might be able to change the music up. One of the owner's friends rented the place out for a private party otherwise you would've needed to be a member to get in."

"Okay, cool, that explains 'The List'. Thanks for getting me in."

"No worries, Mikey. What are you drinking?"

"I'll do a Heineken, man," I said.

"Let's go do a shot too. You game?" Tony uncoiled himself from the two trophy-polishers. They gave me the stink eye when Tony grabbed me around the neck and took me to the side of the horseshoe bar, abandoning them in the aisle.

"Sure, I'll do one," I said.

Tony released me between two women sitting at the bar.

"Hi, ladies, excuse the intrusion," I said.

They smiled, moved their drinks away from me, and huddled closer to one another. I moved out of their space and over to the corner of the bar where Tony was standing.

"Two shots of José, Joey," Tony yelled to the bartender, a lovely brunette. "Joey's cool, you'll like her."

"I didn't get a 'please' with that, Tony? The issue with my sister still needs to be resolved." Joey's brown eyes glared at Tony, the batting of her frozen long lashes and thick mascara told the whole story.

"Yeah, yeah, but let's talk tequila first. I'll make it up to Steph, Joey."

Joey rolled her eyes again and clenched her jaw to trap her gum. She leaned on the bar and made no move to reach for the bottle on the shelf behind her.

"I promise Jo, really," Tony said, with his predator smile, and hand over his heart.

"You better," said Joey. She dipped the rim of the shot glasses in lime juice, dusted with salt, poured the tequila, hung the carefully slotted lime wedge on each, and parked them on the bar before us.

"Thanks Jo," said Tony, smiling with brows raised as if apologizing. "Can we get two Heinekens too, and I'll leave you alone. Oh, and two more shots, please, sweetie."

Joey's eyes rolled back as far as possible. She set up two more shots of Cuervo with limes, and popped the caps of the beers without looking. She was a bartending machine.

"Who's your friend?" Joey said, as she flipped the Cuervo bottle into the speed well.

"Oh, sorry. This is Mikey. Mikey, this is Jo, the best bartender in the state."

"Really nice to meet you, Jo," I said.

"Good to meet you, you're not from around here, are you?"

"Nope," I said.

"Where ya from?"

"California."

"Cool. Well, you guys be safe and play nice." She looked me up and down and all around, snapped her gum, and turned to other customers. My eyes followed her remarkably heart shaped posterior. It was like two carefully placed nautilus shells wrapped in tight black denim cutoffs.

I mumbled, "She seems nice."

"Yeah, she's cool. I should have never dated her sister, anyway, let's drink."

"Let's do it," I said.

"Here's to living the dream no matter where we are," Tony said, as we downed the shots and squeezed the limes.

The first time I had ever shot tequila was with Dana's girlfriend, Carrie, at a party at his house. I remembered it like it was an hour ago. Her light brown hair dropped below her shoulders just above her full breasts. She wore a tan tank top without a bra. It was very revealing and I was shaking. I was not very cool.

"If you're going to shoot tequila, learn to do it right. Can you show him, Carrie?" Dana had yelled.

Carrie beckoned me into the kitchen. She had everything set up on a cutting board, the shot glasses full of tequila, limes, and salt.

She smiled at me like a shark looking at a baby seal. "All you have to remember is the order of doing a shot of tequila. It's lick, sip, and suck."

At first I thought she was talking about something else, which really made me shake. I was a junior in high school at the time.

"Oh…okay." I was trying to be cool, but she saw right through me.

"Just do whatever I tell you and it'll be okay, kiddo." Carrie licked her thumb, her tongue was pretty and pink as a kitten's. Completely mesmerized, I followed her lead. Lick the salt, sip the tequila, and suck the lime.

"Again," Carrie said. And we did another shot each. By the time we went back outside to join the party on the patio I had a little crush on Carrie with her shark smile and kitten tongue.

     James M. Fisher

"How did it go, Michael?" Dana asked.

"It went great, man."

"Figured. Carrie taught me," Dana said. I had tried not to picture my best friend's brother and his girlfriend together.

Tony placed his shot glass on the bar upside down and said, "Yeah, living the dream, I'll drink to that. Cheers."

I looked at Tony and raised my beer up. "Cheers, Tony."

We finished our beers and Tony hopped off the stool. "Now, let's go bribe the DJ."

We walked through the crowd and I heard someone yell, "Hey Spike, nice hair." I blew it off. We kept going and squeezed through the crowd. We maneuvered around the chicks along the dance floor rail who were talking about nothing. No content, just about how they looked, and do my boobs look small in this dress? Why did I wear these pants? My ass looks huge.

We cut through the dance floor and fucking UB40 was playing and before that Wham, Donna Summer, and Boy George.

"I don't wanna complain, but there's something really wrong with the music, man," I said.

"We're gonna fix it," Tony said, eyes fixed at the DJ booth.

We hopped up the steps along the stage to the DJ booth. Tony knocked on the door and the DJ opened up.

"What's happening, Tony?" Gary said.

Gary was not the typical DJ you would picture in your mind. Gary was a young white "Jack Mormon", according to Tony, who mixed pretty good as he slowed and stalled the turntables. He just had a limited point of view of the world, and what people abroad were listening to.

"Hey, Gary, this is Mikey. He's from Seal Beach, California. He wants to hear something other than the crap you've been playing all night. I know your manager told you what to play, but let's have some fun, man."

"No problem," Gary said.

Gary was accommodating and was willing to let us go through his collection. While I was looking, I noticed Tony slipped something from his pocket to Gary, who turned around, and snorted what I had assumed to be cocaine. I didn't care. I was buzzed.

I found Bauhaus's "Bela Lugosi's Dead," and Billy Idol's "Dancing with Myself," "Never Mind the Bollocks album," by the Sex Pistols, a single vinyl recording of "1945" by my favorite Orange County band, Social Distortion, "Only a Lad," by Oingo Boingo, some Clash, X, and the single by the Stooges, "I Wanna be Your Dog." I handed him the records and told him do his best to mix it up. It was a limited selection. I was hoping for some Bad Brains, TSOL, DK, Fear, or The Ramones. But we made do.

The DJ booth was dark, illuminated by a blue light. A two-sided window overlooked the dance floor. I sipped my beer. Gary kept licking the corners of his mustache while he arranged the records I handed him.

"Okay, it's time to do my magic. I might get fired, but for you, Tony, I'll do it. Besides the owner likes you."

"You're not going anywhere, Gary. Don't be so dramatic," Tony said.

"I got you. I'll mix 'em in," Gary said.

"Cool-cool and turn it up," said Tony as he lit up a Marlboro.

The stage went dark and the beginning of Bauhaus's Bela Lugosi's Dead began, with its haunting intro, a soft strobe flickered, a slow throbbing beat was beginning to build as some of the bad girls in the crowd began to take the floor, cigarettes in hand. They didn't give a damn if they had someone to dance with or not, they just went for it.

"Very cool," I said, nodding at Tony.

"Pretty cool for Utah," he said.

Tony and I took to the floor feeling the music and the tequila. One of the girls in the crowd came over to me and looked me up and down. She was a punk chick in a short skirt with ripped tights. Her face was narrow and her black hair was bobbed. She handed me the remaining half of her clove cigarette. I took it and rather enjoyed it, doing my part to keep the cloud going in the place. We danced to the beat as the song went on and on. This chick knew how to move to the darkness of the song. Slowly, building from her hips, twisting her arms upward. She undulated like smoke through a tree. Her eyes were closed, she felt it, she became it. The moment was cool. My buzz was on. Soon the dance floor was packed with mostly females. A couple Goth girls came in from the crowd, which was a huge surprise. I couldn't believe I was in Ogden, Utah.

Most of the guys were unfamiliar with what was going on, and they totally missed it. There were very few women sitting in chairs in the bar. Tony, and I were surrounded. We were instantly hated by those guys. I thought a fight was going to break out after one of the drunk hodads yelled, "Up yours, Spike," and flipped me off. Tony and I returned the favor and flipped him off with both hands.

"I'm going to kick your ass!" yelled the hodad.

"Bring it, asshole," I yelled back.

Tony laughed and lit up another Marlboro. You could feel the tension in the building as the guys congregated in the bar. Sarge was on it. I could see him escort a few of the guys out of the bar. Gary mixed in "Dancing with Myself," followed by "Brand New Cadillac," and "Tommy Gun," by the Clash, then, "I Wanna be Your Dog," by Iggy Pop and the Stooges. Tony and I went crazy. We slammed into each other, and danced with almost all the women who made it to the floor. They were just out for a good time like us. The dance floor maxed out. Tony and I were just grinning for forty-five minutes out there on the floor. I was in a full sweat by then.

"How's the music now, Mikey?" Tony yelled.

"Cool for Utah, bro, It's goin off in here!"

The manager was getting pissed, but enjoyed watching all the girls dancing with each other. He was such a redneck. Gary told me later that he had to change it up, and get back to the pop crap he was playing as soon as the girls left the dance floor. I blamed him for that since he attempted to mix the Go Go's in the middle of "Vacant" by the Sex Pistols. It was a train wreck. Gary caved, and threw in a little disco to boot. No big deal. I had my fill for a school night anyway. I went to the bar and asked Joey for water. She gave me two glasses.

"Why two glasses?" I asked.

"You need to slow down and sober up. You guys really tore it up out there, I'll give you that." She was right on both counts.

"It was a lot of fun. Thanks for the water," I said, slipping her a five-dollar tip.

"Thank you, Michael," she said. She leaned over to whisper in my ear, "How well do you know Tony?" She smelled really good and it kind of turned me on when she whispered in my ear.

"I met him at school, why?"

"Just be careful. See you around."

"Yeah, see you around." She saw Tony approaching and

went back to work. *Be careful of what?* Before I could think about what she had just said the thought of school and then work the next day flooded in. It was getting late and Trophy Wife had zero tolerance for me being out all night unless I was working.

Tony met me at the bar. "You're not leaving are you?"

"Yeah man, I got school and work tomorrow. I gotta be real. I needed this, brudda," I said.

"No problem, Mikey. You need a little bump for the road?" He passed a vial of coke to me as if he was about to shake my hand on the bar rail. That never happened to me before in California either.

"No, I'm cool, man." I passed it back to him. "I gotta get going."

"You sure, man?" Tony asked, as the two chicks from earlier came up to join him, reaching around his waist to polish the trophy.

"I'm totally good, bro. We gotta do this again soon," I said. I waved to Joey at the bar. She was pouring drinks with both hands but figured a way to blow me a kiss. I was stoked and really appreciated her looking out for me.

I made my way to the front door. Sarge was drinking a beer and leaning against the wall by the entryway.

"Goodnight, Mikey."

"Later, Sarge," I said.

I was still a little buzzed, but felt okay to drive. I walked out the door into the fluorescent light of the entryway, and into the darkness of the parking lot. My eyes were blinded as I went toward the deeper, outer lot. The rain had stopped. I could see a field of puddles between the parked cars where the rain had collected. When my eyes adjusted, I could see the reflection of the stars on the water with a faint arc of the moon, trying to move in. Every puddle seemed to contain some of the truth of the night's sky. They were full of stars. The sky was totally exposed, and it seemed to have moved in closer. No haze or smog or atmospheric interference. Clusters of stars were there, like there. Naked. I stared in awe.

Moaning disrupted the moment. A couple making out four or five cars from my space. I was sort of envious. On the other hand, they were totally missing the sky show. I opened my truck door, slid in, and turned the key. I flipped the stereo off and turned my headlights on. My gas gauge read, 'Empty.' I backed up out of the space, and put my truck in gear. A puddle of water in the back of my truck hit the tailgate, swished out the back, like stars in a washing machine. I almost forgot about the rain and the evil weather from earlier. It was getting late, but I had to get gas. I pulled out onto Washington again and drove to a 24-hour gas station and convenience store called KarKwik. I pulled into the first pump. I got out and noticed the temperature had really dropped outside. I paid at the service window. The clerk was reading a magazine and eating a candy bar. He seemed a little put out to take my money. I went back and began to fill up my truck. The dank smell of the deep fried chicken and potato logs that spewed out of the roof top vent of the KarKwik was a bit revolting. They sat on display in the window for God knows how long under a heat lamp. I was by myself except for another small blue Honda a few pumps away. There was a blonde chick inside trying to get her car started. I continued to fill up my truck. I heard the starter grind. She got out of her car and went over to the service attendant who was immersed in his magazine.

"Hey there, excuse me," she said, trying to get the clerk's attention.

He looked up from inside the window. "What can I do for you, lady?"

"I need a jump. My car won't start."

"I don't have any cables. I can't leave the building either," he said. He finished the last bite of his candy bar and rolled the wrapper into a ball.

I finished filling my truck. I inserted the nozzle and hose back onto the pump. My eyes were now fixed on the cute blonde as she turned around in disappointment. She looked really discouraged and it was getting late. She looked down for a moment, and back again at the guy in the service window. He was back into his magazine and opened a bag of chips. The blonde folded her arms, shivering. She panned around in my direction and our eyes met.

I felt I had to say something under the circumstances. "Are you all right?"

"No, not really. My car won't start and I'm a little stranded."

"Well, I don't have jumper cables, but I can look at your car and see what I can do."

"Okay, that'd be great."

I walked over to her car. She followed.

"Do you want to try and start it again?" I said.

"I can try." She got in and turned it over. It sounded like she worked the battery pretty hard by starting it over and over again.

"I think you might have flooded it. I can smell the gas," I said.

"I probably did that." Her head shook in disgust and then looked up.

"Hey, it looks like you have a stick shift. Maybe we can pop the clutch, and get you started. There's not much traffic.

We're on a slope here that leads to the road. It's all downhill. Would you like to try that?"

"That sounds great, thank you. What do you need me to do?"

I talked her through the process.

"I've never had to do that before," she said.

"It's not that complicated," I said.

"What's your name?"

"Michael, what's yours?"

"Danielle. You're not from around here, are you?"

"No, just moved here from Cali. You?"

"Yeah, I'm from here."

What was this girl doing here by herself? Maybe she didn't have a boyfriend? Another car had pulled into the pump in front of hers, and now she was blocked in.

"Looks like we have a few minutes before I can push you out."

"No problem for me, but are you in a hurry, or anything? I don't want to hold you up," Danielle said.

"No, I'm good. I was on my way home anyway."

"I really appreciate this," she said, with a smile. I read it; it was a flirt smile. "So Michael, what are you doing out here this time of night?"

"Just hanging with some friends. You?"

"I was coming home from work and I needed gas."

"I was on my way home, too."

Things were going pretty well so far. We seemed to be hitting it off. Danielle was really nice and cute. I couldn't believe I'd ever thought girls here would be awful. I could be here all night. This chick was awesome.

The car blocking her moved on.

"Try now?" She smiled at me.

"Yeah, hop in." I was disappointed we didn't get to talk much. If I got her car started, and she drove off, then what a waste. The night so far had been about not hesitating and going for it. If I got the chance, I would ask her out.

"Okay, turn on the ignition, ease off the brake, and let's do this." I got behind the Honda, and began to push her out of the gas station parking lot. Faster and faster, down to the slope of the road.

"Now pop the clutch!"

With a jerk and a bounce, the motor started. Danielle put the car in gear and with a burst, was on the open road.

Crap, she was gone.

I turned and walked toward my truck, dragging my feet. I opened my door. A horn sounded and I turned. Danielle rounded back to the pump where I was parked. She rolled down her window and said, "Thank you so much. How can I repay you for this? You really saved me a lot of hassle tonight."

"I hope this isn't too forward, but would you like to go out sometime? You seem cool and I'd like to get to know you."

"I would love too. You do look a little dangerous, I have to admit, but what you did for me tonight was really nice."

"Are you in school?" I asked.

"Yeah, Weber State."

"So am I. In fact, I have an early class. Would you like to meet up between classes tomorrow?"

"Sure! That would be great. Any time after 10:30 works for me."

"Great. Meet you at the quad beside the science building at 11, okay?"

"That's perfect. I'll see you tomorrow." Danielle gave a little wave.

I was stoked. I had a date with a cute chick. Yeah! I couldn't believe she didn't have a boyfriend. I thought a girl like that would have been scooped up for sure. Lucky me. This had been the best day since the move for sure.

We drove out of the parking lot onto Washington. I went right and she went left. The traffic was quiet. I wanted to follow her home to make sure she made it safely, but that might have seemed weird. The streets were high-gloss obsidian-black, polished from the heavy rain. The street lamps and retail signs reflected brightly against the black-mirrored streets. I caught every light perfectly on the way home. The universe was giving me the green light. I turned up my street and chuckled.

Oh shit. The living room light was on, meaning Trophy Wife was waiting up. All I could make out was her silhouette. I felt a tug in my gut. I took in a deep breath, turned off the truck and the lights. I thought of Danielle and didn't hesitate.

We never used that area of the house except when Jock Dad and Trophy Wife had company over. I assumed that's where the women's group had met. The room had a great view with an oversized window. She could have seen me coming for miles. Trophy Wife was sitting in a chair in the living room. The amber glass lamp that sat on the opposite side of the couch was on low.

"Hey, you're up late. Couldn't sleep?" I said in a bubbly manner, which probably caught her off guard. I usually just tried to ignore her and get to my room as quick as possible. Trophy Wife would stop me and light me up for ten minutes. That was our routine. When she finished ranting, I would say, 'Okay, it won't happen again,' and with a little luck make it into my room and miss a full-blown lecture. I might follow up and flip her off from behind the door

    James M. Fisher

depending upon the intensity of the demeaning comments. Tonight was going to be different. That had to piss her off. This new strategy of actually trying to communicate was probably a shock.

"For real?" she said. "It's almost two in the morning. Some of us have to work tomorrow."

"I think all of us have to work tomorrow," I said. "One of us has school too."

"Do I have to treat you like a little boy, Mikey?" she said, imitating a two-year-old.

"Don't you ever call me that! You don't get to call me that, ever."

"I need to know where you are. This smart ass attitude of yours is going to get you nowhere."

"Look, I met up with some friends and hung out."

Trophy Wife stood up from the chair and began to walk toward the stairs that led from the formal dining room to the entryway where I stood. She started down step one and then two, her black silk nightgown hung on each step as she went. Her eyes stared me down. "Have you been drinking? You smell like smoke! You're going to ruin your life."

"What? I'm not drunk. I went to a party, and, yes there was drinking and smoking, but I was cool and careful. I left the party and met a girl afterwards."

"Where did you meet a girl at this time of night? Never mind, I know what type of girls are out this time of night."

"She's not like that. I met her at the gas station."

"At a gas station? Of course you did." She laughed in disgust. "You're making bad decisions. Who parties it up on a school night? You are smoking now, too?"

"You are so wrong here," I said.

"You are going to end up a bum on the street, chasing hookers, and who knows what else! You need to straighten up, and why don't you do something different with your hair? That punk thing doesn't fly here in Utah, and it didn't in California, for that matter. We moved here to get away from all that trouble and give you a new start."

"You and my hair. Look, I didn't need a new start. I was happy in Cali. Maybe I should go back," I said.

"And what, live on the street?" She turned her back and walked up the stairs. "You want to live in this house then you need to abide by our rules."

"You mean your rules," I said.

I walked downstairs to my room. My heart was beating fast. I was about to explode. Why was she saying these things? I was so pissed. I went into my bedroom, set my alarm, and fell asleep in my clothes. My last thought was, I am going to see Danielle in nine hours. Trophy Wife can kiss my ass.

Chapter 9

WHAT'S INSIDE A GIRL?

My alarm kicked and screamed like a lunatic bell—I pressed snooze only to hear it again eight minutes later. Trophy Wife's hurried little feet raced up and down the kitchen floor. She was doing her mad morning scramble which included: grabbing her oversized cup of green tea, and her egg thing in a croissant, and blazing out the front door to get to her six am yoga-aerobics class before work. I remained in bed until I heard the front door slam and her car start. Then I knew for sure she was on her way and out of my hair. No need to revisit the catastrophe that was last night. I jumped up and stepped into the shower. Danielle popped into my mind. I knew nothing about her. Would she actually show up? I was running late and had no time to do the full rooster spike job with my hair. I just let it drop down over the shaved sides of my head, ran some diluted white glue through it to spike it up. I was out the door with books in one hand and a jacket in the other.

I jumped in the truck, twisted the ignition and the Dead Kennedys blasted out the 6x9 speakers in the doors. Before I knew it, Harrison Boulevard was under my tires. I was in a great mood and sung my best version of Jello Biafra at the top of my lungs. That sinister voice of his was not easy to do. Jello had his finger on the pulse of the status quo, and certainly saw right through the illusion of the cookie-cutter-life inside the machine. I liked his views on censorship and the absurdity of the Vietnam War. Don't get me started.

I pulled into the front lot. A layer of ice had formed along the edge of the enormous duck pond in front of the school. Prismatic shards glistened as the sun's rays bounced off the water. It was going to be a beautiful day. A parking space in the front was available. I parked and ran up the stairs, passing the talkers who walked half the speed of those that were just trying to get to class. The crowd was less frenzied than yesterday and it was certainly not my first rodeo. I had gotten my first taste of college when I was still in high school. The opportunity had come along to attend Orange Coast College when I was a senior at Mother of God. It turned out, I had accumulated enough credits to graduate early from the full load of classes I had taken the previous three years at Mother of God. This was based on the California public school requirements. If only I had been given the choice to go to a public school like Los Alamitos or Pacifica in my Senior year. But that information wasn't shared at Mother of God. Thank you, faculty and administration.

Orange Coast was much more dignified than high school. No one cared to be involved with your every move. Nobody complained to you about your hair or what clothes were acceptable, and what classes you had to take. The focus was on learning but with much more freedom. I took computer programming and studied Fortran and Basic. Most of my credits transferred to Weber State without a hitch. However, in a short time, my new knowledge of computers would soon be obsolete.

I was still not sure this school thing was for me, but at least I was more relaxed about it than a lot of the students I had seen so far. After opening the door to the science building, I maneuvered through the dangerous double doors, inning and outing through the crowd. I arrived to the door of my lecture hall only to find a taped note that read, *Physics class is cancelled today. Read Chapters Three and Four by Thursday.* That was a bitch. I was really excited about that class, too. What was I supposed to do now? It certainly explained all the available parking.

Bored, I ended up wandering around the building. The lab and classroom doors closed in unison as I walked through the corridor. The murmurs of classes in session, the suction sound the door made as I exited the building put me right back behind the cage that was Mother of God. I was a floating spirit being pulled into a chasm, like being trapped in a lucid dream. The specter of the outcast I had been in high school was back. In that moment I tasted the loneliness, the grayness of fear and isolation of those early school years at Mother of God again. Not knowing my place in the world, trapped in a whirlpool of conflicting messages from everyone; teachers, parents, priests and nuns was maddening. The worst of it was the fear of not having anything to say and to go through life completely misunderstood.

But why? Why subject myself to that all over again?

My mind always did this crap to me, some sort of defense mechanism, I supposed. Maybe something else was calling me. The problem was, I didn't know its name.

I found myself at the entrance of the Newman Center, the gathering place for Catholic students on campus. Mass was held on a regular basis, according to the sign that was mounted near the door. I sat down on the wood slat and metal bench that was bolted to the concrete alongside the entry. I laughed to myself at the thought of Trophy Wife happening by, and seeing me sitting there. She would have probably thought I was in line for confession after last night. Not happening, not a chance. As I sat there, however, I heard someone sing the Our Father, a prayer that was made example by Christ himself on how we were to pray.

As a Catholic kid, I learned that prayer in second grade catechism class, along with the Hail Mary, and Glory Be. Let's not forget about the Act of Contrition.

I was impressed by the voice of the singer. She sang with such intensity and heart. Beautiful, like I'd heard the prayer for the first time—the way it was supposed to be understood. The blackness I'd just visited about high school dissipated as something peaceful moved through me, though I certainly wouldn't admit it to anyone. Real Mom would have said it was grace. The emotion reminded me of her. I sat in silence and meditation, staring off into the mountainside. In what seemed like five minutes later, the clock tower sounded with its Big Ben wannabe baritone. It was time to meet Danielle.

I stood up, fresh and revitalized. I had shaken off whatever blackness I'd felt. I walked quickly toward the science building; right, left, right, left, right, left. What if she sees me walking quickly like a dumbass? I slowed down and took a breath. Just relax, be cool. Now I was walking with too much awareness. Where did this stride come from? What's next? Sweaty palms? Sure enough, yeah, sweaty palms.

As I neared the meeting point, I realized I hadn't thought of what I was going to say or what tone I was going to use. No plan, no agenda: great! At least last night I'd had the event of her car breaking down, which made it easy to talk and flirt a little—because she was stranded, and in need.

     James M. Fisher

The reality of it just being the two of us last night made it easier. Today felt like the whole world was watching. The traffic between classes was backed up like the 405 freeway in Cali during rush hour.

No problem, talk about the obvious and ease into it, slowly, carefully. There's always the weather, gee you look nice, your hands are…Really, you're going to talk about her hands? Her eyes? No, even worse! I had nothing but panic.

Just be cool and let it be organic. Really? Organic? I was a mess. I turned the corner next to the library, and there she was, sitting on a bench, waiting for me. I felt really significant. Somebody was waiting for me. What a concept. She had on a pale blue angora sweater, tight blue jeans, and white tennis shoes. Her legs were crossed at the ankles. She was reading a thick book that rested on her lap. Her blonde hair was longer than I remembered. Two guys walked passed her and checked her out. Danielle was oblivious to their existence. She was beautiful, for sure, even more so in the light.

I needed to just go for it. Without hesitation, I walked right up to her like Mr. Confident.

"Hey, Danielle."

"Hey, Michael." She tilted her head back to look at me and smiled as I came closer. The sunlight was trapped in her hair.

"How was class?" I asked. An immediate need to swallow along with a mild surge of panic came over me. A huge blank page of nothing else to say parked itself inside my head.

"It was good. I have a lot of reading to do this term, that's for sure." She dog-eared the page and closed the book.

"How was physics?" She was totally focused on me. Her eyes didn't acknowledge anything around us. It was sublime and frightening at the same time.

"It was cancelled."

"Really? On the second day of class?"

People were looking at us as they walked by, trying to nose in.

I laughed. "Yeah, time doesn't matter much to physicists, apparently."

The blank page was starting to fill up. Talking with Danielle felt…I almost said organic, natural was the word.

"What did you do this whole time?" she asked. Something caught her eye over my shoulder.

I decided not to tell her about hanging out in front of the Newman Center listening to the Our Father.

"I just checked out the next couple chapters I have to read by the next class and…" Danielle's eyes left the conversation. She had missed everything I had just said.

Someone was coming up from behind. I turned my head. One of her friends coming to talk to her?

"Hey, Danielle, what's up?" Some Johnny-football-hero type was standing behind me with perfect hair, wearing a pink polo shirt, and tight designer jeans.

I'd been so wrong. A surge of a territorialism flooded my veins.

"Are you going to the fireside tonight, Danielle?" Johnny Football said, barging in on my time with her, flipping back his bangs.

"Rex, this is Michael."

Rex stopped for a second, gave me a brief nod, and turned his eyes onto Danielle—didn't say a word to me.

"I'm not sure what I'm doing," Danielle said, rolling her

eyes back to me.

Rex looked me up and down like he'd never seen a guy without a little pony on his shirt before.

"Who's this dude?" Rex had a bent look on his face.

"I told you, this is Michael," Danielle shook her head.

"What's going on, Rex?" I said.

He didn't seem sure what to say at this point. His chest turned towards me and began to ease into my space. I moved my chest and body forward. I thought, "This is so high school. Maybe I will get the chance to pummel some bullies from high school, just not my alma mater. This guy will do nicely."

Rex took a step back and said, "Maybe I'll see you there tonight, Danielle." He walked away, rolling his shoulders to engage his strut.

"Don't count on it," Danielle said, shaking her head again.

Good answer, I thought.

She stood and swooped up her bag in her hand. We were inches from each other. I took a step back as she pulled the strap over her shoulder. I caught an eye full as her clothes tightened and pressed against her slender body. Her tight sweater accentuated her breasts, and if another second would have gone by, she might have thought I was gawking at her. I couldn't help it: she was beautiful, and I'm talking by California standards.

"I'm sorry about that. He's a family friend." Danielle broke eye contact with me and looked the other way. Grandpa used to tell me that he could tell I was lying to him when I didn't look him in the eye while explaining myself. Like the time I stole one of his cigarettes. I was lying for sure. After that I look people straight in the eye when I'm lying to them. Why would she lie about Rex being a family friend?

My shoulders dropped, and I relaxed a little. I had to admit, I wanted to hurt that guy and not just because he was a stupid jock. I was in a new place, first time on the planet with this emotion. I didn't like feeling jealous or territorial and I certainly didn't like the way he looked at Danielle. I had a bad feeling about this guy.

"No worries," I said. "Would you like to go and get a coffee or something?"

"That'd be great," she said.

The corridors of the quad emptied and the classes resumed. It became mostly quiet for the walk back to my truck.

"You really are different, Michael," she said, smiling, looking at me, up and down.

"And, really tall too," she added.

That came off a little freakish. *Am I back in middle school?*

"Only a foot or so taller than you," I said. Compared to me, she seemed tiny, but she was actually fairly tall for a woman, like five-foot-five or six.

"I should probably wear heels around you," she giggled.

"You're very different from the girls back home," I said, with my "I'm so wise and been around" voice. I guided us down the path toward the parking lot.

"I think different is good, don't you?" I added.

Danielle stopped for a moment to adjust her book that was slipping. "I don't know, is it?"

We didn't elaborate on whether or not different was good. I looped into my own quandary. She aligned her books in the same direction under her arm. I couldn't help but notice how that sweater hugged her body. She smelled so good, sweet but subtle, like gardenias.

I was a step ahead of her and said in a John Wayne

voice, "Well, can I carry your books for you, little lady?" It was such a cornball thing to say, but she seemed to like it.

"No, I think I got this," she said, chuckling.

We walked down the concrete stairs, through the lot, and finally to my truck.

I let Danielle in first then went around to get in.

"This is nice. I didn't get a good look last night," she said, rubbing her hands on the leather interior, and giving it an approving smile. "It has a stick shift, too. No wonder you could get my car started last night."

"Okay, you caught me."

Her smile quickly changed when "It's a Holiday in Cambodia!" came blaring out of the speakers. If Jello Biafra's voice was water, we would have both been soaked. I quickly turned it down.

"What kind of music was that?" Her nose actually wrinkled as if the song had a bad smell.

"That's DK, one of the best bands around."

"It sounds dangerous and angry. I guess it goes with your clothes and your style," she said. She looked horrified.

"Hold on. I got other stuff."

"Do you have any Journey?" she asked.

I laughed in contempt and could have thrown up at the same time. "Journey?" So far it seemed that music might be the deal breaker for both of us.

"Yeah, you know, Journey or REO Speedwagon."

"I…I would like to just hear your voice right now. We can explore our musical tastes later." I didn't want to hear any more requests of music from the mainstream or the bubble gum generation. I didn't want to disappoint her either.

"You don't like Journey?" she said.

Here we go.

"It's not that. Those guys are talented." *Great, now I'm a spokesperson for Journey.* "I just don't relate to the music. It's not where I'm at right now. It doesn't describe my world or what I'm feeling or thinking. Punk dares to go there."

"Okay, that's fine." She said raising her voice an octave, almost condescending. "Like I said, you're different, cute in a dangerous way, and kind. That's why I decided to meet up with you."

The smile was back and she scooted in closer to me. I'm sure Journey had a song for that moment. Instead we had only silence.

So was different good or not? We never finished that conversation. I dropped it since the difference in musical tastes had worked out so well.

"Where are we going?" she said. She turned the knobs on the radio tuner.

"This little coffee place called Urban Grounds. It's downtown. I go there a lot."

"Okay," she said, staring out the window.

"Just What I Needed," by the Cars came on. I turned up the radio and Danielle sang along. I joined her. Dave and I had our own version. It was, "You're just what I needed, I needed someone to breed." I pronounced the 'L' carefully. No slip ups.

Danielle giggled. "You're pretty good."

I was into it and trying to impress her with my pitch control.

"Not too bad yourself, little lady." I said, John Wayning again.

"Are we on Twenty-Fifth Street?" she asked.

"Yeah, almost, it's right down here."

"Okay…" she said. She sounded vaguely disappointed.

The buildings were old, some in disrepair, some in outright dystopian ruin. Ogden was fixing up the street, and new businesses were moving in, but it had a long way to go.

I pulled around to the alley. The parking lot in the back had a few chuckholes. You could see the decades of wear and tear on the bricks in the walls of this old building. The aroma of fresh roasted coffee beans filled the air. You might assume that parts of the town was wrapped in old newspaper and left forgotten. Twenty-Fifth Street has its myths and secrets. I felt quite at home there.

"Is this place okay?" I said, parking and setting the brake.

"This is fine," Danielle said, but she looked tense. "I've never been here before. I was never allowed to come down here as a kid. They said it was dangerous…" She bent forward to look out the windshield. Her eyes widened and moved up and down and left to right, like she was looking for flying monkeys or something.

"The place has a certain vibe and it's mysterious. I feel right at home here," I said. "Seriously, it's fine. Let's go get a cup."

I ran around to her side of the truck and opened her door. She stepped down like a princess in a carriage onto the broken ground of the lot. As both feet landed, her eyes moved panoramically about the street. She smiled the way a child does the first time they see a Ferris wheel.

"The coffee's great and they roast their own beans. You don't see many places like this, especially not in Utah," I said.

I took a deep breath through my nose and smelled the wafting layers of fresh roasty goodness. We walked toward the front door. The entry was a beautiful glass door with a dark wooden frame. The letters of Urban Grounds were proudly displayed in gold leaf, black and white pin striping. I pushed the door open, bumping to life the dangling brass bell. Danielle entered first and reached for my hand. I was so excited to bring her to a place she'd never been. The aroma of the coffee and the intimacy of the dimly lit dining room were instantly inviting and calming. The high backs of the wooden booths were private, each slightly different. They seemed to have come out of an array of old diners or bars. The lighting was an eclectic group of chandeliers also from different places. They were carefully placed and set at different heights. Nothing matched but somehow it all worked. The candle shaped bulbs flickered and didn't match, either. Some were clear, some milky white, and a few yellow ones.

A deep voice with a Jamaican accent greeted us from behind a chalkboard. "Welcome to Urban Grounds. I be right wit you." A Rasta-looking fellow with a big smile came from behind the newly hung chalkboard, which displayed today's specials.

"Michael, how are you?" he said, with a smile only successful immigrants have.

"Good, Noel. How about you, brudda?" I said.

Noel came from behind the counter and gave me a hug. "Good to see you. And who is this beautiful ting?"

She was looking up into the tin ceiling not paying attention.

"This is Danielle," I said.

"I'm sorry. I've never seen a ceiling like this. It's beautiful," she said.

"It's okay. Nice to meet you, Danielle," Noel said. He held out his arms and gave her a hug like they were long lost friends.

"Nice to meet you too, Noel." Danielle was trapped inside Noel's woven pullover that smelled of patchouli and ganja. "I love your accent," she said, still muffled.

"Thank you. I love yours, Danielle."

Her head popped out and her face lit up when she discovered she had an accent.

"Okay, Noel can we talk coffee, bro?" I said. His hugs could last for days.

A couple of women walked in and were checking out the chalkboard.

"Yah, man," Noel said, releasing Danielle from the purple drape of his pull over.

"Jamaican Blue, Michael, large yes?"

"Absolutely," I said, turning toward Danielle.

"And for you Danielle, my little flower?" Noel asked.

"I don't really like coffee, but it smells wonderful," she said with a twisted expression, like a child who's just broken their mother's vase.

"Do you have any Journey?" I said, jokingly.

Noel stared at me as if I just erased the chalkboard in his mind.

"Just kidding," I said. I looked at Danielle who made an awful face at me like we were in first grade.

"I'm sorry but we didn't have coffee in my house growing up," she blurted.

"No worries," Noel said. "How about a nice hot chocolate with island vanilla?"

"That'd be great" Danielle said. Happiness swept over her face like velvet summer. We sat down in a corner booth. The vinyl cushions were diamond-tucked and brown like old leaves. The table was old and scratched like old 45's tossed around in an antique store. The stories the tables told with their etchings, carvings, and gouges. Some resembled the intrusive marks of battered whales.

Danielle ran her fingers along the wounds. "This place looks like it's stuck in time" she said, sipping her hot chocolate. Her eyes danced around like she was in a museum. The walls were brick and where the tin ceiling ended, heavy wood beam skeletons began.

"Yeah, it's a special place," I said. "During World War II GI's came here in droves. There are myths about what really went on then. Even before that there was prostitution, bootlegging, opium dens, and gambling like crazy. Chinese mobsters and members of the Tong worked, lived, and died above and below 25th Street."

Danielle's eyes fixed on mine. "I heard about tunnels under the street," she said.

"Yeah, that's part of the myth. Secret tunnels below the street ran from Union Station to the Ben Lomond Hotel. The basements below the bars could also be accessed from the tunnels so bootleggers and mobsters could get around. Drinkers and speakeasy-goers had a way to sample every vice imaginable."

I sipped my coffee. The ladies at the counter were quiet, as if eavesdropping on my story. I raised my voice, playing for the audience. "There was this woman, Dora Topham, but everyone called her Madame Belle London. She was the Dragon Lady and she ran a brothel on Electric Alley. Hookers operated just a few doors from here between 24th and 25th. Al Capone said, 'Twenty-Fifth Street's too wild for me,' after he got off the train at Union Station."

Danielle was wide eyed. "I lived here all my life and never heard half of that. How do you know so much about this place?" Her hot chocolate cup was pressed against her bottom lip, and ironically, the whipped cream swirl floating in her hot chocolate was in the shape of a question mark.

"No wonder I was told never to come here," she added.

"I come down here to think and walk around the train tracks. Some of the tavern owners, like over at the Kokomo, love talking about it. The owner is really nice. She showed me the door and the stairs that led to the basement under the bar." I grinned.

"Why would she show you that, and how did you get in there in the first place?"

I shrugged. "I applied for a job and she showed me around. I almost got it too, but I wasn't old enough. There is such a bizarre energy on this street. I asked the other people who work down here a lot of questions, too. The guys that own Junction City News down the block gave me all kinds of info. I went exploring and became intrigued by the place. One question led to another. I even talked to a couple of the bums a few weeks ago. They've been here since the hay-days."

"You talked to bums! Oh my heck," she said, and the "O" formed perfectly on her pretty little mouth. I laughed.

"Oh my heck?" I said. I was stunned. It was the politest form of swearing I'd ever heard.

"What do you want me to say?" she said. I could see I had kind of pissed her off.

"Nothing. I just have never heard anyone say that before." What a waste of words. If you want to swear, let it fucking rip.

She took a long drink, shifted, and eyed me as if determined to figure out some mystery. "So you were talking to bums. Weren't you worried about them pulling a knife or something?"

"No, not at all. Most of these guys just don't have a home and society turned their backs on them. They're just people who, for whatever reasons, have lost their way. I worked construction with quite a few of them in Cali, but they were mostly Vietnam vets. War can steal your soul. One of the guys I talked to here was a vet. He was pretty harmless and a little drunk, but he told me his story."

"You seem to be full of stories."

"Everybody and every place has one. It's what makes us all significant, I think. Do you wanna hear it?"

"Yeah, you're so bizarre. I wanna hear more. I love these stories," Danielle said, as she captured the curve of her whipped cream question mark with her tongue.

I motioned Noel to bring her another cup and a warm up for my coffee. He brought them in seconds.

"Here you are. You two enjoy." Noel winked at us as he left the table.

"Thanks, Noel," Danielle said, winking back.

"Okay, this guy's name was Jack. He was from a small town in Iowa. I can't remember the name. Like Danville or something. He was a kid when he went into the war, lied about his age, said he wanted to get outta of his shitty little town and away from his old man. All he could think of was this girl he met, about some promise he made to a girl he hardly knew. Without her face in his mind and the vision of their night together, he wouldn't have survived the war. He went on and on about that. She was kind and gentle. After all, he was only seventeen. This guy was going to war and was scared shitless." Danielle's eyes got big when I said 'shitless'. I didn't know the non-swearing Utah version.

"She was twenty-one or twenty-two, he said. He didn't have a girlfriend and no one at home would miss him. How sad is that, right?"

"Oh my heck, really sad." Danielle held her cup close to her lips while she listened.

"She was all he ever had, even though it was just one night. Jack had fallen ten stories in love with a hooker he barely knew who he'd met down here in a bar. She stayed with him the whole night without charging him extra. It sounded like she, at the very least, had sympathy for him. Anyway, GI's were pouring in that week. Jack said he felt lucky to have met her in the crowd."

"Go on. I hope it's a happy ending."

"The next morning, Jack had to board a train and go off to war. He promised to come back for her when the war was over. So off he goes and gets a chest full of medals and a leg full of lead. Anyway, Jack kept his promise and returned."

"What happened, did he find her?"

"He searched and searched for her. After months of searching hospitals, police stations, jails, he finally got his answer. A drunk off duty cop named Callahan told him that she was strangled by some maniac john, only two months before he returned. He said Callahan saw the look on his face and bought him a couple rounds."

"What? That's awful," Danielle said, eyes welling up, a renegade tear streamed her cheek.

"Oh my god, I'm so sorry. I know it's really sad. Imagine her anguish in those final moments, her will to live, snuffed out, and his disappointment of his dream; gone like gone. He wanted to save her and give her a new life, like he promised. He kept on drinking in that bar down the street where the Kokomo Club is now. Back then it was the Pioneer Tavern. He's never stopped chasing her ghost. Before he realized it, forty years went by. Whenever he gets his social security check, he bellies up to that very bar."

"That is the saddest story I've ever heard," Danielle said, wiping her eyes. "I'm so mad at you right now."

"Sorry, that's the most passionate story I've ever heard. After hearing Jack's story I dug into the past here even more. I even wrote a ballad about this place."

"Wait, what? You write songs and play an instrument or something?" she asked, sniffling.

"Yeah, I play guitar and sing a little. I've never told anyone I do that, until now."

"I feel special," she said, looking straight into my eyes. It was a mushy moment, cotton candy, and stuffed animals. She reached out for my hand. "What's the name of the song?"

"The Ballad of Twenty-Fifth Street."

"How does it start out?"

"You are putting me on the spot here."

"Oh, c'mon," she said.

"Okay." I felt a little shy, but after what Jack and his luckless ladylove had been through the threat of minor embarrassment didn't seem so bad. "I'll tell you the lines:

Trains used to blow through my old town,
pushing the snow like smashing a house of cards,
That train used to be my dream,
so it seemed, in my backyard,
No wishing well in my old town,
Pennies were just scrap to those old tracks,
Then you're off to war, and never coming back,
Hey, that's my back, my backyard,
This was the place where the GI's got off,
Looking for Belle,
On the corner block,
Looking for love, in the time of war,
You might not have your girl,
you might have found a whore,
Just inside, electric alley doors,

Hey, that's my back, my backyard,
Two five drive was my old street,
Two bits on the railroad track,
Then you're off to war, and never coming back,
Hey, that's my back, my backyard,

Danielle clung to every word. I was impressed. "That's the first few verses," I said.

"Wow, that's really good. How does it end?"

"Okay, um, the bridge is:

Dirt is free, a dusty brown
stacking up in that old town.
The dirt will remember the day Jesus came,
with a badge and another name.

"And the final verse is:

Sometimes at night, I hear a sound,
seeping from the cracks of that old town,
Though I'm a thousand miles away,
Hey, that's my back, my backyard.

I felt totally naked and discovered. What was I doing? It must be the caffeine in this Jamaican Blue. It's like truth serum. I had just blabbed away, out of control.

"That's it." I smiled, trying not to feel self-conscious as she stared at me.

"Michael, that's great. I don't know what you meant by 'the dirt is free' part. I was never good at deciphering poetry."

"Well, thanks, that means a lot. The dirt represents the ones that were trapped here after the war, like Jack. The rest of it is about the change that took place here after the Union Pacific Railroad no longer carried passengers."

"Oh, I get it," she said.

I avoided telling her the rest of the line was about the Mormons and their influence on the culture here. I also realized I hadn't asked any questions about her.

I'd never shared that stuff with anyone. I gave into her blue eyes that led to a place that gave me a glimpse of something genuine and true. I was all in at that moment. "So, what do you have planned for the rest of the day?" I said.

"Nothing really set in stone. I was going to the fireside tonight with some friends, but we could go together if you are up for it."

"Fireside sounds cool," I said.

"I told a couple girlfriends I was going to show up tonight. It's not the coolest thing in the world, but it's something to do."

"That's what Rex talked about earlier, right?" I said, with a slight tone in my voice.

"Yeah, it's a church-driven get together. They're pretty popular around here."

The hairs on my neck stood up like the extended palms of the SS.

Danielle kept talking, oblivious. "They are, like I said, not that cool but a way for people to get together and socialize."

The thought of Rex hitting on her drove me nuts. I didn't trust it. My gut was telling me it was going to be lame.

"Is this something you really want to do? We could blow that off and do our own thing," I said.

"I committed to my girlfriends that I would be there, but we could do something else."

She said it like she had mixed feelings, like she really did want to go. The last thing I wanted to do was to go to a church function. That meant any church, any function that

     James M. Fisher

had to do with a church. It also meant that I would have to call out sick for work. I'd always covered for the other flakes I worked with. My turn now. I still had time to work that out.

<hr>

THE THOUGHT OF THE MACHINE WENT THROUGH MY mind. Churches, military, and government are all part of the machine. Many churches preach that life here on Earth is a temporary misery pit. That we're selfish, unclean, scum-sucking sinners, and must come to the water, bow down, and give ten percent of our earnings to a righteous god, with a fist full of consequences, if you don't heed to the creed. Many believe we are being put to a test, and by passing it, the hereafter is going to reward believers with a special membership into a beautiful country club resort, full of like-minded individuals who passed the same test. Those who don't pass the test and the judgment will find themselves perhaps smoking cigarettes, while feeding a furnace fueled by their own flesh, for eternity. Constant burning forever. But our god is a loving god who cares about his children, believers would say, shortly after talking about their take on Heaven and Hell. I didn't know what god they believed in, but I'm sorry, even the most dysfunctional father would never allow his children to burn forever. Maybe an hour or two, but that would be it. So why worry? We're going to end up in the great country club in the sky when it is all over anyway.

Danielle was still talking about her girlfriends and why they go to firesides. That led me to another memory from my childhood, as if that cerebral rant wasn't enough.

I was eleven years old and had agreed to go to a Baptist revival meeting with a friend from school, Jeff. He invited me with the promise that it was going to be fun. I was bored and grounded when he asked. My parents gave me permission since it was a church function and told me to have fun. I had been grounded for toilet-papering a neighbor's house. I was sure Trophy Wife thought a revival was a fine idea, and that maybe I would stay out of trouble for five minutes. Jeff the Baptist's dad picked me up in the family station wagon full of people. Besides his Boy Scout leader dad, his sweet, soft-spoken mom, his sister and brother, there were a few other kids from the neighborhood packed into the car.

It was uncomfortable. It was a hot summer evening, and the car had no air conditioning. As we turned off my street, dread immediately took over. Everyone started singing "Onward Christian Soldiers" at the top of their lungs. They really got into it. The kid sitting next to me elbowed me in the side to start singing. I had no clue of the words, nor was I going to chime in with the rest of them. I elbowed back.

We finally arrived to the church, which was more like a big auditorium than a church. It was also packed. They started with music and reciting random bible verses. Every-one there had PHS—Parrot Head Syndrome. After saying how wrong the Catholics and the Jews were, the pastor signaled for the movie to start about the Rapture. I had never heard of such a thing.

They believed the Rapture was true and could happen at any moment. It sounded threatening, like the promise of a good horror flick. If you don't believe, then you will be left behind, was the theme. There was a stretch of film where a kid, who was the black sheep of the family, came home from school. He entered his house and nobody was home. He noticed right away there was steam coming out of a coffee cup, the newspaper was on the floor, water was running from the faucet with a glass broken in the sink, and the phone was dead. Hours went by with him running through the house calling for his parents. It was as if the entire family had vaporized, and had been taken immediately—whole-body—into Heaven by none other than the Lord Jesus Christ himself. This kid could not find his family anywhere. He had been left behind. The North and South Vietnamese survivors probably had a similar experience when over two million of their people disappeared during the war.

Any hoot, the kid ran down the street only to see his town burning with his sinner neighbors being rounded up, and taken to what looked like prison camps. They had the mark of 666 on their wrists and forehead. It scared the shit out of me, and it must have had the same effect on half the crowd in the church because they stormed the altar to accept Jesus into their hearts. Frenzy swept through the place.

I remembered how I felt watching those people getting suckered in because of a horror flick. It was hysteria with all the crying children and emotional parents.

"He's speaking in tongues!" someone cried.

"The Holy Spirit is with us!" someone else cried.

It sounded like gibberish coming from a guy standing behind me, mumbling and crying. I couldn't help but think about all the Jews and Catholics the preacher had just mentioned were wrong for what they believed. Immediately, a cartoon with a Bugs Bunny retort came flooding into my mind, "What a maroon." Ole Bugs said this describing those who acted like ignoramuses. He constantly mispronounced his own words.

I asked Jeff the Baptist if we could leave. He asked me if I wanted to go to the altar first.

"Heck no," I said.

"We are going to the cafeteria for cookies and punch after, and then we could leave," Jeff said.

I finally made it home and didn't sleep for a week after that. It felt eerie when I came home after school and had to wait for my parents to come home from work. When they were later than normal, I panicked a little. I found peace several days later when Jock Dad said we didn't believe in the Rapture. That was a Protestant belief. I was overjoyed.

A few days later, I was reading about Giordano Bruno in my encyclopedia. He was killed by the church we attended on Sunday. During the Inquisition, he was burned at the stake for a theory that supported a Copernican model about the Earth orbiting the Sun. I didn't dare grab the "I" volume for obvious reasons. New nightmares emerged.

I was ranting wildly in my head, while Danielle went on and on about going to this fireside thing. She was still talking about it. The thought of Rex hitting on her trumped my better judgment, even though I would rather play pool or anything else. Despite my misgivings, her green eyes and pouty coral lips got the best of me. I relented. She smiled like she had won a poker hand. I half smiled back at her like I captured a snake.

"Are you ready to go?" I asked.

"Yes, this was great," she said, sliding out from the table. "Thank you for bringing me here. I like this place a lot."

"Cool, I'm really glad." I helped her with her coat. Danielle took a final look at the tin ceiling. I grabbed her hand, and we made our way to the front.

"Later, Noel." I said. He was in the back checking in an order.

"Later, Michael. See you soon, Danielle!"

Danielle smiled, waved, and said goodbye. We exited out the door, sounding the clapper that dangled inside the little brass bell.

Chapter 10

WELCOME TO THE MACHINE

Winter rode in on a broomstick, across a half-naked sky. Heavy winds prevailed, clouds resembled tired gourds, remnants of an early Fall fell, leaving leaves along the streets scattered in odd clumps, their intense colors of fire trampled to death, old news. They seemed to have disappeared as soon as they hit the ground. October's end was near and it was only September, a dead ringer.

The air dipped into the thirties when I dropped Danielle off to get ready for the fireside. Toward the end, I found it harder to keep up my end of the conversation than earlier in the day. It had everything to do with going to this gathering tonight with this girl I was falling for. It was against my better judgment. I hated the idea that this event was going to infiltrate my time alone with her. The thought of going to another unknown church event made me shudder. I had a tight schedule, and my time was important to me. There was a lot going on with my part time jobs, tonight's shift had to get covered, not to mention school, songwriting, working out, and my guitar practice. I would take one for the team this time. Besides, how bad could it be?

     James M. Fisher

I got the spikes in my hair looking sharp. I wore the black leather Buzzcocks jacket that I had won playing pool against a sadistic skinhead punk in Long Beach a couple years ago. He didn't have the twenty bucks that he owed when he lost, so I took his jacket instead.

I jumped into the truck, cranked the ignition and backed out of the driveway.

"What You See" by Oingo Boingo, blared from my speakers on the way to Danielle's house. I was pumped up again to see her and could hardly wait. That smile and laugh, her blonde hair bouncing softly when she talked, a young angelic face, her body carefully fashioned by a god, and in all her brightness, I sensed some darkness, and I think I liked that most of all. It made attending a church event seem worth it.

I pulled into her driveway, got out, ran up to her door, and knocked. An attractive, older version of Danielle opened the door. She had a lit cigarette in her mouth, a beer in her hand, and she squinted her eyes like she was trying to figure out a puzzle.

"Hi. Is Danielle home?" I said.

"You must be Michael-from-California," she said, exhaling her smoke through the screen door.

"That's right. Are you Danielle's sister?"

"Her mom. I'm Nora," she said, with a side smile that nearly made her cigarette fall from her lips.

"Nice to meet you." I was confused. Mormons didn't smoke or drink, right? Either way, Nora seemed pretty cool.

"Nice to meet you, too. Come on in. I'll get her." Nora pushed the screen door open for me, turned and sipped her beer, and led me into the next room. The screen door rattled shut. Danielle and Nora really could have been sisters. Nora was really hot. Runs in the family in this case.

I heard Danielle moving around in the kitchen. She emerged, swinging her purse behind her hip and gave me a big smile, her eyebrows raised. She was wearing a floral pattern dress under a sweater complete with a white lace choker at the neck, knit tights, and kitten heel shoes.

"Is everything okay? You seem dressed up for a casual night by a bonfire," I said.

"I should've explained better; it's a more of a formal thing. Do I look okay?"

"You look great. The only thing that's missing is a spiked dog collar," I said.

From the look of surprise on Nora's face and shocked horror on Danielle's, I appeared to be alone in my humor.

"That's not funny, Michael. Let's get going." Danielle marched past me to the door.

Not funny? Oh well…

I opened the truck door and she hopped in. I backed out of the driveway and had the radio down low. Danielle was quiet, like she was preoccupied.

"Everything okay? You seem a little distant," I said.

"No, I'm okay," she said.

"Your mom's real nice."

"I hear that a lot," Danielle said, matter-of-factly.

"Is she Mormon?" I asked.

"She became a Jack Mormon ten years ago when we heard my dad was shot down in Vietnam. He was assumed dead."

"Oh, my God!" I said. "What's a 'Jack Mormon'?"

"Oh, it's a person who was a member of the church but no longer follows the faith."

"Sorry to interrupt, I'd just never understood the term before, go on."

"She thought he was dead and never coming back so she got a divorce. She met up with my step dad, who's not a Mormon, and returned to the person she was before she converted to the church. She only converted to the church so she could marry my dad. As the years went on she became unhappy in it and it affected their marriage, not to mention he was very critical of her. My dad was a fanatic about the church. You could imagine our surprise when my dad turned up alive in a POW camp. When he returned home and found out his wife hadn't waited for him and there was another man sleeping in his bed, he was…not happy."

"That's heavy," I said. "You've been through a lot."

"Yeah, I've adjusted, and my stepdad has been very good to us. They are separated right now. He still makes my mom laugh. My dad soon became a war hero and the church played on that. He ate it up and became very popular, and he wrote a book about it. It didn't take him long to find a Mormon wife either. My dad got remarried immediately, and now they live in Arizona. They had kids right away too. It's a little complicated."

"Wow, I guess."

We pulled into the campus.

"Where do we go from here? Where's the fire?" I asked.

Danielle laughed. "I've been trying to tell you: there is no fire. The fireside's in the church hall." She shook her head.

"Okay, no fire. Fine," I said.

What the hell am I getting myself into? This felt like a set up.

We got out, and walked through the cold. I was a little disappointed because a fire not only sounded good and romantic, but we could have possibly escaped unnoticed if this thing was a dud. We could have attended without feeling trapped or obligated. I like to have a backup plan.

Now we were going to be stuck inside a church. That sucked! I thought it was going to be casual and low key. I was trying to be open-minded, but the vibe was way off.

It got worse.

"Hey, Danielle, over here!" It was Rex with a couple missionary-looking boys with shiny black name tags on their jackets. They made their way through the crowd toward us. My jaw clenched. We were outside the church with a crowd of thirty or more people, hanging out.

"Hi, Rex. You remember Michael?" Danielle smiled politely and set her hand on my forearm. Good.

"Yeah," Rex said, looking me up and down.

I nodded, and said nothing. I looked at him like he was a putz. One of the two missionaries that walked up with Rex was 'Elder Chase Hanes', according to his nametag. He had glasses, short sandy blond hair, and an athletic build like he played basketball. He was my height. He walked behind me and I could feel his awkward presence. I turned to look at him over my shoulder.

"You can't wear that jacket in the church," Chase exclaimed.

"What a random thing to say, Chase. Why not?" I asked sarcastically.

"It's…" he lowered his voice, "pornographic."

"How can the name of a band be pornographic?" I said.

My back was now turned on Rex, Danielle, and the other missionary.

"Oh my heck! What are you wearing?" Rex asked, as if he had some authority.

Danielle was speechless. She must not have noticed the back of my jacket earlier. The disapproving look she gave made me think she was just as shocked as they were. She appeared to be on their side.

"You are definitely not wearing that in the church," Rex said.

"I don't know what your problem is. This is a band jacket. The band is an English band called the Buzzcocks. It's not pornographic. There are no pictures of anyone having sex on my jacket. Are you an idiot, Rex? Why are you so threatened by a jacket? Does the word 'cock' offend you? In English 'cock' refers to a young male, not a penis like you're being right now. What's your problem?" I stepped forward, moving in to his space.

"You're the problem, and you're not wearing that in here!" Rex said. He was six inches from my face. Rex and I were almost bumping chests.

"Here comes the bishop," said Danielle.

I turned around and looked for a red robe and pointy hat, or some version of that, but the man who came up to us was wearing a suit instead.

"How's it goin, Dr. Townsend?" I said. The bishop was my dentist? Go figure.

"Hi, Mr. Price. I'm surprised to see you here," Townsend said with a guarded smile.

We shook hands.

"Not as surprised as I am," I said. Danielle came up to my side and latched onto my arm, turning her back on Rex and the other two. Dr. Townsend started into the building.

"I'll see you all inside. Tell your folks I said, 'hi.'"

Rex grimaced like he had something to say, but the words took a detour and got lost. He stomped up the stairs and the other two missionaries followed as he walked toward the fluorescent glow of the doorway leading into the church.

"Later, Dr. Townsend," I called with a shit-eating grin on my face.

Danielle squeezed my arm and smiled. "You are full of surprises. None of us knew who the Buzzcocks were. I'm sorry about Rex."

"He just wants to get into your pants. I know the type."

Danielle blushed, and slapped me in the gut. "We are going into a church. I can't believe you just said that." She lowered her voice to a whisper.

I felt a cold presence as I crossed the threshold into the starkly lit entryway. I was expecting to walk into a version of a holy place like a mosque or a cathedral. Instead it was an auditorium, like where you would have a business meeting. No crosses, candles, or saintly pictures. No flowers or sacred scrolls, not one baptismal font, or statue. There were a few portraits of men in suits centered in the middle of the entryway wall. They looked like they could be Amway salesman or bankers. What kind of church was this?

The blinding fluorescent light buzzed overhead as the believers walked in and sat down on benches that resembled pews. No chance of sleeping or praying in this light. The place felt cold and vapid like a detention hall. Escaping unnoticed would be impossible as the whole congregation could see you. Two doors in and two doors out.

Danielle and I sat down three rows from the double door. Two missionaries pulled the metal doors shut. The doors latched like iron jaws and echoed throughout the room. Rex and his buddies sat two rows in front of us. Rex looked back and gave me a sneer, shook his mason jar shaped head and said, "Gentile" in some kind of twisted whisper, then he immediately turned around like he was hiding from the teacher.

I leaned forward with my elbows on the bench, nudging between two blonde girls, and in my own twisted whisper said, "Hey Rex, only my Jewish friends can call me that."

Rex said nothing.

Danielle tugged the "B" on the back of my jacket and pulled me back into the bench.

I smiled and whispered, "Sorry" to the two cute girls I had nudged between. They smiled back, and giggled. I rested my back on the bench and looked over at Danielle. She gave me a what-the-heck look. It was gone as quick as it surfaced. She poker-smiled and tried to bury a split-second look of displaced jealousy. In my head I was yelling, 'Yeah! She had a little jealous moment!' I poker smiled back and a rush of emotion moved between us. Danielle looked away into a space that was beyond the fluorescent lights, and back again. She slid closer to me, making contact, and at that moment half the lights in the room were turned off.

The bishop began to speak into a microphone, attached to a portable podium. His voice was low and slow. "Good evening. For those visiting and those whom I have not yet met, my name is Bishop Townsend. Over the last week I have felt a rumbling, a disturbing darkness, stirring in my heart. I have had an evil reveal itself to me that I must share with you tonight. But first, I ask all of you to bow your heads in prayer and ask our heavenly father to bless us and give us the ears to hear, and the heart to listen to this very important message."

There was a rustle as heads bowed. I kept peeking during the prayer.

"Heavenly Father, thank you for all who have come tonight. I pray we all embrace this message and take it into our minds and hearts, and I say these things in the name of Jesus Christ, amen."

The bishop paused after his amen, kept his head down as did everyone else. He seemed to dip deeper and deeper into some indulgent void.

"I am going to be sick," I thought. "The king of the parrots is about to go into a sermon."

Danielle was fixed on every word of Townsend's introduction and prayer, as was every single other person besides me. PHS! This was the worst case of Parrot Head Syndrome I had ever seen. There was a terrifying moment as if sound was being brutally murdered in my head, gasping and bleeding in the corners. I couldn't hear anything, not even breathing. I was beginning to hear my own heartbeat rise above the dead silence. Time felt stretched out like cosmic taffy. The bishop was still, head down, face pious. Everyone was motionless, frozen, like a snake before striking.

Finally, slowly, as if taking aim, Townsend's head rose up and in unison with him, the believers did the same. The bishop looked out to the congregation, panning left, and across the middle, and to the right, fixating on the room with his machine gun eyes.

What the fuck am I doing here?

I looked over at Danielle. She half smiled. When the bishop leaned into the microphone to speak, she was gone in his words like a retriever chasing a tennis ball.

"I received a revelation this week. I was contemplating a message by one of our past Presidents from over a decade ago. It was a theme that would not let go, that kept me up at night as though I was chosen to deliver this message again. He is speaking to us now. My brethren, we live in a wicked world. The time has come when the defilement of society has become so great that it has put undue pressure on this generation. It is hard to choose the right path and to distinguish the way of the light and the way of darkness."

"Here it comes," I thought. I felt a train roaring in from the distance and I was not alone. There were a few others twitching in their seats, looking around at the congregation like I was. The two girls in front of me locked eyes with each other.

"I feel the spirit already," the one on the right breathed.

"Me too," the other replied, pressing a hand to her chest.

I sat there thinking, "I let this guy put his hands in my mouth." They all saw a prophet delivering a message; I saw a dentist talking out his ass.

"The Devil is well organized. He has emissaries. Through his many agents, his satanic majesty has proclaimed his intentions to destroy one whole generation of our young people. The Devil-inspired destructive forces are present in our literature, in our art, in the movies, on the radio, in our dress, in our dances, on the TV screen, and even in our modern, so called popular music."

Rex turned around to sneer at me. I sneered back like Elvis—cocky and young Elvis, not fat old Elvis. Rex turned around, shaking his head. *What an ass hat.*

I could not help but think, "The train's getting closer and louder." I was not sure where the bishop was going, but his words were starting to make my jaw tighten.

Rex, of course, was quickly back, on the edge of his seat. Danielle was fixated on the tennis ball.

The bishop went on. "Satan uses many tools to destroy the home and our youth. The Devil's thrust is directed at you, the young, the future. I have a letter from a concerned father and teacher about the evil effects of popular music. 'Music creates atmosphere. Atmosphere creates environment. Environment influences behavior.' What are the mechanics of this behavior?" He paused to scan the congregation again like someone was going to raise their hand and answer him. When no one did, he went on. "Rhythm is the most physical element in music. It is the only element in music that can exist in bodily movement without benefit of sound. Loudness adds to muddling the mind. Sound magnified to the threshold of pain is of such physical violence as to block the higher processes of thought and reason. Turning the volume down does not remove the other evils. Repetition to the extreme is another primitive rock device. Gyrations, a twin to rock rhythm, are such that even clean hands and a pure heart cannot misinterpret their insinuations. Darkness and dimmed lights are facets of the rock scene."

He shook his head. "When your identity is lost in darkness, it's easy to tempt the spirit from the normal, moral behavior and responsibilities. Strobe lights split the darkness in blinding shafts like an interrogator's third degree or the swinging pendulum of the hypnotist who would control your behavior. Combined with the screaming obscenities of the lyrics, this mesmerizing music has borne the fruit of filth."

I was frozen. *This can't be happening. People are buying this crap?* I was amazed and shocked at the same time, feeling like I did when I read about Hitler's propaganda methods.

The bishop just ranted on. "Our religion is one of absolutes and cannot be mingled or watered down by relativistic philosophy. The Church must not compromise standards before popular demands. Surely tobacco, coffee, and alcohol users have been alienated by uncompromising standards as much as today's miniskirts have been by the Church. The rock music scene is a doorway, a trap for our youth. Rock music festivals are one of Satan's greatest successes…"

Who is this guy? Is this the fifties with Joe McCarthy in charge of the festivities? I want my MTV! The train was too close. The private recesses of my mind were on fire and quickly filling with smoke. I turned to Danielle, but her eyes were bright, fixed on the bishop—a dog slathering over its tennis ball. I reached over and grabbed her shoulder, moving her in towards me. I almost had to shake her, like she was in a trance.

I whispered, "Danielle, I can't listen to this anymore. I'm leaving."

She looked at me, "You can't. It'll embarrass me."

"Stay in your seat then. Nobody believes you're with me, anyway."

She had a frantic look on her face. I stood up, worked my way out of the pew, and into the aisle, headed toward the metal double doors.

The bishop stopped. I could hear the entire crowd turn around in their benches. I felt a thousand eyes on me. The Buzzcocks were now in everyone's mind with my back toward the hoard. A gasp swept through the room. The insane silence that had filled the room before was back. My hands were pressed softly on the bar of the door to make my exit as quiet as possible. Just before I pushed the bar, I heard the bishop breathe into the microphone.

"The thing about the truth is sometimes it's hard to hear, Mr. Price." Townsend's voice was low and slow again.

"Happy Halloween," popped into my head. I relaxed my shoulders, and turned around. I exhaled, zipped up my leather jacket and said in my own low and slow voice, "No, Mr. Townsend, these lies are hard to hear. I'm not drinking your Kool-Aid, Bishop."

I turned around, pushed the door open, and walked out

into the cold night air. I drank it in, sucking the chill into my lungs. The sky was clear. There was no moon, but the stars were almost obscene in their beauty. Before I could start thinking about what a serious mess the night had become and blowing it with Danielle, I heard the skipping, and chatter of high-heeled shoes kissing the pavement behind me.

"Dang it, Michael! Were you just going to leave me in there? You left total disarray in there. Everyone started talking over the bishop. Rex started to come over to me. The look on his face made me sick. Like he was coming to rescue me, hold me, comfort me, save me, from the mean and nasty Gentile wearing a black jacket. I'm not some pitiful little girl."

"Apparently not," I said. I couldn't help it. I broke into laughter—gut breaking, bone cracking laughter, partly because I was so happy to see her and at the same time I was on the verge of sinking into a black place, an emotional abyss of depression or some other unknown emotional void. I had felt it coming on when I thought I lost my chance with Danielle.

I saw the look of distress on her face and immediately went into an apology. "Listen, I'm sorry. I guess…"

"Why are you laughing? This isn't funny! You embarrassed me in front of my entire ward. The bishop just took the opportunity to run with your little stunt. He used you as an example of what the outside world was like. He even said you were an example of the Devil's handiwork and that you were under a spell and couldn't hear any of his truths or feel the presence of the spirit. That was when I walked out."

"I'm sorry for laughing. I'm just really happy to see you. I take music and art seriously. Townsend is a good dentist but a foolish holy man. He can thank Dante for his image of the Devil."

    James M. Fisher

"Who?" She sounded lost in the forest—crickets. "I wasn't ready for that speech, either you know. This was not the best idea for a date, at least this early in our relationship."

"We're having a relationship?"

"Well, something…" she said and crossed her arms over her chest.

I looked into her eyes and put my hands gently on her shoulders, pulled her close. For a moment she was stiff, then she relaxed against me, put her arms around my waist, and drew me in toward her. I could feel the shape of her body against mine. I squeezed her.

"You were quite the cowboy tonight." Her voice was muffled against my chest.

"What do you mean?"

"In all the years I've gone to church, I've never seen anyone leave in the middle of a bishop's talk. You basically called him a liar in front of the whole ward. That was so… so outlaw," she chuckled. A little darkness broke through her brightness.

"Yeah, well, I couldn't take it anymore. I probably should get a new dentist."

Danielle looked up and gave me the biggest smile of disbelief.

I grinned down at her. "You were pretty outlaw yourself, skipping out in heels."

"I'm sure I'm gonna to hear about it tomorrow." Her lips pert, eyes widened as she peered across the parking lot.

"Well, let's get outta here, little lady," I said.

"Whatever you want, cowboy."

Whatever I want? My mind ran wild. I went searching for a relative memory that wasn't there. I was writing it in the moment. My mind, my heart, and my lower extremities seemed to come to an agreement about what we'd all like to do with Danielle.

The church doors opened, the faithful pouring out like pressurized cheese from a can. Danielle and I looked at each other like a burglar alarm had just gone off. We had to escape the crime scene.

The next thing I knew we were running back to my truck, laughing all the way like juvenile delinquents. I opened her door and she hopped in and landed with precision. I went around the truck and slid in. I put the key in the ignition and fired up the engine, turned the music down. Danielle was tugging on her seatbelt, which was stuck. I slid over to assist her, reached across her to release it. She took a deep breath as my cheek lightly grazed hers. My hand fumbled to find its way to the stuck belt. I felt the warmth of her face and could smell the perfume in her hair. A profound silence came between us, the world around us was gone like gone. Our eyes met, and sent out an invitation. We slowly found a path that led to a soft kiss, my hand pressed her hip, and her hand was around my neck. She held me tightly. I don't remember breathing at all. I do remember my heart beating like a swinging sledgehammer. I thought she probably heard it. Other cars in the parking lot started up and roared away as if the anxious drivers wanted to escape after my confrontation with the dentist. Outside was a symphony of revs and flashing lights. Inside, Danielle and I were in our own space, a cloud made of glass and fog, hidden from passersby on their way to join the orchestra. I had completely forgotten about the seatbelt when I finally drew away from Danielle.

She smiled and half closed her eyes. "That was an outlaw kiss, Michael!" She relaxed her shoulders and settled catlike into the seat.

 James M. Fisher

"That was amazing," I said, shaking my head.

The windshield had fogged up and was beginning to sweat. I reached over to the dash and turned the fan on. We remained in the parking lot until all the other cars had gone. The fog on the windows danced away like a fading ghost. I leaned over and put my arm around Danielle. We watched the remaining trace of the phantom disappear with the burst of night air brought in by the fan. I didn't want to leave, but it was starting to get late, and the windows were now clear.

"It's a shame, but we should probably get going," I said.

"Yeah, probably, but it doesn't have to end here," she said.

"I like the sound of that. What do you have in mind?"

"Let's get something to drink and go back to my house."

"Sounds great. Should we stop at KarKwik?" I said.

She laughed and said, "Aren't you the romantic all of a sudden?" I teased her, then added a little more seriously, "This is all new to me."

"Oh right. I bet you said that to all of your California girlfriends."

"No, really," I said, with some shame.

Danielle had a puzzled look on her face. I backed up the truck, flipped the lights on, and began to drive out of the parking lot onto Harrison Boulevard. There was silence, her mind appeared to be turning over and over like her car the night we met. She seemed lost in deep thought.

I turned off Harrison, down 36th street to Washington, and the next right took us into the KarKwik drive thru. Danielle remained silent.

"Only one car ahead of us. This should be quick," I said.

I looked over, and Danielle half smiled at me. I interrupted her train of thought.

"What do you want to drink?" I said.

"Just a diet Coke," she said. A smile made way to her face.

We had to wait. The person in the car ahead of us must have brought a shopping list. The service window was packed with a case of beer, a carton of cigarettes, a gallon of milk. The attendant was stuffing a foil bag with chicken thighs and potato logs. The fried smell seemed to thicken the cold night air. All we wanted was a couple of Cokes.

"So, Michael, were you saying that you never have had a…?"

"Hey, look they're finally done," I said. I let my foot off the brake and eased up perfectly centered, in the take-out window. The know-it-all attendant from the night Danielle and I met was working. It was nice to see him get his butt handed to him by a busy flow of customers after his lack of decent service the last time.

He approached the window with his head down and said, "Welcome to KarKwik, what can I get you?" His words were garbled and swished around like he had marbles in his mouth.

"A large diet Coke and a large regular Coke with extra ice, please."

The cashier totaled up our drinks and handed them out to us; his eyes were that of a dog looking for a new home.

"How's it going tonight man?" I said, sincerely. I knew his pain well with my own job at 7-11. Understaffed and underpaid was a popular song most of us sang who worked at a convenience store counter. I was grateful for the job, at least. Being with Danielle made life painless and happy. I felt I could do anything. I was very much at ease in my own delirium as some of this felt like a dream. I looked in my rearview mirror and could see that four cars were behind us. The pain for Mr. Know-It-All was not going to relent anytime soon. His only response was a groan as he placed our drinks in the window and slid them forward.

"Two forty please," he said.

I gave him three dollars and told him to keep the change.

I handed the diet Coke to Danielle. She rested the drink on the edge of the seat and gently held it between her knees. I slipped mine into the cup holder.

"Mmmm, I'm so thirsty," she said, as she stabbed her straw through the lid and sucked down a few big gulps.

"I know, me too. We'll be floating soon," I said, as we guzzled. I pulled around the corner of the building and parked with the motor running.

"What are you doing?" she said with a sexy smirk.

I smiled and reached over to plant a kiss on her mouth. I could feel the m's vibrate on her lips as she gave a little moan. We made out for minute. She smiled and bit her lower lip when I pulled away. I lowered my voice and said, "Would you like a little rum in your drink?"

"Rum! Are you trying to get me drunk?"

"No, I just thought we would finish the night, toasting like the outlaws we are."

"I don't drink…but I will have a little taste. How'd you get a hold of a bottle of rum anyway?"

"Noel gave it to me. One day we were talking about where we came from and how different living here was compared to living near the ocean. I guess we bonded that day. I gave him my favorite Harbour Surfboards T-shirt from Seal Beach. He gave me this bottle of dark rum. He told me that several of his family worked for Appleton Rum Distillery in Jamaica. A few members of his family started working for Appleton in the late 1700's. Some of his ancestors had been enslaved by Christopher Columbus. Anyway, they brought him out a few bottles when they came to visit.

He said to save this one for a special occasion."

"I would say this is a special occasion. You and your stories Michael," she said as she lifted the cup and un-squeezed her knees. She popped the lid while I poured the rum into her bubbly froth. The ice hissed and crackled as the rum flooded in.

"I've never had dark rum before," she said, swirling her straw in the mix.

"I had a little taste to check it out a couple of weeks ago. I almost forgot it was under the seat." I removed my lid and poured myself a strong one. I figured it would taste better with a couple shots since the Coke was oversized. I snapped the lid back on and stabbed the straw through. I took a sip and I looked at Danielle. She was busy with her drink. She went from a thirst-quenching guzzle to a petite girly sip. I put the truck in gear and we were off, heading toward her house.

Danielle rested the drink between her legs, looked over to me, and asked, "So, were you saying before that this romantic stuff is all new to you?"

"Yeah." I must have had a look of panic on my face. I was catching every green light and we were getting close to her street.

"Does that mean you haven't had a girlfriend?"

"Oh, shit, here it comes," I thought. The inquisition, that uncomfortable talk of experience and past loves in our lives. The awkward rite of passage of the newly dating. I was sure I did not want to engage in that conversation, but I had to say something. It was going to come up sometime. I had a little rum hitting the bloodstream, so I jumped in.

"I had girlfriends, but no one special to go steady with. I was always busy with my friends. We surfed a lot and hung out. I never found anyone yet to slow down for. I'm only nineteen. Besides if it was just about getting laid, I could've made that happen. I'm looking for The One."

"The One, huh? Wow, you are definitely a romantic," Danielle said, taking in a few sips of her diet Coke and rum.

"Your street is coming up," I said.

The neighborhood was asleep. Most windows in the houses were dark and dim. We were the only ones on the road. The sky was clear and full of starlight. The moon was hiding behind the scenes. The shadows of the parkway trees were frozen on the wooden fences that divided the houses and properties, illuminated by carefully placed lights. We were a couple of houses away from Danielle's place.

"Just pull into the first driveway and let me out. I'll go in and make sure my mom is asleep. She usually has a few beers before bed and then she's out for the night. Just around the corner, up the hill is an empty lot. Park there and double back. Go through the side gate of my yard. The neighbors are pretty old and they turn in early so you should be able to get in the gate without being noticed. The den is in the basement and there is a sliding glass door where I'll meet you. Sound like a good plan?"

"Yeah," I said, "I think I got it." I was opening my door to come around, but she put a hand on my arm.

"Don't worry about walking me up to the door, I'll see you in a few minutes," she whispered, slipped out of the truck, and ran off to let herself in. The porch was dark. Her mom hadn't left the light on for her. It took her a few extra seconds to get the key into the door. I waited until she was in before I backed the truck out, went around the corner, and parked in front of the empty lot.

The empty lot was covered in scrub oak and buckthorn

bushes. Somebody had dumped an old water heater into the brush. There was a creepy looking oak tree in the middle of the lot. Its branches extended out like ancient arms. At one angle it looked as if the Big Dipper rested on one of them. In the distance, a dog barked.

I stepped out of the truck, grabbing the huge bottle of rum. It wasn't easy sliding it into the inside pocket of my jacket. I took my large Coke. The buzz of the rum rushed to my head as I stood up outside of the truck. The cold air was sharp when it hit my lungs. I was on a mission, sneaking around like a spy, or maybe a derelict, in my case. It felt like the first time I toilet-papered a house. The cops here would love to throw my punk ass in jail.

I rounded the corner. The streetlight was almost blinding against the dark pockets of the neighborhood. There was no place to hide until I could get to Danielle's gate. I heard a car coming. I could see the silhouette of the car at the end of the street: it was a cop! Just my luck. I put my drink down behind a bush and ran to Danielle's neighbor's house and jumped their fence. The fence was cedar and I caught a splinter in my right hand. The rum swished and tumbled in my pocket. The cop slowed down, shining a spotlight between two houses. I thought he saw me. Perhaps a nosy neighbor had seen me park and walk around the corner and had mistaken me for a prowler.

The adrenaline and the rum were becoming a volatile mix. I waited, thinking that at any minute the neighbor would come out and find me hiding. The minutes passed, the cop turned his light off and sped away as if he had an emergency. I wasn't going back for my Coke. I guessed that about twenty minutes had passed. Was Danielle worried by now? She must be thinking I had chickened out. I looked around to see if there was anyone. It seemed clear. I hopped over the neighbor's fence and ran across their lawn to Danielle's gate.

I looked around again to see if there was anyone or anything lurking about. I lifted the latch; it was stuck. I tugged the wooden gate from the bottom and it released the latch. I was in. A gravel trail led down the side of the house. Each step seemed to echo between the fence and the house. I might as well have been walking on potato chips. It was insane. How could I arrive without anyone hearing me? I inched along and could finally see a light in what I'd hoped was Danielle's bedroom. As I turned the corner of the house I saw the sliding glass door. It was dark inside, curtains closed. I approached the door slowly.

I could hear voices and bent down to get a closer look. It was still too dark to see between the curtains and the voices were coming from the next room about ten feet from the slider. Maybe that was Danielle's room. I edged along the patio. The light from the street lamp was, again, inescapable. My shadow danced along the wall of the house as if it was trying to expose me. There was a fire pit and outdoor furniture.

We could have had our own fireside here tonight!

I made it to what I believed to be Danielle's room. The drapery was closed, a vague glow of light shone through. Voices grew louder. I could hear Nora's loud bowling alley voice. She talked about the fun time she had out with her friends. I assumed that Danielle was also talking about her night. It was hard to understand her muffled voice. I was stuck outside, and started to freeze my ass off. Finally after ten more minutes or so, I heard, 'Goodnight, Mom," and "Goodnight, Danielle." After a moment, I tapped the window with my finger. No answer. The light went out in her room.

What the hell?

I started making my way back toward the sliding glass door. It was still dark and the curtains were closed. I was going to give up and begin making my way toward the gate when the curtains rippled slightly. Slowly the curtain widened enough for Danielle to peek through. She put a finger to her lips as if to shush me like I was in a library. I thought, "No shit, I know enough to not make noise right now." Danielle's blonde hair poked through as she carefully opened the sliding glass door without a sound.

"I'm so sorry. You must be freezing. Come in. I have some warm blankets over here."

I loved it when she whispered. It was hot. The whole situation was hot. She led me through the darkness to a large couch with blankets. I was shivering. She placed me on the couch and told me to take my shoes off. I did and I wrapped a blanket around myself.

"I'll be right back. My mom made some hot chocolate."

"Oh, that sounds great!" I said, as my eyes were slowly beginning to adjust to the dark room. I stretched out on the couch and tightened the blankets around. The cold, the adrenaline, the rum, and the holy-shit-what-have-I-just-done emotion were all competing for a front row seat in the theatre of my mind. I took a deep breath and smiled. I felt so alive. My eyes were adjusting to the darkness of the room. I could see portraits on the walls but not the faces. There was a TV in the corner, a small roll top desk, and a coffee table in front of the couch. The couch faced the sliding glass door. The curtains were half drawn, allowing some of the streetlight in. The silhouettes of lawn furniture outside on the patio looked like sleeping prehistoric animals. I could hear Danielle making her way down the stairs.

"Here you go," she whispered, handing me a mug of hot chocolate.

"Thanks, this is great," I whispered. I took off my jacket, pulled the rum out, and added a shot. I took a sip. It was the best hot chocolate I'd ever had. I could not get it down fast enough. Danielle curled up into the blankets with me and watched as I finished the hot chocolate. I started to feel really good and tried hard not to slurp. It was so quiet. I felt self-conscious every time I took a sip.

"How are you feeling now?" she said.

"Really good, how about you?" I said.

"Great. I had a fun night, despite how weird the fireside thing was. I have a little buzz from the rum and Coke. I finished it while I was talking with my mom. If she only knew."

"Would you be in trouble?" I whispered.

"If it was my dad, yes definitely; her not so much. What about your parents?"

"It would be intense for sure." I sat up a little. "Hey, you're wearing pajamas."

"It took you long enough to notice," she said with a smile.

"Sorry, I was too busy freezing to death."

"I think it's really great that you are waiting for The One." She studied me seriously. "So you haven't been with anyone, like slept with a girl?"

"I told you I was waiting for the right one and I meant it. Do you want me to say the 'V' word? I'm not ashamed."

"I think it's awesome."

"What about you?" I said.

"I'm waiting for the right one, too."

"Are you a 'V' like me?"

"Just like you." Her whispered reply was almost a purr.

I closed in, and searched for Danielle in the blankets. I

kicked the coffee table out toward the sliding glass door to untrap my legs and lie down next to her. She moved in closer to me and we began to kiss on the lips. I kissed her neck, and touched her lips with my fingers. I ran my hands over her silk pajamas. She wasn't wearing anything underneath. Her body was warm, sultry, in places more delicate and hidden.

I moved along her neck with my mouth and along the contours of her body with my hands. It was new territory and wonderful. She unbuttoned my shirt and slowly removed it, rubbing against me with her breasts. I unbuttoned her shirt, kissed her up and down her naked chest. I put my arms around her back and held her close, her warm breasts brushed against me. I could feel a part of myself begin to slip away. Her body felt unimaginable in my hands. The pajamas were lost in a sea of churning blankets. I had never been this close to a naked woman before. Touching her felt more natural than her touching me. She removed my belt, and unbuttoned my jeans. My blood pumped and I trembled uncontrollably, and kept going anyway. Every part of me wanted her. I rolled over on top of her nude body. The lamplight illuminated us. I couldn't drink enough of her in. We moved into danger.

"Michael, is this what you want?" she said. I wanted in, I wanted it all, we were ready, her legs tightened around my waist. Suddenly, my Catholic damage staggered in like Friar Tuck, mumbling mortal sin, mortal sin, and I hardly knew her. This wasn't how I had imagined it would be the first time.

"Absolutely, but maybe not now, maybe not this fast."

I had to slow the passion down. All I could think to do was hold her until our bodies calmed down. It was really late, and exhaustion was kicking in. We rocked ourselves back to Earth in a lovers clinch. It was too early in the journey to go any further. I wasn't sure how I stopped, I just did. She fell asleep in my arms. I let her down on the couch and covered her in blankets, and kissed her on the lips. I felt her smile when she slipped me an "m," and whispered a faint goodnight. I put my coat and shoes on and made for the door. Feeling passion drunk, but totally sober, I opened and closed the sliding glass door, moved toward the gate, glided over the gravel like a cat, and got back to my truck with my shadow behind me. The rum swished and bobbed like a hurricane in a bottle. The storm quelled in my hands as I tucked it carefully back under the seat. It was a surprise to see that the bottle was still nearly full. In minutes, the most beautiful images of Danielle danced in my head. I slipped into my own room through the basement window well without a sound, and arrived undetected…

Chapter 11

ORGASM ADDICT

Lightning splintered through the early evening summer sky, like branches from electric trees. It was so close you could smell the clouds burning. Each flash looked like cracked glass across a pane of purples and grays. I watched from the basement and counted to ten before the first rattle of thunder. The next count was to fifteen and the crescendo of its enormous cannon like boom, knocked the power out through Washington Terrace where Danielle lived. I imagined everyone in the neighborhood rushing to keep their kids and pets calm while looking frantically to find a flashlight that worked, somewhere in the belly of the kitchen junk drawer. At least, that was our story. Danielle jiggled and shook the kitchen drawer upstairs. I was watching the weather outside and tried to nudge open the locked roll top desk to see what secrets might be buried inside. I really had no business doing such a thing, but my curious side took over in an obsessive kind of way. I'd spent about a year seeing it always closed and locked and now I couldn't let it go. Was there a prize inside the Cracker Jack box that was this desk? The cloud cover made the room darker than usual, but a bit of grayish light found its way between the spaces in the curtains that hung on the sliding glass door. Danielle was still in the kitchen mining for a flashlight and candles. At any moment the storm could easily snuff out whatever light remained in the sky. Trophy Wife and Jock Dad had called an hour before and cancelled dinner with us due to the storm report on the local news. It was pouring down on the upper bench. They told us to stay put and not drive in the storm.

I stretched out on the couch and reminisced about our journey and the struggles we had early on. It was hard to believe Danielle and I had been quite the item for well over a year now. It felt like I had it all. In the beginning my grades dropped after we started having sex. Needless to say, I had become preoccupied. I also wanted to work and save money for whatever might happen in the future. The first three or four months, my appetite for lovemaking was over the top and had become my main priority over anything else, including my three jobs. I loved it, Danielle loved it.

Apart from sex, our relationship had moved very fast and reality arrived like an unwanted chaperone. Where was this going? We had fun together, watched movies and went out; but as things became serious, so did our conversations. The wedge between us was our beliefs, and the different cultures we'd grown up with. We couldn't have been more different.

It was Contextualism verses Literalism; the Vatican verses the Mormon Temple, punk verses pop music. By this point in my life, I was over religion. It was bad for humanity and a dangerous place for kids. I had no interest in joining what I suspected was a cult, either.

Unfortunately for me, this Mormon thing was important to Danielle and I cared for her deeply. The thing she knew about her church was her father's fanatical influence, and the peer pressure she'd had all her life. Her life seemed planned and arranged, which was great if she wanted to be a Stepford Wife.

At first, my impression was that the Church of Jesus Christ of Latter-Day Saints was just another watered-down version of Christianity that had trickled into another Protestant sect. No big deal. I had even considered getting married in Danielle's church at first, temple and all if that was what she wanted. Until I researched it. I picked up book after book including: *The Book of Mormon*, *The Pearl of Great Price*, *Doctrines and Covenants*, and *No Man Knows My History* by Fawn Brody, which was the most enlightening. I studied like I did when I was in my religion class at Mother of God; questioning everything, the science and historical facts, and the motive behind it all, seeking the truth. The more I read the more it became apparent to me that this was a cult devised by a couple charlatans to make money, have a little power, and get laid.

The doctrines seemed like a male-centric fantasy; secret society-ish, Masonic, a fraternity of sorts with secret handshakes, bizarre rituals, things that could only go on behind closed doors, constructed out of ignorance and then played off like the emperor's new clothes. I had no idea how messed up all this was, and my biggest concern was how to talk about these topics with Danielle. It was tough.

After the fourth month of dating, and things were going smooth, I caught Danielle in a lie. She told me she was covering a shift for another aerobics instructor who was sick and working late. I decided to show up around closing time at the spa where she worked and surprise her with hot chocolate from Urban Grounds. They told me she was off and they hadn't seen her. I gave the nice receptionist at the front desk the hot chocolate. I was a little perturbed and went home and did homework.

The next day Danielle called me. "Hey," she said.

"Hey," I said, dryly.

"So, they said you stopped by last night," she said, like she was creeping into a mysterious cave.

"Yeah, just thought I'd bring you a hot chocolate from Noel's, but you were off."

"Yeah, they didn't need me after all."

"I see." Silence bled out of my veins, converting into heat.

"Look, Michael, I met up with some friends and went to a Fireside."

"Really? That's pretty disappointing. Was Rex there?"

"No, he wasn't. You don't like going to them so I didn't want to tell you I was going. I just wanted to see my friends."

"We need to talk about this. Lying to me is not cool. I'm not keeping you from your friends. Maybe we should just slow down." That killed me to say, but what the fuck?

"I know. I'm sorry," she said, in her kitten voice. "Do you wanna come over?" she added.

"I do, and I really want to talk about this." Who was I kidding? Were we really going to talk or just have sex? I really wanted to have sex, even if I was still mad at her.

Oddly enough, when I arrived at Danielle's house, she guided me to the couch and we sat. We were really going to have a talk. I rolled with it.

"Hey," I said, giving her a hug.

"Hey, Michael," she said, smiling back with an extra squeeze around my waist. She looked sad, forlorn. "I'm really sorry about last night."

"Look, we need to talk about what we want in this relationship. It's moved really fast and I'm really falling for you, I gotta be honest," I said.

"I'm falling for you, too," she said. We both smiled, knowing the elephant in the room was something we couldn't outrun forever. It was scary, I assumed we both felt something for each other, and knew it could be crushed in a heartbeat.

"What do you want to be when you grow up Danielle?" I said, awkwardly trying to get the conversation moving.

"Oh, you know, have a family, a bunch of kids," she said, like giving a correct answer in class.

"What do you want for you?" I said. "What are your dreams?"

"I'm not sure," she said, really stumped.

"You are funny, talented, you supervise people in your job, you're smart. Don't you want to do something…more with your life?"

She shrugged, her words dammed.

"I bet most people want to have a family someday, kids and all that, but we can also have a life, too. Everyone should have their own authentic life, right?" I said, struggling to get to my point.

"Yeah, I'd really like that," she said. She didn't really seem to be getting my point.

"I know we've had different upbringings and the expectations that go with that, but we have choices, too." I said.

Danielle's eyes beamed.

"Mormons are groomed early in their childhood like Protestants, Catholics, Jews, and Muslims. It's all about family and tradition, which is wonderful and happy. But then there's this history you have to accept, with its atrocities against life—all done in the name of God. All the visions, miracles, myths, and tales are also in the stew for all walks of faith."

"Where are you going with this, Michael?" Danielle asked nervously.

"I've been doing my homework, trying to get to know your church, and it's a hard doctrine to follow. My question is, as a woman, what's in it for you?"

"I want to go to the Celestial Kingdom and live with my family forever," she said. "And what do you mean, 'as a woman'?"

"According to the doctrine, a woman's salvation is in the hands of her husband. He has to live a perfect life in the priesthood in order for his wife to get into the Celestial Kingdom. When you get married in the Temple, he's given a secret name that you're going to be called in the afterlife. In fact, he will summon you from the grave with it."

"Come on, where are you getting your facts? That's absurd," she said.

"It's in the doctrine. Don't you know this?" I said.

"So, your telling me that my salvation is determined by the life my future husband lives and I lie in my coffin until he calls me? And what's wrong with *my* name? How am I supposed to answer to some secret name if I don't even know what it is? This is so sexist! I'm calling my dad tomorrow." She was almost in tears.

"Danielle, I'm sorry. I thought you knew all this. Actually, I'm relieved that you didn't, cause it seems, well, crazy."

"Crazy" was clearly not the right word. Danielle's tears turned to a glare. "At least we didn't do the Spanish Inquisition," she said proudly, as if quoting her bishop.

"Fair point. No religion is perfect, which is why I'm pretty skeptical myself. Still, you gotta admit the blood atonement practice, the Mountain Meadows Massacre, and the whole thing about becoming gods on your own planet and practicing polygamy in order to populate your planet with spirit children is freaking weird, right?" I said.

"Oh my God, Michael, this is ridiculous. I will clear all this up with my dad," she said, red faced in shock, with the fear that these things might be true. I felt bad for her, but cults and religious institutions that pretend to be your friend with all the answers, and their hand in your wallet, are nothing more than a con, and manipulative to the core.

"Okay, fair enough. I'm only a gentile here. Let's talk some more tomorrow," I said.

"I will prove to you how wrong you are, I promise," she said.

"I want to be proven wrong more than you know. I care about you," I said, holding her hand.

The next day, I called her. She was upset and in tears. "My dad pretty much confirmed what you said was true."

"So?"

"So he was pissed I was upset and ashamed of what we believed, and above all, questioning the faith. He told me to go straight to the bishop with this. He said you twisted all these facts around and confused me. He also said you were a smooth talker, and the Devil has corrupted you."

"I'm sorry. He confirmed the facts because they are the facts. I looked into your church because it was important to you. I wanted to share that with you, but the Fireside we attended was revealing to me. I needed to know more about what I was getting into. I'm sorry about all this."

"It's okay. It's really okay. The church is not for me. I'm my own person. No man is going to rule my salvation, and no way in hell am I spending eternity watching my husband do a bunch of other women to populate *his* planet. That's the craziest thing I've ever heard. I'm so dumbfounded and pissed right now. Can you come over and take me out or something?"

"I'm on the way."

I was flying high. I'm sure her dad was raging mad that she had heard all this from me, a gentile punk, instead of some missionary boy who could have made it a pleasant fairytale and unicorn story. The fact I prompted her to ask questions and get answers must have really pushed his buttons. I didn't care. I was on a mission to save her. Danielle started attending church about one Sunday a month after that all went down, when she succumbed to pressure from her friends and her dad. After a few months, the religious conversations between Danielle and myself had tapered off. It was like we were reading a badly written fantasy comic book, or that we discovered a perverse map of a fun house designed by Ripley's Believe It or Not.

The innocent moments of childhood are probably the only period of time in our lives when we could witness the true virtues of faith and see them represented fully. That is what we really want and selectively, remember. We wanted Santa Claus, chocolate, Jesus, and warm fuzzy feelings. Then reality set in if we studied the history, the doctrines. It turned the tables on who we thought we were, and where we came from. With deeper knowledge, the Kool-Aid became harder to swallow.

I questioned everything about my childhood faith. I struggled with it, as I always had. The things we did in the name of God. Shame on us. The priests I talked to growing up always told me to keep asking questions and seek answers, unlike what Danielle's bishop told her. "Embrace the spirit," he would tell her. "Remember the promise of the Kingdom." The Force, Luke, remember the Force. Translation, exhaust all practical and rational forms of thinking then become a believer. The Felonious Baloneous detector, for Danielle and me, had gone off the Richter scale.

Unfortunately, my questions about my own church were never answered, which led to more questions. They were summed up as a mystery, like clever theories in quantum physics only less believable. I had my suspicions about Danielle being confused and still wanting to get married in the temple. Even with her newfound knowledge about her childhood church, there was a lot of pressure from her family, friends, and her fanatical dad.

Her best friend, Jan, an Ogden native who had been on the cheerleading squad with Danielle in high school, could sum up a good example of this. I couldn't get over the fact that she spoke like a valley girl from Hollywood Hills and had never been there.

On a trip to the grocery store, I ran into her in the cereal aisle. There were boxes of Count Chocula faced nicely behind her when she decided to unload on me. It was a funny moment considering how much she resembled the face on the boxes of cereal. She could be the daughter of the Count, I thought. Despite the humor of the moment, I ran right into a trap of her lecture. I could relate to her angst and rebellion but not the cause or the reason. She was simply a twit.

"Ya know you're screwing with Danielle's chances of getting married in the temple," Jan said, without so much as a "Hey, how you doin'?" first.

"Ya know, it's none of your business, and is that really a bad thing, Jan?" I said, mocking her valley girl accent.

"You don't have to be so rude," she said.

"I care about Danielle and what makes her happy, not what you have to say. Let her figure things out for herself."

"Whatever, Michael, you just don't get it."

Jan walked away with her Fruit Loops in hand. What a maroon. We weren't even engaged yet. I assumed the topic of her ending up with me had come up.

Things with Danielle and me moved faster. As a few more months passed, she seemed more secure in her own skin. The more time we spent together, the more I fell for her.

A storm rattled the windows at Danielle's house, the rain hit so hard it sounded like birds hitting the clear panes, *thump, thump, thump, thump.* Her mom was out of town. Fortunately for us, Trophy Wife and Jock Dad had cancelled our plans for the night. If they only knew what we had in mind for the evening. I had a whole new appreciation for hunkering down for a storm.

"I found it!" yelled Danielle from the upstairs as the sound of a hammer and nails hit the floor.

"Great! Are you okay up there?" I asked.

"I'm fine, I'll be right there," she said. I heard the sound of various tools, perhaps box end wrenches, a pair of pliers, and maybe, just a guess, a tape measure hitting the floor.

"Are you sure you're okay?"

"Yeah," she said, slamming and cramming the drawer back into place.

In my leisure on the couch, my eye caught a small object hanging on a string attached to the underbelly of the roll top desk. I leaned forward: it was a tiny key. My curiosity flared as I could not help but become slightly obsessed with what was underneath that roll top. Why was there a hidden key? Danielle would lean against the desk, talk around it, and never acknowledged that it was there. It was an unspoken mystery between us.

I heard her speedy footsteps on the stairs. The beam of her flashlight bounced along the wall with each step. As soon as she came over to me, I forgot all about the mysterious roll top desk. I grabbed her by the waist and scooped her up into my arms and laid her out on the couch. The flashlight flew from her hand, the beam staggering along the walls and ceiling like a drunken buckyball. It bounced off the couch cushion and rolled under a chair. When it came to a stop, the beam went out.

"What are you going to do now?" Danielle said, in an overly sweet baby doll voice.

"I'm going to remove your clothes." I moved on top of her with a knee on either side of her hips. She smiled and bit her lip at the same time. I slowly began twisting the buttons on her shirt as she reached up and undid mine. The second the buttons were undone; the rest of our clothes became airborne. We went at it like beasts. I was on top, she was top, we were on the floor, then back on the couch, changing positions, inning and outing, pulling and sucking, lifting and twisting, the moans, the sighs, the sweat, the locking hands and letting go, the loss of reality, like two serpents devouring a strawberry. Then the release, exuberance, a soft flop, leaves falling from a tree, resting on the ground, we became still, a quiet simmer.

A quilt hung along the top of the couch. I pulled it over us. Danielle's grandmother had made it. The stitching read, "Families Are Forever." We fell asleep like a pair of spoons inside the hand of the oversized couch.

     James M. Fisher

My sleep was interrupted. My imagination drifted in, like a dream you are partially awake for. Outside the thunder cracked like an orchestra of bullwhips. It rained buckets of cats and dogs. The sky caught fire. The streets disappeared; cars were up to their exhaust pipes in some watery concoction from the gutters that spewed everything that lined the stomach of the city. Street lamps flickered like lanterns in a mineshaft. I floated above us and saw us lying together on the couch. I closed my eyes. We slept through it all, and escaped into the deep recesses of our own private ocean.

Several hours later, I felt Danielle move around, and abruptly sat up.

"What time is it?" I asked.

"I'm not sure. I'm gonna get a shower and some food, though," she said, groggily.

"I'm with you on that one," I said, stretching and yawning. "That was certainly the best nap I've ever had."

"You seem really proud of yourself," she said, sarcastically, as she attempted to find her bra in the layers of our discarded clothes. I was enjoying the view as she hunted and gathered.

"Why, yes, little lady, mighty proud," I said. I set back on the couch with her grandma's quilt between my legs and thought, "Man, I could do this forever." I felt on top of the world. I was so in love with Danielle.

"You were pretty awesome, and that was amazing," she said, kissing me with her lips and tongue on my cheek.

"I'm sorry, I didn't quite hear you." I tried to hold on to my serious voice.

"I'm inches away from you, I think you heard me," she said, smiling and turning in the direction of the stairs, with a bundle of clothes wadded in her hands. "For a person who was new to sex and a recent virgin, you sure know your way around a woman's body."

"I just love you, I guess. I've had a lot of practice, too, this year."

"No, you actually know what a clitoris is. I'm astonished that's all."

"I grew up in California when the sexual revolution was on. Women were burning their bras and discovering themselves. Everyone was talking about the clitoris including my friends, like it was a secret gem recently found in a pyramid. I'm glad I was finally introduced."

"Oh, my heck, Michael, you didn't just say that?"

I chuckled. She blushed.

"My stepmom had a book called *The Joy of Sex* hidden in her nightstand. I was a curious nerd with books, read everything I could about sex. I was shocked to find out how many women didn't know about their own orgasms. Some actually thought they needed a man for that. Okay, I did a paper on it for my Human Sexuality class too, I confess. It ended with the understanding that women have been horribly mistreated, things still need to change, and men kind of suck. Not exactly in those words."

"I just never knew anybody that knew what to…" Danielle paused, like she wanted to start over.

"Knew what to…?" I said.

"Never mind. Anybody who knew so much. I'm just impressed with you, that's all," she said hurriedly.

"I just know I love you. That's what makes it all work. That's the connection, and the real secret here."

Her butt dimpled as she took to the stairs and stopped. "Are you showering with me or what?"

"I'm right behind you," I said, holding myself like the

Devil with a pitchfork.

"Be careful with that thing." She winked.

I showed up late the next morning at my house. I told Trophy Wife and Jock Dad that I had just got off the graveyard shift at 7-11. They bought it.

Things escalated with Danielle. My life was hitting a huge crossroads and the only person I could think of sharing all this with was Dave. He was always in the background of my mind, taking a backseat in the circus that was my life. He was there like comfort and security, just a phone call away. Or so I thought.

I had called his mom several times over the last year and a half. She was really distant and curt with me like she had taken up drinking or narcotics or something. We were approaching two years since Dave and I had last surfed. It was completely absurd, since up until I moved we had talked everyday. Was moving a deal breaker, a cut of the cord? Confusion bled.

About noon, I called Dave's house again.

"Stark residence." His mom's voice was impatient, all business, sad.

"Hi, Mrs. Stark, this is Michael. I'm still trying to get in touch with Dave."

"Michael," she said my name as if it tasted bad. "Dave has moved and I don't have his new number. I told you before."

"You don't know how to reach him? You're his mom and-"

Silence, white noise, held underwater, churning bubbles, still, clear water, quiet.

"There has to be something you're not telling me. Something is wrong. Are you okay, Mrs. Stark? Hello?"

"I'll let Dave know you called when I see him."

Click.

What the fuck? She hung up on me. I called back, and got a dial tone.

I grabbed a paper and pen.

Dave,

Where the fuck are you? I called several times. I'm sorry I moved away, but really, no callbacks? Is Trophy Wife not telling me that you called? That would be her style, but I just called your mom. Bro, she's out of it, man!

She acts like I'm a pain in the ass or something. She won't give me your number, says she doesn't know how to reach you and you don't have a phone…Really? I'm sending this note to your mom's house and hoping she gets it to you. I'm hoping you guys are just going through something. I've saved some money and I'll come visit at some point.

I never thought I would have to write you. I thought we would always be at least a phone call away. I really could use a phone call right now.

Anyways, here's what's up with me:

Utah is a trip. You and I have got to hang in SLC and check out the underground punk scene. Not as cool as LA with Henry Rollins and John Doe dropping in when you least expect it, but it's cool. Ogden has hardly any scene at all but they party hard. Dana would love it here. You just have to turn your watch back fifty years if you decide to come out. You have to have a membership to get in to bars and you have to buy liquor from a state liquor store. Lame!

I can't believe we haven't talked. Time flies when you're getting your ass kicked with school and work and chicks. That's my story right now. You know how you always gave me hell all the time about never getting laid and looking for The One? Well, it happened. Her name is Danielle. She's a student at Weber State. Are you at SC or Poly?

Don't laugh, but Danielle was a cheerleader in high school. I can hear you laughing, bro. She's blonde, drop dead gorgeous, and works as an aerobics instructor. She's not the type of a girl I would have dated back at Our Mother of God. She's not like the girls we knew. She's really kind, fun, smart, and has a great laugh.

She's not into drinking though, but likes my company and to top it off she was waiting for The One, too. Yeah, I said it, was. Not that I could give a damn about being in the "I got laid club." Being with someone you really care about and in love with matters. I don't care what you say: I think it's better. Sex is the most awesome thing. I have a whole new respect for women and their amazing bodies now.

This last year, my grades have dropped, partly because I wonder why I'm even there. Eventually I want to go on the road and play music, but sex has clouded my entire life. I can hardly function. All I want to do is have sex with her. How were you so cool about it all the time? I'm a freak show! Haha. All I can see is her. I'm hoping someday I can be as cool as you are about it.

Now for the big news, I'm looking for a ring. After this last year, it seems like the right move. My parents got married when they were twenty. Is this my Catholic damage surfacing? You would know. Dammit, I wish we were talking right now. I have no one to talk this over with. Am I rushing this?

Moving on. Remember all the crazy talks we used to have about science, philosophy and how religion and quantum physics should have a baby and all that? This reminded me of you and the tangents we would get on. This would have been a classic. Anyway, I ran into one of my physics professors at this coffee shop and decided to ask him about this weird watch he has with no hands while we were standing in line.

He said, "The watch without a face represents the things we don't see (microscopic world) and also to not get too attached to the things we do see (macroscopic world). The wearer represents the observer himself, which is a quantum system that also reacts to other quantum systems with different possible versions when seeing a particle or object in different positions. I apply the idea to my own life. These different versions exist concurrently in different parallel universes. So, when these quantum systems interact, the wave function does not collapse but splits into many alternative versions of reality, all of which are equally real. It's a silly reminder that life is truly special and the secrets held within are on the verge of being decoded. Isn't it great to be alive?" Remember that time Father Bernacki rolled a steel ball on the podium during his sermon? It hit the floor and echoed through the church. The whole student body was dead silent. In his monotone voice he said, "Gravity invisible, God invisible, isn't it great to be alive?"

We laughed hysterically and nearly got kicked out of mass. Fun times.

I know what you're thinking, and yes, I smoked a little before writing that. I knew there was going to be some super-cheesy moment at the end of his Many Worlds Theory love story. But what also grabs me here is that I am not seeing the whole picture and we are living in two different universes right now. Two separate realities. I imagined our lives in the moment and at the same time in the unknown, drifting, awaiting entanglement.

I live in a different place now, with strangers really, where I now get laid, the surroundings and geography are alien, and in another universe there we are, going to college together and surfing our brains out.

I miss you, bro, and our adventures. Nobody knows me like you do. I feel transparent at times. Danielle is different, and I have my concerns about her and all this. I feel this other voice inside my head that is really on the defensive and it feels like a warning, self-protection or something. You would kick my ass right now and say something nuts to pull me out of this weird funk. I haven't told you everything, either. I'm still living at home but I'm moving out soon. Trophy Wife is still a she-devil and I can't stand it here anymore. Besides, I want to be able to have my own place and come and go as I please.

About Danielle, she is a Mormon. I did some research on what I was getting myself into. Remember how much I questioned Sister Anne Therese about Catholicism? Well, bro, Mormonism is a crazy piece of work and it creeps me out. I actually went to their church to learn more. Its secretive, women are objectified, blacks couldn't enter the priesthood until a few years ago, and most Mormons have no idea what they believe, what their doctrine says and how absolutely impossible the history in the Book of Mormon is.

Your eyes are really big right now aren't they? After I showed Danielle the things I learned, she stopped going to church every Sunday. Her friends tell her I'm the Devil, but she doesn't seem to care, so maybe the church thing between us won't be a problem.

I'm rambling. There's so much to catch up on. We got to meet up soon. Please call me. Your mom has all my info.

Love you man,

Mikey

THE KKK TOOK MY
BABY AWAY

The V-Twin motor of my bike was opened up like a skull being prepared for brain surgery. Gaskets, bolts, wires, cylinder heads, pushrods, flanges, seals were laid out next to the body. The headlight and taillight were off to the side by the battery and wiring harness. The wheels were off and the frame stood up in the corner on its own like a monk kneeling in prayer. I had many more parts to purchase before final assembly. The bike looked like an art project by Picasso. The money I had saved to refurbish and finish it was now in the palm of my hand in the form of an engagement ring. This was no promise ring. This was big league serious. I had to put up with a lot of crap in my jobs to be able to do this.

The ring sparkled wildly in the spotlight in the jewelry store. My wife would always have the best. Jock Dad, however, was going to be pissed when he finds out that it would take another year before I could afford to put the bike back together. He was forced to park out in the snow, with Trophy Wife's car taking up the rest of the garage. Maybe he would understand. Maybe not. More than likely, not. Trophy Wife would have some opinion about it.

I couldn't waste my time worrying about things that were out of my control anyway. As I pulled out of the jeweler's parking lot I felt really scattered. I was somewhere else as I moved into traffic. The music was off and doubt moved into my mind like dark clouds with teeth. I couldn't help it.

We had made love so many times, but never in Danielle's bedroom, never on her bed. Always on that couch and once in a while in my room when the parents were away. I was always the one sneaking into her basement late at night. I was about to ask her to marry me and yet I'd never seen her bedroom. She had never taken me in there, always too embarrassed because it was 'an incredible mess.'

Plus, that roll top desk was always locked. Danielle had never opened it around me. She leaned against it, talked around it, but never opened it. She had seemed really comfortable about having sex with me that first time, too. I was scared to death. Surfing double overhead waves never made me feel as scared as I had been that first night. I trembled afterward. I was so nervous, but Danielle appeared anxious and ready. She guided me in like an air traffic controller. I must have been naïve or something.

My own preoccupation with those details played on through my head in a never-ending loop. This was not how I imagined I would feel, but at the same time I had never done this before. In surfing, hesitation can get you killed or pound you into a reef. I was hesitating and not going for it like I should. I need to be "all in." I was manufacturing my own fear. Perhaps.

Tonight was the night. I was asking Danielle to marry me. I had it all planned out. I called Noel at Urban Grounds and set up the details. It was fitting to ask her there versus all the other places we had gone. That obscure little cafe was definitely special to us. Noel had become a good friend since I had moved to Utah, and tonight he was in on every detail. His place had really caught on and business was good. He prepared a special petit coconut cake for Danielle that he would later drizzle with a creamy rum sauce. The ring was hidden carefully in the center.

I told Danielle a little white lie to set the night up. I told her that Noel wanted us to come by and try out some new coffees and desserts he was considering to add to the menu. She obliged since it had been a couple weeks since we had stopped in. We entered and Noel popped out of the back as soon as he heard the little brass bell clank the glass when the door swung open. The place was empty, but he must have been busy just before we arrived because most of the tables were dirty and needed attention.

"Hi Michael, and hello, Danielle," he said giving her his usual over the top hug. Her head disappeared as his dreadlocks poured over her.

"Would you two like to sample my new Kona coffee? And I have a new hot caramel with dark chocolate for you to try, Danielle."

"Sure, I love caramel," she said.

"Kona it is, brudda. Thanks, man," I said.

Noel headed behind the counter and returned in a minute with our drinks. As he passed me he whispered, "For the nerves," and smiled his big island smile. After my first sip, I realized what he meant. My coffee had a huge shot of coconut rum in it. Probably a good idea. I winked back at him and raised my cup when he caught me taking a sip. He reciprocated with a thumbs up.

Danielle and I talked about school and work, and she laughed at my off-humor. About half way through our drinks, Noel brought out his homemade dessert. He sat it down in front of Danielle.

"What is this?" she said.

"A very special surprise just for you," Noel said, with his accent turned up to island overload. The sound of his voice could have come out of a coconut syrup bottle. It was so sweet, he almost gave the night away.

"You two enjoy." Noel danced off to the beat of Peter Tosh singing, "Legalize It" through the speakers in the background. He slipped behind the wooden saloon style doors into the kitchen.

"You can have the first bite," I said.

"No, go ahead. I'm not sure I like coconut," Danielle said.

"Really?" I thought, "The most romantic moment of my life and she says, 'I'm not sure I like coconut.' Ah fuck my life!" I wanted this moment to be harmonious and smooth and perfect. Instead, it felt awkward like a freshman dance. My mind went spinning, like an investigator desperately searching for clues as he reviews the evidence, or a shark smelling blood in the water. The dark clouds with teeth were swirling again. The evidence built: the damn locked roll top desk, the fact I've never seen her bedroom, the elephant in my gut.

I felt like I had gambled my heart, my soul, at that moment. I was too honest about my virginity. Why had I even brought that up? Was she really The One? Was I just naive or a sucker? All this inner emotion moved in over a bite of coconut cake. I was losing it. Not only was this plan a flop but…And then I'd had enough with the doubts.

I took a deep breath and blurted out, "It has rum in it and Noel is watching from the kitchen. Do it for him. He made it special for you. For God's sake, take a bite!"

        JAMES M. FISHER

"Okay, already, just a bite," she said, as if I was selling her a used car or encyclopedias. She planted her fork through the middle of this beautiful little cake and felt something solid the first time through. She angled the fork to cut a triangle shaped piece. As she slid the pie shaped piece with her fork, a gold shoulder of the ring became exposed.

"There's something inside of this cake!" she said, amazed and confused.

No shit, you are a genius.

I needed to calm down. I was overthinking everything. I was being too critical. I sipped my coffee. The warmth of the coconut rum channeled down the back of my throat. The clouds with the teeth began to dissipate. I watched Danielle work the fork gently. She picked the ring up delicately with her fingers. She brushed the cake and a morsel of shredded coconut off the ring, exposing the diamond solitaire. It shone like fire even under the dimly lit bulbs of the cafe.

"Oh my heck!" she said, looking into my eyes.

I reached for her hand that was holding the ring. I placed both my hands over hers and said, "Will you marry me, Danielle?"

I'd said it. After my mini panic attack, I'd said it. Her face was in total shock. Her eyes were wide as moon rims on an old Ford, and it seemed she lost the ability to swallow.

"I...I don't know what to say," she said.

The truth scattered into fragments, increasing in every second she hesitated.

"Yeah, you do," I said, as I sat back a little and tried to relax.

Another minute passed as the color came back into her face. "You're right. Yes. Yes!" she said, with a big smile, covering her mouth with her right hand. I took the ring and slid it on her finger.

"It fits. How did you know the size?"

"Your mom helped me with that one," I said.

"That's surprising. She usually can't keep a secret," Danielle said and nodded, agreeing with herself.

Noel came by with his congratulations and hugged Danielle again; she nearly drowned inside his woven pull over and patchouli scented dreadlocks. He gave me his nod of approval. His smile was as wide as the Caribbean, exposing his gold-capped canine.

"I'm so happy for you two," he said, in a slight hurry as several customers came walking in. His sweetness went from sugar syrup to a rich caramel. He was truly the warmest and most genuine human being I'd ever met. I think he was happier than the two of us combined. He made the entire night very special.

"Here. I'll go rinse that off for you," I said and Danielle handed me the ring. I ran to the back sink and washed it off. I caught myself in the mirror. I saw uncertainty and a strange look on my face. I almost didn't recognize myself. It was fear again, but now I saw it. Okay, she said yes, and that should have been enough for me. It was going to be fine.

I returned to the table. Danielle was smiling as I approached. I slipped the ring on her finger, kissed her on the lips and asked, "Are you ready for forever?"

"I'm ready for anything," she said, as she gazed at the ring.

"I love you," I said.

"I love you," she said.

I kissed her softly on the lips. I thought, "Skyrockets will be firing off in my chest." It was more like a nuclear scare. Certainly, it was my first time being engaged and I was young and all the bullshit that went with that. *This must be a natural stage. Everyone goes through this sense of doubt and disbelief. I'm going to roll with this. She says she loves me. I love her. It's a natural progression.*

I finished my coffee, tasting the last swallow of the coconut rum. Danielle finished her caramel cocoa. She never took her eyes off the ring from the moment we left Noel's place until we arrived at her house. For the entire drive home, she held it up close to her face, and then with her arm stretched out. She even placed her hand on the dashboard and watched it sparkle as we passed under the streetlights. We didn't say a word all the way home.

The lights were off and no one was home. Her mom was going to be gone for a couple days at her sister's. The thought of having sex with Danielle put me at ease, and as I relaxed the dark clouds in my head began to melt away. Maybe we could do this in a bed for once. I imagined her naked body on a bed sprawled out, ready for me.

As I opened my truck door, she said, "This was an incredible night."

"Yeah."

"I'm so tired," she said.

"What?"

"Can you come by in the morning before you go into work and we can have a little, you know, fun," she said, with a little pouty mouth, flashing her eyes.

"Sure," I said reluctantly. I felt like I should have ducked for an oncoming flying brick. I didn't see that coming. "I guess so," I said in disbelief and total confusion.

"Bring me a hot vanilla cocoa from Noel's, will ya?" she said, laughingly.

I was speechless. We just became engaged. Nobody was home for two more days and she said to come by for a quickie *in the morning*?

I said again, "Sure, fine. I have stuff I can do tonight. I can do that."

Maybe I'd just heard her wrong. I tried again. "Do you want to hang out for a bit? It is not even ten o'clock. I don't have to stay all night or anything."

"No, I'm exhausted, and I need a good night's sleep. I will be ready for you in the morning," she said in the same baby doll voice that Trophy Wife would do with Jock Dad if she wanted something. It made me nauseous.

"Okay, no problem. I'll see you in the morning," I said.

She gave me a nice kiss, with a little tongue. "See you in a few hours, Michael."

She opened the truck door, and along with the diamond, went into the house like she was in a hurry. I put the truck into reverse and slowly left her driveway in total dismay. Something didn't feel right. The dark clouds in my mind began to roll in with elongated fangs. We should be locked in passion about now. I slowly passed a few of the neighborhood houses illuminated by the TV light. We should be sealing the deal, so to speak. Instead, I was cut loose on a Friday night. We had never done this. Maybe I could find a party to go to. Tony was probably hosting one right now. Not too smart on her part, but oh shit, I was engaged!

This was the complete opposite of how I thought I would feel after presenting the ring. Maybe Danielle was just scared, or maybe she was really exhausted. She invited me back in the morning. The hairs on the back of my neck raised, my hands had become sweaty, my heart clenched in my chest like an angry fist. The clouds with the teeth had arrived with a mouth like a killer shark waiting to gnash down hard. Something inside me would not let this go. *Am I pathetic or is my entire being trying to tell me something?*

I turned the corner slowly and then moved into the right lane, hugging the curb, made a U-turn. I slowly drove up the hill and parked up on the vacant lot like I always did when I would sneak into her house. I couldn't help myself. *Why weren't we together tonight?* I was nearly out of my skin before I opened the truck door. I climbed out of the truck knowing I was not invited this time to sneak into her backyard, but I proceeded anyway. I was going to trespass and really break the law this time. Didn't I have any special rights now that we were engaged?

I opened the gate, carefully, quietly like I always did. I crept along the wall to the step near the sliding glass door. There was a slight crack in the curtains. I could see in. The TV and the desk lamp were on; the roll top desk was open. That was a first. I stepped to the left a bit to see more and slipped on a small stone, causing my knee to bang the window slightly.

Danielle walked into the room. She had a drink in her hand, and looked right at the window where I was squatting. She turned to look at something on the TV when the phone rang. I looked at my watch: 10 o'clock on the nose.

Danielle picked up the phone quickly, like she knew it was about to ring. She was standing over it and smiling. Her hands moved up and down like she was excited. Her voice was loud, but I could not hear what she was saying. She talked for forty-five minutes. I couldn't hear a damn thing with the TV on. She finally hung up the phone, sat down at the desk, pulled out some paper, and began to write. After half an hour, which seemed like a day, she finished. There were at least four pages that I could see. She picked up the pages and reviewed them before folding them and placing them in an envelope, which she sealed.

What was going on? I asked this girl to marry me and she gets on the phone fifteen minutes after I drop her off and then she has to write a letter? What could be that urgent? I was dumbfounded. I looked into the window between the curtains. Danielle closed the roll top desk and locked it. She rehung the key, turned the light off, and shut the door. I left through the back gate and made it back to the truck. I didn't remember the trip at all or how cold it was. I was at boiling point.

Maybe she had to write a friend or a relative that she was engaged. Who made a phone call precisely at 10 pm? The fact I had to fill in the blanks furthered my frustration. The bottom line was, what the hell was with that roll top desk? Why was it locked all the time? Why hadn't we consummated our engagement? My heart wanted one thing, and my mind was not putting up with any bullshit. This seemed unreal and I was starting to feel foolish.

One thing was for sure; I was getting into that roll top desk.

I could have done lots of things that night. Tony was always partying. He would say, "Lots of chicks, man. Don't miss this." I could have worked a late shift, but instead I arrived home early. I heard Trophy Wife and Jock Dad banging the headboard upstairs. Like things could get any worse. I flopped down on my own bed, turned on the stereo, and put my headphones on. It felt lonely and pathetic to be lying there alone on the night I became engaged. I stared up into the ceiling and plotted my next move.

The next morning, I knew Danielle was going to work at the spa at nine o'clock. I was supposed to be there at eight for a quickie before work. At seven-thirty, I called her and told her that I had to go into work early and would have to see her later in the evening. She said, "Fine," in that little voice of hers. At 8:30 I parked two blocks away, opposite the route she would take to the spa. I walked down to her street and huddled between two oak trees, bent over like I was tying my shoe. At 8:45 Danielle came out wearing her work clothes. She walked around her car and went to the mailbox at the curb. She opened the mailbox door, slipped a letter in, and pulled up the flag. She paused for a moment, looked at her ring finger, turned and walked to her car and sped off in a rush.

The neighborhood was quiet. It was overcast and a little on the cool side. It would have been a perfect day for sleeping in but it was time to engage the plan. I was breaking in. *Fuck it, I'm doing it.*

Could that be the letter she had written last night? So along with trespassing, breaking and entering, I added postal fraud to the mix. After Danielle made the turn out of her block, I checked the neighborhood out. Dead quiet. Change of plan. The first target was now the mailbox. I just needed to see who the letter was addressed to. It be could be an aunt or a girlfriend. If so, no worries. It would save me from having to break into her house. All this would be ridiculous and I would be wrong. I could live with that. I laughed a little at how stupid and insecure I was being. I felt relaxed again because this was really, after all, a dumb idea. I would just walk over to the mailbox and peek in and be off.

After a minute or so, I clenched my jaw and went for it. I walked carefully like I owned the place in case somebody happened to look out their window. If anybody said anything, I would just tell them that I am slipping a love note in the box for Danielle. I made it to the door of the mailbox, and took a final 360-degree look of the neighborhood and yanked down the door and grabbed the envelope. It was face down. I flipped it over.

It was addressed to Elder Kirk Lisbon in South Africa. I shut the door of the mailbox, and walked to her side gate with the letter in my hand. I stepped into the yard and closed the gate, resting my back on the weathered splintery planks of the redwood chair. This could be a Dear John letter. After all, we were planning on ripping each other's clothes off later, and we'd been engaged for 12 hours! I did that laugh thing again as I thought how really dumb this was getting.

I opened the envelope. Immediately I caught the faint scent of her perfume on the letter. My heart threw a punch as I opened the three-fold, four-page letter.

It started with:

My precious Kirk,

It was so wonderful hearing your voice last night after not hearing it for so long. I know you had to sneak out to make the call. I have missed you so much! I'm excited that our wait is almost over. Two years seems like forever. I'm so glad your mission has gone so well. It sounds like it has been a real blessing. I knew you would be very successful no matter where you went. I am excited for our temple plans and being married forever to you. I long for your touch.

Emotion electrified my body. It was flight or fight mixed with psychosis. I ripped the letter in half and stuck it in my pocket. I would burn it later. I had never experienced a leveling of my being before. The only thing getting married now were my rage and pain. I wasn't done. I went in to finish the job.

There was a bathroom window that didn't shut all the way. There were plenty of bushes and trees to give me cover. I could only get the window to come out four inches. I could cut the screen and roll out the window but I didn't have my knife. I was surprised I didn't throw the redwood chair or a rock through the window. I moved on to the bedroom windows. They all had blinds that you could not see through.

I was dying to see Danielle's bedroom. Used to be I was mildly annoyed and curious that I'd never seen it. Now I was just angry that I didn't even know what my supposedly future wife's bedroom looked like. All the bedroom windows were secure. I would have to break glass to get in. I paced around and ended up on the patio where I sat down on a splintery redwood lawn chair. I could hardly breathe. I was trying to get my bearings and navigate through this hurricane.

I got up to leave. I had enough evidence to move forward. I really didn't need to go any further. I stood up not able to think straight with the hellish rage. Just in case, I tried pushing the sliding glass door open before I took off. I looked around for any neighbors peeking over the fence, it was clear. I placed my fingers on the handle and it slid right open. She must have forgotten to lock it after our last romp. I slipped between the red curtains and I was in.

Looking at the couch made me ill with anger, guilt, and shame. I went to the desk. I sat in the tiny little wooden chair and felt for the key. I pulled it from the nail, and placed the little brass key into the tiny keyhole, and turned. The roll top released and went up easy, like a skirt at a drunken prom. I was in. There was stationary, a letter opener, pens, envelopes and stamps placed carefully, systematically, like the military, at attention to order. I pulled an inner drawer. There was a folded piece of paper with some writing on it.

A note from her mom.

Danielle,

Kirk's mother called and said he was going to be able to sneak away and call you Friday night. The bishop made the arrangements. He will be calling at 10 pm our time. Good luck with all this.

Love, Mom.

The bishop, what a bastard! Her mom knew I planned to ask Danielle to marry me: what a bitch. Danielle took my ring, said yes, then did all this. My mind was blown. There was another box. It was full of perfectly opened letters with a yellow ribbon around stacks of three and four. They were nestled into the order they arrived. I reached to the bottom of the pile. The postmarks went back fifteen months, all from South Africa.

Really, the Mormon missionaries were in South Africa? How fitting. Mormon President Kimball had this revelation a couple years ago that allowed people of African descent to enter the priesthood. Ever hear of the civil rights movement, Utah? What a revelation in the midst of apartheid. Why would anyone be a member of anything with segregation and prejudice, greed and false promises at its heart? Just more money for these white supremacists.

Noel even challenged a few missionaries who were trying to convert him. He was well read and had a college degree in philosophy. Prior to the "revelation" he told me that he asked the missionaries that barged into his cafe one day, why he couldn't take endowments in their temple or join the priesthood. Clueless, one of them spoke up and said that it had to do with the mark of Cain. Noel laughed hysterically at their ignorance and told them to leave and never come back again. A week later a few more showed up.

Our whole relationship had been a lie. Danielle had been writing to Kirk the entire time we'd been together. My hands were shaking, I was breathing hard. My eyes were on fire. Streams of violent thoughts came pouring through like wishes from a satanic well. I used to be peaceful surf punk. I was losing myself.

I carefully placed the letters back in the order they had been in. I had no need to read them; I knew enough. I locked the roll top and rehung the key. I stood up carefully, thoughtfully, put the chair back where it belonged. After all, this was now a crime scene. I walked up the stairs. I had one thing left to do. I was going to her bedroom. I needed to see it, the mess she was always too embarrassed about. I needed closure. We laughed and loved just the other day. How could all this just go to shit so fast?

The carpeted stairs creaked a bit. The happiness of the other day played over in my head like a film reel spinning in that twisted theatre of my mind as I took each step. I made it to the hall. Family pictures blurred as I walked past. The kitchen was just a glowing mirage. The bathroom smelled like her perfume. This was probably the last time I would experience it. Her mother's room was on the right, the one on the left must be Danielle's. I approached the door and turned the knob. It was locked. It had the cheap privacy-locking knob. I could open it with a small Allen wrench, or a heavy paper clip, or my boot. The key was in the universal hiding place, on top of the doorframe. I reached up and slid it into my fingers, poked the key into the little hole and, *pop,* the door was open.

I really didn't know what I was going to see. From the way she talked about it, the room was going to be a hoarder's den. At this point, I felt I was doing something wrong, but not as wrong as what she had done. Without hesitation, I flipped the light on. The room was immaculate. It was a flash of white. In the middle of the room was a beautiful bed with a white silk and satin bedspread between four white wooden bedposts with a white lace canopy. The bedspread was taut and made elegantly, for royalty or a young couple who are destined to be gods. There was a matching dresser and armoire. Certainly a girly room. I walked in a few steps more and the walls were covered in high school memorabilia: pom-poms, cheerleading trophies, a school newspaper clipping showing a picture of her and Kirk as Homecoming King and Queen, gymnastic awards, ribbons, medals, paper certificates of awards, pictures of her and her quarterback at a game. This was her missionary. It was a shrine of sorts with scented candles nestled below a collage of Danielle and her high school sweetheart. Kirk's high school ring hung on a chain hanging from a lamp, his football jersey in a glass case on the wall. His letterman's jacket was hanging from the post on her bed. There was a framed picture of Danielle and Kirk with Bishop Townsend, my ex-dentist. The etching on the bottom of the frame said, "Temple Bound."

This was a fucking nightmare! This guy was everything I wasn't, and everything I despised. Sure, I hated high school but for the right reasons. The phony educational system, the bullies, the fights and the games between the popular and the insignificant. It was ridiculous to praise and cheer for a team who didn't give a shit about anybody but themselves. It was not a fair level of exchange across the board in high school. But we were told to have spirit and support our school. Most of us were treated as insignificant and we didn't care, because we refused to enter the mouth of the machine like the rest.

I felt I was going to overdose with all the emotional poison pumping through my veins. I had to get out of there. I made sure everything was put back where it belonged. I locked her door and placed the key on top of the frame. I realized Danielle or her mom could possibly show up here any minute, and I was late for work. I slipped out the sliding glass door. I felt like I had been hit with a thousand clubs when I took in a breath of fresh air. Before I reached the gate, I threw up into the bushes. I couldn't stop. I dry heaved bile and still it wouldn't let up. I ran to my truck, gasping and dry heaving. I sat in the cab and started breathing heavy. I had to get a grip; I had to make a plan. I was going to be late for work. I drove to 7-11. I walked through the front door. My manager looked at me as I walked in.

"Michael are you okay?"

"Yeah, just a little sick. I'll be okay. I won't let you down," I said.

I ran to the restroom and still could not stop the dry heaves. After ten minutes my manager knocked on the door.

"Michael, I can cover your shift. Why don't you go home and take care of yourself?"

"Thanks, I'll do that as soon as I can get out of the rest-room without puking."

Moments later, I stumbled out of the restroom and made it back to my truck. Making it home without tossing it was going to be a challenge. Fortunately nobody was home. My body shook uncontrollably, making it hard to get the key in the lock. Upon entering my bedroom, I collapsed on the floor.

Chapter 13

THE BITTEREST PILL

A few hours went by and I woke up with my face on the floor. The carpet of my room had imprinted what looked like hideous formulas of complex quantum algorithms on my face. If I was able to unlock their meaning then maybe I could have understood how to get back to happier times. My mind had been really stretched. I was hoping it was just a bad dream. Instead, a dark chasm of fear and loathing and heartache moved in. My guitar was in the corner, neglected. The dust revealed the truth. I crawled across the floor, reached for my guitar, and sat back on my bed, moved my thumb over the strings. It was clearly out of tune, but felt good in my hands. I tuned the guitar to my ear and wiped it down with the corner of my bedspread. I began to free play and all I could do was find the A minor key. A song began to write itself as I played…

> *There's a devil in the trigger and*
> *an angel in the lead,*
> *beside a smokin barrel, there was*
> *redrum in the bed.*
> *A quick bridge followed.*
> *It was the jilted lover, twisted spoons*

My eyes welled a little as a new darkness came flowing out of me. I rested the guitar on the bed and stared at my four walls, feeling displaced, broken. After a half hour or so, enough of that shit! I got up and went to the garage. I sat down next to the scattered bones of my motorcycle. I told it that it was going to be okay, and promised to put the pieces back together. I would do it, but how? I walked back to my room and flopped on my bed to think. The ceiling revealed a skull that was never there before, the clown, the claw, white ceiling, white noise.

Part of me wanted to cry; rage cut in on the dance. The anger was too perfect, pressing me down as if an enormous stone gargoyle was perched on my shoulders. Danielle would be home soon and would probably call. I needed to talk to Dave, but I only had his mom's number. He would be so cool in this situation and would tell me to get it together. Then it hit me, I needed to get that ring. Maybe the jeweler would give me my money back if I returned it brand new. I wanted to reveal what I knew to Danielle so badly, to let her know it was over. She might do something crazy, like not give the ring back or destroy it. She would figure out that I had illegally obtained the information. Breaking and entering. Could she prove it? I couldn't just start the conversation with "Hey, you lying bitch…," I had to have a plan to get the ring back and move on with some dignity.

The phone rang an hour later.

"Hey, Michael. How's it going? How was work?" Danielle said

"Fine. I left early. How was your day?" I said. I sounded normal, like nothing had happened, like I didn't know about her and Kirk.

"Great. I can't wait to see you," she said.

"What would you like to do tonight?" I said.

"You for starters," she said, giggling.

"Sounds great, I'll be there in an hour," I said.

"Perfect, I will be waiting for you," she said in her seductive voice.

It was like the perfect crime. The idea of playing dirty pool with her felt soothing to my train wrecked heart. This dog was going to have his day. I would have an opportunity to have sex one more time, snag the ring, and blow her mind with the truth. I might be riding on the Devil's tail, but why not?

I took a shower, washing off layers of gunk, but not removing the stains of guilt, hurt, and anger. She was clearly not The One. The One was somewhere else. The algorithms disappeared, my face had returned to a blank page. The plan was to go out in style. I got in the truck and slid in "Mean Machine" by The Cramps. I cranked it up and punched it. I couldn't wait any longer.

I pulled up into Danielle's driveway, got out, and walked up the step. Then mourning poured over me, total sadness. I thought I was going to weep or something. *Get a grip, man!* I took a breath and regrouped. This was going to be good-bye and she didn't even know it. The enemy was on the other side of the door and assumed we were going to have sex and a fun night together. I nearly choked up again and blew the whole thing. I couldn't veer from the plan. I had to get the ring back and some dignity. Before my knuckles hit the door, it creaked open and Danielle was standing there in very sexy black lingerie. I swallowed hard.

"Wow, Danielle, you look beautiful," I said. *Holy shit what do I do now?*

"Come in," she said. She closed the door with her left hand, fingers splayed out, flashing the ring of fire.

She went right for my shirt and started taking it off. I moved in and grabbed her waist bringing her into me. I smelled her hair and her skin, freshly showered and perfumed up. I moved up and down her neck with my mouth inhaling her for the last time. We went to the couch and our hands moved up and down each other's body. As she moved her left hand down my spine, the ring caught on the cushion. Now was my chance.

"Take the ring off so you won't lose the diamond," I said.

"Good idea," she said.

She took the ring off and placed it on the end table. She proceeded to run her mouth down my chest and was removing the belt from the buckle on my jeans. My eyes fixed on the ring and drank up the last image of her body. Her breasts were bare and she rubbed them across my mouth. I sat up and laid her back on the couch. I could feel the heat of sorrow build in my heart. I couldn't do this. She was not just a fuck. She was going to be my wife. For a brief moment in time she was The One, my one.

I stood up and grabbed the ring from the end table.

"Hey, what are you doing?" Danielle pulled the straps of her lingerie and placed them back on her shoulders.

"This is over. I'm leaving," I said.

"What? Why?" she said, eyes blinking.

"You know why." I said, looking into her eyes as deep as she would let them go.

Danielle flinched, turned away as our eyes met. I lost it.

"How could you do this to me? You told me you were a virgin. I know there is another. You being a virgin was never an issue. If I fall in love with someone, that wouldn't have mattered. Why the lies?" I said.

"It wasn't like that," she said.

"Of course it was," I said. "It made me feel like we had something to share first with each other. Why would you lie to me about that?"

Danielle burst into tears. "I can explain," she said through her sobs. "My bishop said that I was like a virgin again when I confessed to him about my relationships. It was like I was forgiven and I was made new again."

"Relationships! There were more than your missionary-quarterback Kirk? Did your bishop give you a new hymen, too? The guy's a fucking dentist! Are you for real?" I said, clutching the ring tightly in my fist.

"How do you know about Kirk?" she belted. Her eyes smoldered.

"This is a small town, Danielle. Everyone knows your temple plans!'"

"What?" She said. She glanced at the roll top desk. "You bastard."

"Is there something inside the desk you would like to share, and why haven't we ever gone into your bedroom?"

"You asshole, you invaded my privacy."

"You bitch, you broke my heart, and stole an experience I was hoping to share with someone who actually gave a damn."

"I gave a damn, Michael. You were different than all the rest."

"All the rest? I knew it. I just knew you lied, Danielle.

Were you just going to keep on lying to the both of us?" I said. I turned my back on her. "I'm done. This is goodbye. It's over."

"I'm the best you'll ever have!" she said.

"I can do better than a lying and cheating bitch. Take a good look, you're watching the best leave your ass." I slammed the door and could hear her crying as I left. Her sobbing was phony. She was upset because she had been caught. The hurt I felt was deep, penetrating and intensified by the minute, like burning poison pumping in my veins. The emotion was new and didn't have a name. Anger and rage no longer mattered. I gave that girl everything and took in all the lies she told me. My body and soul had known the truth all along. Though the doubt had been there, my heart had just wanted to believe. I burned rubber out of her neighborhood. I was independent again, a rogue.

 James M. Fisher

Chapter 14

HANG DOWN YOUR HEAD

Several weeks had passed. Not only had they been the loneliest weeks of my life, but I tried several times to reach Dave, only to get his mom's answering machine. Something was seriously wrong. The drama and the emotional state that had gone off the Richter scale, leaving me to feel I was going to need some miraculous healing, a lobotomy, and probably a heart transplant. I was wrong. One conversation with a certain jeweler changed everything.

Mr. Oscar Lorenz was also the owner, and he was really taken in by my story. A classy European guy from Northern Spain, with a suave accent that could melt the female heart. From my conversation with Mr. Lorenz, I learned that he had seen a few things. He seemed to have been to every exotic place on Earth. Certainly handsome for an older guy, he seemed like the type to make shit happen. I liked that about him and failed to see that trait in myself at the moment. I liked he got my story, tearing up like he did up when I told him the whole thing. "The saga of Michael and Danielle," sounded cool when he said it. He had been jilted too, by what he termed "the romance of a lifetime," which nearly cost him his entire business as his ex-cheating-total-bitch-of-a-wife, as he put it, made off with over half of everything in the divorce. He took a slight loss on me, too. The important thing was, I got my money, he got my situation.

I realized for the first time, I too had a story, a discarded personal piece of sheet music perhaps, rocking and rolling down a broken highway destined for nowhere, and certainly outside of the mouth of the machine. Before I had always reveled in everyone else's history, ingested it, spreading it onto my skin like war paint, their myths seemed to be my mission to perpetuate. I pined for it, truly I did, but this time, my preoccupation would be my own. Into the mirror I would go, arms wide, to free-fall where the only ghost to be seen would be mine. I would not be fooled again. A schmuck, I was indeed.

I planned on taking a trip to California to see Dave and my bros again, surf, and most importantly forget Danielle. I started writing again and played my guitar every day until my fingers bled. Really, I bled like Pete Townsend at Woodstock but without the windmill, the theatrics, the audience. It was just me, four walls, and my voice into an empty void. The heart finished the set as the brain left the building. It won't be fooled again.

I got the motor put back together on my motorcycle. I mounted it on the frame. It was brain salad surgery—setting up the rest as the parts came in. I would be road bound soon. Sunsets and leathered maidens and other secret fantasies snuck into my vault of unwritten schemes. Who knew, maybe a three-breasted alien with turquoise skin. With each bolt I tightened and twisted, carefully positioned into place, I felt I was repairing myself, too. Twist by twist, nut by nut.

Trophy Wife was nice enough to point out that Danielle posted her impending temple marriage to quarterback Kirk in the paper. She had actually planned to juggle us both at the same time. What a circus act. After reading their letters, I knew he was coming to town soon. At some point I wanted to kick his ass, mercilessly, and go western on him like the Mountain Meadows Massacre, but at the same time, I felt bad for him. He was totally unaware of the truth, and was about to enter the lion's mouth.

It was Sunday; Christmas was in the air. Frozen crystals, frosted panes, with a silence only death could hear, still like still and over a month away. Pine and peppermint scents permeated Twenty-Fifth Street as the truth of yesterday's past was further swept under the carpet and into the bowels of the steam tunnels where opium and bootleg whiskey had once pumped through the veins of downtown Ogden, only to be replaced by tiny boutiques and bistros, a fancy mall, fine coffee, and festive holiday colored balloons. The few surviving bars along the drag still smelled like the piss and vinegar of the forties. God bless them and their will to survive beyond the threshold of death, though they appear to have died a couple times along the way.

As much as I despised Trophy Wife, the woman could bake. I found myself in the kitchen mesmerized by trays of thumbprint cookies with preserves from Knott's Berry Farm, Texas ice box brownies made with sour cream, caramel bars with nuts and chocolate fudge crinkle cookies. I was in Heaven, and no one was here to witness what was about to go down. It wasn't even Thanksgiving yet!

I took a plate out of the cupboard and a gallon of milk from the fridge. I stacked a mound of those cookies and bars on that plate, keeping the thumbprints quarantined, as the preserves were not going to play well with others. I went downstairs, and cranked on the stereo, and wolfed down that plate of holiday dainties. It was so good that I nearly totaled an entire half-gallon of milk. I replaced it carefully back into the fridge. I was fat and happy for the moment.

I sprawled out on the couch like a sated suga-holic, ready for a nap. Life tasted pretty damn good for the moment. I had the day off and had picked up a new tail-light and headlight assembly for the bike. Pure fun was on the agenda for the day. I pulled the throw over myself and my eyes slammed shut. I slipped into a deep sugar-crash for about an hour. The phone rang. It rang and rang and after the sixth time it stopped. I turned over, pleased the raging sound had died. Five minutes later, it rang again and again like a bad version of Poe's bells. I got up, knowing I had to work on the bike anyway. I picked up the phone. "Hello."

"Hi, Michael. It's Danielle."

I paused and wiped the hardened chocolate from the corners of my mouth. Blinked a couple times.

"What do you want?" I said.

"I need to see you," she said.

"I'm kind of busy. Aren't you getting married?" I said.

"I need to see you. It's really important," she said again.

My chin dropped to my chest. I ran my hand through my hair. I paused. In my heart, I missed her and I wanted sex in a bad way. Once you have had it, it is like vampirism. You need to feed. My mind went haywire. I couldn't keep a straight thought.

"Where and when?" I said.

"I'm at the spa. Ring the bell at the back door."

"All right. See you in twenty minutes."

What the fuck was I doing? This could only end badly.

 James M. Fisher

Danielle was getting married and should be at church or something, not meeting me at the spa. What did she want with me now? I jumped into the truck and headed her way. This was insane. I should just blow her off and go back to the bike, get some things done. I remembered the oh-shit feeling, when I realized that I was almost there. What the hell did we have to say to each other? I entered the parking lot of Feminine Fitness. I drove slowly, creeping, as part of me was starting to die all over again. I saw her car. It was the only one in the parking lot. I parked two spaces away and turned the truck off, feeling certain doom. My hormones raged; I wanted her badly and didn't care about the outcome in that minute. I took a breath and made a pact with myself to keep it at five minutes no matter what happened. I walked up to the door. The Feminine Fitness logo was hard to miss. It was black and pink. I felt I was knocking on the door of a giant tampon box, with its swirls and girly floral exterior. I rang the bell. No one answered at first. She was going to make me stand there. I was in no mood, and I was certainly not going to ring twice. As I turned to walk away, the door opened.

"Hey, Michael," Danielle said. I turned back.

Danielle stood inside the door, wrapped in only a towel. I stepped inside and she closed the door. I swallowed hard, like a pelican devouring a giant fish. I was stunned seeing her that way. Behind her, the hot tub was bubbling away like a witch's cauldron. She dropped her shroud, exposing everything. Yikes, what was she doing? Her breasts were odd, larger, and out of proportion to the rest of her body, nipples displaced.

"What do you think of my new breasts, Michael?" she said. "I had them done the week after we broke up. One of the spa member's husbands is a doctor, and he gave me the family deal."

"I can see that. You gotta boob job like your friend Jan?"

"Not exactly. Different doctors and mine were inserted from the side, hers under the nipple," she said.

"I liked you fine before."

"So what do you think?" she said. She swayed slightly so her breast bobbed. "They feel real, you can be the first man to touch them."

"What? Who are you?" I said.

She looked surprised.

"I would have never asked you to do that."

She walked up to me and started to unbutton my shirt.

"I'm not going through with this, Danielle," I said.

"Come on, Michael. I know how much you like it," she said, nipples pointing north and south. How could the doctor get the alignment wrong here?

"I used to, when I thought it was real between us. Now things are faker than ever," I said.

"We deserve at least one more time, don't we?" she said.

"I'm not doing this. You need help. You're getting married." I stepped back. "We're done! We've been done."

"You don't really mean that," Danielle said with a confident sidewinder smile, clasping my wrist.

"I was in love with you. You're getting married in that church with your high school sweetheart. This was never just about fucking for me." I pulled away.

"Damn you, Michael! You spoil everything," she snapped as she reached for her towel.

"I can't believe you," I said.

"Just get out!" she said as she wrapped back up.

"I'm leaving. You're nothing but sad!"

"Leave!"

I had my hand on the doorknob, so it seemed absurd that she would say that again. My heart was ripping apart, dumbfounded. I wanted her bad, and she was right there in front of me. I couldn't believe she was already getting married—we had just been engaged a short time ago. Insane, insane. I slammed the door of the tampon box and left quickly. Danielle latched the door. It was good-bye all over. I blew out of there thinking, "This was supposed to be an awesome day." I chirped the tires in second gear, flooding the carburetor, dropping the clutch. Back to square one with all of this.

That whole time was nothing but a fling for her. I was a boy toy to her. A gentile-slave. Who did she think she was? Madonna? I laughed for a second. The loss of her crept in slowly and started to build. As badly as I wanted sex, I needed to have all of her. The real thing. This was too much.

My mind went to Dave. He could talk me off the ledge and turn this into something silly and small. He hadn't checked in once, and his mom had lost it; as far as I knew, he was completely unreachable. A phone booth was coming up on the right. Tony's constant promise of a good time triggered an impulse. I pulled over and dug some loose change from the ashtray, his number from my wallet. With the truck running I got out and pushed the folding doors of the booth open. Piss, perspiration, an aura of helplessness and depravity waited inside, cigarette butts, lipstick stained, beer cans with their bellies punched in like fetal discards on the floor *tink-tinked* as I barged in. The door closed, clumsily with my shoulder pressing, adjusting, pressing, adjusting. *Ding, ding.* The phone chimed as my quarter dropped. I was hesitant to call Tony. We'd had a great time at the Gimlet, but it had been a long while since we had last talked.

I dialed most of Tony's number and paused. Fuck it! I pressed the last digit, the number three. The connection seemed to take extra long. The booth had a certain vibe about it: threatening graffiti, a flickering fluorescent light above, and what appeared to be dried blood on the inner door. The glass was cracked where somebody's fist might have hit, the street—elongated, blurred, sepia, in the afternoon sun. The receiver clicked, the connection was being established. A recorded voice said, "Twenty-five cents for the next three minutes."

I had already put money in. I dropped another twenty-five cents. *Ding-ding.* The voice again, "Thank you." Tony's phone began to ring. What would he think of me calling out of the blue like this? His answering machine picked up. The voice on it was a very provocative female. "Tony is tied up right now and cannot come to the phone. But leave a message at the beep and I'll make sure he gets it, Hahahaha" *Beep.*

"Hi, Tony. It's Michael. I know it's been a while-"

"Mikey, is that you?" Tony, said, as he picked up and cancelled the recording.

"Yeah, man, how's it goin?" I said, sounding a little pathetic.

"Great man, what are you doing?" he said. "It's been a while bro, you okay?"

"I broke up with Danielle and-"

Tony interrupted. "I knew it was a chick. I thought we hit it off pretty good, bro"

"We did. I got caught up and almost married her."

"Holy shit, it's really bad then! Come right now, Mikey. Do you know where the Canyon Condos are by the golf course, on Twelfth?"

"Yeah, at the mouth of the canyon,"

Tony gave me the code for the gate and I told him I'd be there in ten minutes.

The phone booth doors crackled and stuck as I yanked and kicked my way out. That was the first and last time I would ever use that booth. I was really caught in that thing for a moment. Like an insect that narrowly escapes the teeth of a Venus fly trap. By the time I hit Harrison I had forgotten the whole thing. Tony sounded excited to see me, and when I heard the welcome in his voice, a bit of weight seemed to have lifted. The afternoon light looked amazing against the mountains as I drove onto Twelfth. The Canyon Condos were expensive. He must have several roommates to make it work, along with a really good job. I pulled into the front gate and entered the code. The black wrought iron gate opened slowly, retracting from large sandstone walls. The condos were modern, multiple terraces with amazing views of the golf course and mountains. A creek flowed between the golf course and the condos. The designers here really pushed the envelope using all the natural elements found here. Large boulders, giant wood beams, carved stone and floor to ceiling glass windows seemed to be reimagined and placed in a clean and sophisticated way. "This can't be where Tony lives. No way," I kept thinking. "He's a punk like me."

I parked the truck and followed the sign toward Tony's unit. The pathways were beautiful, green, rectangular ponds, woody, massive carved stones placed in clean lines and tight angles that made the aesthetic simple and a feast for the eyes. Who was this guy? Stone steps framed in wood led me to the door of his place. On the other side of the door was laughter. Tony wasn't alone. I rang the bell. It had six tones to it. Dave's mom's house in Huntington Beach had one. The more tones the wealthier you are, I randomly assumed.

Tony yelled, "Mikey's here," then opened the door. "Mikey!" He pulled me in and hugged me like boa constrictor.

"So good to see you, man. Shit," he said.

"It's good to see you, Tone," I said.

"You remember Sarge and Gary? We're getting ready for a night out, setting the mood so to speak."

The entryway opened in two directions. To the right led to a staircase and up to a loft. The left led to a huge open floor plan. Three of the four walls were mostly glass windows from top to bottom. The fourth was a wall dedicated to Patrick Nagel and the female form. His art was everywhere. Female nude sculptures were displayed on glass tables throughout the room with careful thought. The floors were stone, and in the corner was a fireplace with a seating area that was carpeted with a tight woven pattern. All colors were neutral, the main wall was white which made the Nagels stick out with their black hair, white-skinned, art deco forms. In the sitting area was a large, black leather sectional, and three black leather high-back chairs with large metal brads surrounding a large glass table. Sarge sat in the sectional and Gary in one of the chairs. Over in another black chair across from Gary sat a woman with black hair that was cut in an angled bob like an Egyptian princess. She was wearing only a terry cloth robe. On the table was a wood framed mirror about the size of a sheet of paper with several lines of cocaine on it. A few feet from the fireplace was a Guild hollow body guitar. Faces turned in my direction as I entered the room.

"Mikey," Sarge sighed like he was relieved I was still alive or something.

I was truly happy to see him. I had been so intimidated by him when we met the first time. He seemed even bigger.

   James M. Fisher

He gave me a bro hug followed by a smack on the back. He looked good, dressed in black with a black leather jacket. He could have been anybody's lovable mafia hit man.

"Hi, Sarge, good to see you," I said.

"Hey, Mikey," Gary said, still licking the side of his mustache.

"Over here is Monique, one of our models. She also poses for me on various projects."

"Projects? What kind of projects?"

"Sketch work, photography." Tony shrugged.

"Oh, wow. I didn't know you were an artist."

"I dabble. Monique, show Mikey one of your poses."

Monique dropped her robe and went to the dining room table, sat in a chair, crossed her legs, folded her hands, looked into my eyes, said, "Guess what's for dinner?" and froze.

My mouth dropped. Her body was like a piece of art. The guys just broke in laughter. I was gobsmacked. What was I walking into?

"What the fuck, man?" I said.

"Mikey, lighten up, this was for you. It's funny. You're going through a hard time, and brother, we are going to help you forget Danielle."

Monique got up and walked over to me, still nude, and kissed me on the cheek. She said, "It's all going to be all right." Without a backward glance, she went into another room.

"Jesus, guys, you have no idea of what my day was like."

"Yeah, Tony told us," Sarge said.

"What are you drinking, Mikey? Let me get you something," Tony said.

"Okay, Jack rocks, double," I said. I needed to calm down. Two nude women in one day? Certainly I was living two lives at once: multi-worlds theory goes out the window if I'm the observer in both worlds.

"Here you go," Tony said.

"Thanks man," I said, gulping the drink with two enormous swallows. I took a deep breath and looked around the room.

"Whose house is this, Tony?" I asked, careful not to sound crass.

"It's mine," Tony said, smiling like a predator.

"How?" I said.

"I have a couple businesses that do very well," Tony said.

"I thought you were a punk like me. No one our age could afford all this," I said.

"I figured a few things out, that's all. Who wants a line?" he said.

Both Sarge and Gary agreed.

"Mikey, you want the honors?" Tony asked.

"I've never really done coke before. I smoke a little pot every now and then," I said.

"It's like a depression eraser," Gary said. With his demeanor, he would probably know.

"I'll try it. It's safe right?" I asked. I wished I hadn't just said that.

"Try a little and see what you think," said Tony. He handed me the glass straw off the table. He told me how to snort a line by closing one nostril and inhaling through the other.

"Whatever you do, don't exhale or the coke will go flying. Like this," Tony said, taking in the entire line like a pro. "Your turn."

"Here goes," I said. I took in half a line. I felt a slight burn in the sinuses and then I was flying, amped up like ten cups of Noel's Jamaican Blue coffee hitting my bloodstream. Minutes later, I was ready for the other half. Sarge and Gary followed. Monique came in from the bedroom, wearing a little black dress and heels.

"One for the road," she said, snorting her line and out toward the door she went. "See you at the club later, boys."

"So, what kind of business are you in, Tony?" I asked.

"I'm in the party business, party supplies, event planning, I even have a love-a-gram business. It's for people who want to send a message to a loved one, friend, significant other. It depends what type of message they want. I even send strip-o-grams where my actors or actresses show up for birthdays, anniversaries, and so on. It's all entertainment."

Sarge and Gary chuckled.

"Right, 'party supplies.'" Sarge was trying to hold back his laughter.

"We deliver the supplies when the orders come in," said Gary, nearly losing it himself.

"Okay, I get it. Sorry for asking," I said. *Oh my God, he's a dealer!* Was that what Joey had been trying to warn me about that night at the Gimlet?

"I'll fill you in later. In the meantime, let's party," Tony said, opening an envelope full of coke.

"Sarge, why do they call you Sarge?" I asked.

Gary rolled his eyes. "Here come the war stories. I'm heading out. I'll meet you guys at the Kokomo later."

"Later," said Tony.

"I was in Vietnam, took a few a bullets, got a Purple Heart," Sarge said.

"Jesus, my worst nightmare. So were you a sergeant?" I asked.

Tony was lining out the coke on the mirror.

"It's funny, considering I was just a private when I went in and when I was discharged. I was in a jungle near Cambodia. We were holding our position when all hell broke loose. My team took fire from every direction. Some lived, but most of them died. I took three in the chest and one in the hip. I thought I was dead. I woke up in a hospital in Saigon and was sent home. My CO gave me the Purple Heart on my last day there. He saluted me and tucked it in my shirt. I actually got my name Sarge when I started bouncing at the clubs. I look the part I guess."

Sarge poured himself another drink and went silent for a minute. Tony slid the mirror to him. Another line disappeared.

"Jesus, Sarge. I don't know what to say. Ah, thanks for what you did, man. Glad you made it back," I said.

Silence snuck in.

"Who plays the guitar, Tony?" I said, attempting to break the heaviness of my last question.

"I play a little," he said.

"Can I check it out," I said.

"Sure, knock yourself out," Tony said.

I picked up the guitar and strummed it. It was way out of tune. With a few turns of the pegs and plucking a few strings, I got it tuned up. Normally, I would have been shy and would never have picked up someone's guitar like that. I felt fearless. The cocaine or something else?

Tony and Sarge watched me and sipped their drinks. The neck felt nice, the action was fast, strings set just right. The hollow body sound was deep, dark, and beautiful. I muffled the strings and was searching for the rhythm to Folsom Prison Blues. I did the bass intro and Sarge went nuts.

"I know that song! It's Johnny Cash! I love that guy,"

he said.

"Do you hear the train coming, Sarge?" I said, feeling a huge rush coming on.

"I do. Play it man," he said. I played through the song, and Sarge and Tony sang along with me. It was cool.

"Play something else," said Tony.

I played "Invisible Sun" by the Police next.

"I like your version of that song better than the original," said Tony.

"Thanks, man," I said. I felt wired, my heart beating fast.

"We should introduce him to Spyder Blue in Salt Lake," said Sarge.

"Ever think of playing live, Mikey?" Tony said, picking up the glass straw.

"I dream of doing that. I think that's all I really want to do. I want to perform my own stuff though, maybe change my name, I don't want to get stuck doing covers," I said.

Who am I?

"I got a friend in Salt Lake and he books everything in downtown. We'll hook you up," Tony said.

"That would be awesome, really."

"Play one of your own," Tony's face was serious like I was in an audition.

"Okay, this is a rockabilly punk song called "Baby, Won't You Ride in My Car.""

I started with a quick lick intro, then went right into the rhythm bounce of the song and started singing:

> *Baby, baby won't you ride in my car?*
> *Baby, won't you ride in my car yeah*
> *We won't go all the way, but we'll go real far*
> *And it'll be all right, and it'll be all right yeah*

I ended with the same licks I started with. Sarge and Tony both applauded. Sarge threw in a couple hoots.

"You're full of surprises," said Tony.

"That made my day," said Sarge.

"Thanks, guys. I appreciate it. You're my first audience."

"No way," said Sarge.

"I can see you playing live soon, Mikey." Tony grinned.

"I hope this isn't the coke and whiskey talking," I said.

"No, you're the real deal man."

I placed the guitar on its stand. "Thanks for having me over. I need to get going." My heart raced and I felt a little paranoid.

"Meet us at The Kokomo later," said Sarge.

"Mikey, you don't have to go. Are you sure you don't want to hang out a little more and talk about Danielle?" Tony said.

"I'm good, man," I said, actually feeling really lost inside. The whole day was like a freight train coming at me. It was too much. I was done.

"Okay, brother. Meet up with us later. I mean it. We'll get you in."

"Okay, see you guys there," I said.

I made it back to my truck still spinning about Danielle, and what the fuck was with Tony? I felt wired beyond belief. The Jack rocks double didn't even touch the effect of the two lines of coke I had snorted. What was I thinking? There was no way I could go home like that. I rolled the windows down and drove off. The fresh air felt good, but I was higher than a kite at the same time, feeling like I was in full control of my faculties and hyper-aware of it. Tony was some sort of eccentric character from the punk underground, some sort of a drug dealer or something. Party supplies? There was so much to take in. He treated me like a best friend, and he really didn't know me that well. I just got up and performed in front of people and entertained them, and now I had a chance to play live? *I'm snorting cocaine now? Who am I?*

I drove my truck up to a pass near my parents' house. I needed to be alone to think things through and to straighten out, calm the fuck down.

Driving up to enjoy the sunset seemed like a good idea. I imagined being in Cali again. The cliffs in Huntington and Laguna were popular spots to see the sun go down. People would pull their cars over on highway 101, get out, and just watch. The sky, periwinkle and fire, would put on a show to end the day with the final curtain of oranges and reds folding into the crescent remains of the sun, dissolving like a communion wafer along the salt water tongue of the ocean. What followed was most extraordinary, applause.

My anger and rage with Danielle was meaningless at that point. I was drained, exhausted. How could anything like this exist within me? I had been on a road to healing, and now I was an ocean away from the closure of it all, again. I pulled off the pass near a bluff that overlooked a small river to the left and a farm below on the right. It was nestled in the basin, between the broad shoulders of the Wasatch Mountains. The pine trees skyed and stood like taut arrows, waiting for a target. At the fringe of the bluff I put the truck in neutral and parked with my foot on the brake. I kept the motor running as the temperature was starting to drop. I only needed a couple minutes, a place to throw my mind into, and flush it if possible.

I fixated on the sun that sat on the shoulder of the mountain. Just a tiny break to collect for a few minutes. The incredible beauty gave me a little peace as I thought things through until the sun faded. The Cramps album "Flamejob" was playing low. "Mean Machine" came on again. I was not the mean machine that I thought I was. I couldn't just screw Danielle, take the ring and run away that night, or just do her at the spa one last time. I wanted her to know that I went down loving her and respecting her, though it meant nothing. In my head, it was some sort of premeditated rape to do her and then steal the ring off her finger, at least in the court that resided in my mind. I was not capable of such things. I wanted the real thing and that was not it. I wanted the Danielle that I thought was in love with me. Where had the laughing outlaw in heels gone?

I took a deep breath. The stew of this new emotion boiled and churned inside me, misery loitering, its black, withered hands squeezing my beating heart. The coke continued to rattle my cage; dry mouth followed. Was I ever going to come down? I remembered that bottle of Appleton rum was underneath the seat. It was two-thirds full. The reality of actually marrying Danielle sunk in. I had actually been going to marry someone. How weird was that? I was still so young. None of my friends in Cali would even be considering the notion.

I popped the cap and took a swig. I turned the volume up on my cassette player. I fast forwarded the tape to "Let's Get Fucked Up" by the Cramps. I smiled and swallowed again. I tasted one of the first dates we had together. I turned the stereo up again. Lux Interior howled the emotion I was feeling. Yeah, let's get fucked up.

     JAMES M. FISHER

It seemed like yesterday at KarKwik, we were filling up our drinks with a little rum. She had called me 'outlaw' after the Fireside. I took a huge gulp. I remembered her body and how beautiful she was as I took her all in. The twisted little theatre in my mind opened its door and began to roll the film on the torn screen of our lives together. I drank another swallow. I was just a toy. I drank another. I was an asshole because I wanted to know the truth. She did this. I drank another. I felt the rage, and I was yelling the lyrics. I drank another. I couldn't feel myself crying, but I knew that I was. One more for the road. I drank another.

I closed my eyes for a second and took a deep breath. The flames of cocaine were extinguished. I felt the truck ease forward. Before I could hit the brakes, I was over the edge and falling downward into blackness until I couldn't hear the music any…more.

Chapter 15

BALL AND CHAIN

There was a green glow in the midst of total darkness. Everything was blurry, random. I was twisted up, contorted. I could not feel the left side of my face. Music was playing. I was barely conscious in the early moments of coming to. Everything was a motionless fog. I swallowed, tasting liquor and puke. Oh, shit, I was in my truck, the green blur was my stereo. My mind raced, eyes tried to focus. Flashes of memory knocked at the door of my skull, pounding like metal fists. It felt like I'd been hit in the head by an aircraft carrier. My right eye was swollen shut, numb. My twisted torso was wrapped in the seat belt; my face hugged the floor on the passenger side. The floor had an inch of water in it mixed with my own vomit. I wormed around to get loose, which freed my arm so I could unfasten the seat belt. I used my shoulder to wipe the swill off the side of my face. My heart raced faster, pulsing far into my head. I inched myself up onto the seat toward the driver side, dragging my face, and catching a hint of Danielle's perfume on the cushion. Our last moment together intruded in like epic failure in clown shoes. Pain shot through my ribs as I inched over, sloppily, to the driver's side. My left foot slid over the empty rum bottle, kicking it to the passenger side. It was all coming back to me.

I was high on the bluff and must have passed out. I had gone over the edge. I was afraid to find out where I had landed and could see nothing out of the windshield. Total blackness filled the void, no moon, no stars, just a silence intensified by the darkness. I hesitated to turn on the headlights. The clock on the stereo illuminated the cab with an eerie green lantern glow, 2:00 am. My hands were on the wheel, right hand shaking, left hand clutching. The truck was still idling. Everything was running together and so surreal. My only option was to open the door of my truck to see where I had ended up, because the windshield was cracked, covered with who knows what.

The rain trickled through the cracks in the glass and dripped over the dash, onto the floor. I was spinning and reached over to turn the stereo volume down. "Naked Girl Falling Down the Stairs" played on. The cassette deck was in a loop.

I slurred my words when I said, "Every time I hear the Cramps play, I will remember this moment." My wit was coming back even with the doldrums of the day and the wicked pounding in my head and ribs. The adrenaline kicked in as I opened the truck door. Cold mountain air rushed in. The darkness hindered visibility again. Rain thudded against the ground like it was landing on dead meat.

I stepped down from the truck into a muddy, broken field. The driver side door was heavy, covered in what felt like seaweed and wet hair. I staggered forward to see what had stopped me, or slowed me down; feeling my way along until I reached the left wheel. A solid object, round and broken was caught under the tire. It felt like something from a Halloween horror house. I carefully touched it. It was sludgy, wet. Had I hit an animal or, God forbid, a human being? I panicked as I touched what felt like wet guts on the top of the hood just above the wheel well. I wanted to scream like a little girl. I ran back to the driver's side to look at my hands. There were long vein-like strands on my trembling fingers. I opened the door and checked them under the cab light with my one good eye. The veins were orange and the gutty pieces were crushed pumpkin shell and seeds. I was in a vegetable field. Thank you, Lord God! I was bleeding pretty good, getting blood everywhere. I pressed my hand over the wound along my ribs to slow the bleeding and turned the wipers on. The rubber of the windshield wipers caught in the cracks of the windshield, which made an irritating sound like a dog gnashing at a bone. I watched the rain hit the windshield and trickle in. It was hypnotizing.

I looked in the rearview mirror. My face was swollen, nose bloody, and my right eye looked like a black mussel. Blood had rivered down my neck and dried to a crust. I saw someone else in the mirror. Michael was gone. The universe I landed in was noxious, the planet, knocked off its axis, imploding, reforming. The atmosphere, bad acid, fractal, splitting. The truck was spinning, I hung from the door handle. I was getting weaker. I held on to the door, ready to pass out. Then I was on my back, and the mud held me down, the rain riddled my face.

Danielle snuck into my mind uninvited, the intruder she now was. The memory of our tragic end rushed into my aching head, mad-rapids. I remembered again, the murder in the cathedral that was my heart. I was spinning like a drunken top. When I read the letters in the roll top desk, it was as if a great heist had taken place from the most guarded vault inside my soul. Innocence was snuffed like a candle in an ape's hands. The heart silenced like a church bell, macerated by a speeding train, left splayed on the track, devolving into a nightmare only pennies have: Forever enslaved into the gravel, the dust, only ringing again when it rains the hammers and the nails deep inside the twisted chasm of my soul.

From this chasm, a shadow emerged, a presence, hallucinatory and familiar, a voice I could no longer run from. Like risen ashes of Pompeii, with the strut of Pan seeking sirens in the forest, neither man or beast, blessing or curse, a traveler in the wind, a fixer of broken bells, a muse for the confused, a thin white duke, a song for the songless, a vitamin B shot for the soul, the original Freudian slip, the person in personae, the Prufrock, the Sweeney, the Cantos, the names and aliases are many but not limited to, comes from a place where too much is not enough and you would never just settle for more, no such thing, possibly responsible for the fall of Rome, the middle finger gesture toward authority, early punk music and definitely not hair bands, but maybe, certainly, the black in Johnny Cash's hat, a sort of friend when you should have more enemies, seldom seen but always heard like the licorice syrup voice resonating from the Twilight Zone, he is and isn't, present and past, and rides the shadows at the speed of light, a friend and faux pas, and in this particular moment in space and time he arrived and called himself Jimmy Crane.

The spinning was the worst of it, soon replaced by a killer headache, and muddy grit in my mouth. I felt I was really dying, blood everywhere. I was barely awake and lying in the mud, and I didn't remember hitting the ground.

I pulled myself up and looked at the clock on the stereo: 3:00 am. The truck was still running. At least the rain had finally stopped. I got up, touched my swollen eye and patted my forehead to snap out of my half-sleep, the spinning and the nausea slowed way down, but I was cold, wet, and covered in muck. I climbed into the truck and turned the headlights on to see where I landed, and if there was a way out. After putting the truck into four-wheel drive, I rocked back and forth to free myself from the apparent cornfield that kept the truck from going any further. I backed out of the cornfield for thirty yards and found myself two feet deep in a pumpkin patch.

In the headlight beams I could see the carnage of my descent. The truck had pummeled first through a cabbage patch, then through broccoli, cauliflower, and pumpkins, which must have exploded like bombs on impact. The truck had finally stalled in the arms of a half-acre crop of late season silver queen corn. The vegetable debris must have scattered like starlings after a shotgun blast. I was one lucky son-of-a-bitch. After breaking free from the pumpkin vines and eight foot stalks of corn, I could see a farmhouse about a thousand yards away. Realizing I was trespassing on private property, I quickly turned my lights off. Around here it was likely someone could open fire on trespassers. Was I in danger? After this clear miss of death, was I going to survive or was I going to be killed, like the way Danielle had murdered my heart?

"Shoot me now!" I cried.

In my delirium, my half breaths, my blood loss, any-thing was possible. Through my one good eye, I could see the farm was fenced in by barbed wire and chain link. The road out was barely visible. I wiped my eye again, attempting to focus. Getting out undetected was impossible, since the road ran alongside the farmhouse. I was soaked in blood, rain, and puke, completely exhausted, and probably needing medical attention. My only plan was to creep slowly and then punch the shit out of my gas pedal. I neared the house. I put the truck in first, and held my breath. After a hundred yards or so, a dog barked, another fifty yards, another barked, and then another.

"Okay, slower," I thought, "good idea." Another bark followed. The final straw broke. The hellhounds were aroused. They sounded like they were chained beasts behind a fence or door, and bloodthirsty. Cerberus had awakened. I eked along a couple more feet and the lights went on in the farmhouse. Fuck this. I held my ribs, and punched it, roaring past the farmhouse. Two large men came running out in their underwear with shotguns, yelling the things you would obviously say in that situation. I was gone like gone, the truck fishtailing through the muddy broken ground. I was free. Pieces of dripping corn, pumpkin, cauliflower, broccoli and cabbage trailed behind me for a quarter mile as I watched through the rearview mirror.

I laughed a little because that was all that was left to do. Looking in the rearview and seeing the empty road was satisfying. I was definitely not the same person who had dropped into that field and nearly rag dolled to death in the process. The rearview mirror did reveal that a death had taken place, but I knew that from this point forward, I would never be the same. For whatever reason, the universe had intervened. Perhaps the same force that had resurrected Dave from his coma?

From the edge of the pass, I could see a lake and certain death if the truck had gone along that path. The trail was rock, the lake deep. It would have drowned my ass in my stupor for sure. On the other side to the right was the farmhouse. Just below the edge was a drop, full of large boulders and buckthorn bushes. The truck should have rolled for sure. But it hadn't. It had landed on all fours and nobody had witnessed it except the eyes of the universe. I had to have been travelling fast. The truck probably looked like a redneck torpedo as it achieved momentum. If the corn hadn't been planted late in the season, along with the rest of the pumpkins and vegetables, to slow me down, I would have plowed into the farmhouse and who knows what the outcome would have been. I was glad to have landed in the parallel side of the universe that allowed a second chance. Who'd had the wheel? I certainly hadn't. I felt like an experiment from Schrodinger himself.

Ironically, as the lights of Washington came into view, I stopped at the KarKwik where I first met Danielle. I was nearly out of gas, and it was the only place open. It felt like time suspended itself for me. I stood in the lane where we met, now alone. I had loved the mystery that was her. It was like walking through a dream. I might have believed it too, if it wasn't for my closed up eye and the fact I could hardly breathe. My truck looked like it had crashed into a salad bar.

I went to the window to pay for my gas and the attendant said, "Dude, what happened? You look like you were punched out by the Terminator."

I laughed, and said, "Blonde chicks, stay away from blonde chicks, man."

I filled up, and as I replaced the gas cap, out of the corner of my good eye, saw pumpkin slop was still falling out of the bumper and wheel wells. I jumped in, started her up and was finally on the way home. I was in anguish, hurting in every part of my body, still drunk. The night attendant's face was priceless. I was surprised he didn't call the cops. I felt I was barely alive as I drove myself home. I just wanted to crawl into my bed, hide in the covers, and sleep. There were things about the drive home I had never noticed before—the new construction on Washington, and a newly lit parking lot on Thirty-First, a new music store. I had been so into Danielle that nothing else around me had mattered, just her.

I made it up the steep hill to my house on Jefferson. It was so late that I had no option but to go through the basement window well to get into my room undetected. I closed the truck door quietly. The street lamp exposed the vegetable debris that remained, and the cracks in the windshield looked like frozen lightning. The blood from my side and head had crusted over. I staggered and stumbled up the steep side of the yard that led to the back. The grass was long and moist, and its sweet dewy scent almost made me throw up. I collapsed to all fours, carefully dropped into the dark steel well, and slid my window open, moaning with every awkward move. I couldn't tell which was worse, my fatigue or my physical pain. I lowered myself feet first moving slowly and carefully, hugging the wall until I could feel the give of my bed. I slid the window shut and flopped onto my bed, finishing in a fetal position toward the wall. Safe.

Gravity took over and sucked my body deep into the bed. I felt punched full of holes, my eye numb and heavy. I was so ready for a long, deep sleep. I whispered out loud, "No changing my clothes tonight, just crashing, crashing, hard." My body succumbed to the exhaustion, like a slow death. I relaxed; the sweet silence of the room became intoxicating, until it wasn't.

Flick, flick. The room illuminated for a second. I heard someone inhale deeply, then exhale. A cloud of cigarette smoke swirled in close proximity to my bed, and into my lungs, my heart pounded, the last bit of any energy I had was consumed, and then I heard a sipping sound. Holy shit, I wasn't alone. Somebody was there.

In great agony, I turned my head slightly to the right, and with my good eye barely made out a partial female silhouette. The light went on. Trophy Wife sat there with a cigarette, sucking down a martini, just waiting for me, vulturous. I hid my face.

"Where were you tonight?"

"Are you smoking?"

"Yes, yes I am, thanks to you."

"Is there really no God? Of all nights, Jesus God, please!" I said.

"So where were you this time, Michael?"

"Michael is gone." Couldn't she see I wasn't that boy, that pathetic kid who'd been made a fool of, who'd had his silly heart broken? Could she not recognize the man who drove out of that field? The man who walked away from the temptress Danielle? The man I had become barely recognized the boy Michael. I closed my eyes and growled. "Leave my room."

"Chasing whores and getting beat up? You are a filthy mess. You tracked in mud and there's blood on the wall! Who's going to clean that up?"

I tried to listen, but I struggled to breathe and was ready to fall asleep, even with her ranting, riotous, fucking madness.

"So what do you have to say for yourself? You're going to end up in jail, like your buddy Dave," she said, sipping and smoking in between her words.

"What? You talked to Dave?"

"A letter came from the Chino Jail in California. It's on the bed."

"Great. Now get the fuck out." Much as I wanted to rip open the letter and figure out what had happened to Dave, I was too tired, and I certainly wouldn't give her the satisfaction of watching me read Dave's letter…from jail. From jail? What the fuck was he doing in jail?

"No, Michael, you're going to get the fuck out." Trophy Wife's voice was low and slinky like a cat about to pounce.

"Can we just talk tomorrow, please?" I begged, holding my chest.

"No, we can't. You need to be out by tomorrow."

I pried my good eye open enough to see the smug smirk on her lips. Her lipstick was smudged and little kiss marks dotted her martini glass like she'd been making out with it.

"Give me a break. I broke up with Danielle and now Dave's in jail? Jesus!" I said, coughing blood into my hand.

"Of course, she broke up with you, with all the sneaking around you do. And Dave's a loser, just like you," she said.

"You really don't get it, do you?" I was lying there in pain, bleeding, maybe with internal injuries or a concussion, and she picked now to confront me?

"I'm afraid I do, Michael. You don't appreciate anything," she ranted on. "I'm sick and tired of your crap."

I could barely hang on to be further abused. I was on the verge of passing out. I kept my face turned to the wall to avoid the blaring light and her cigarette smoke that had no place to go but my lungs. My side burned with every breath; there was a deep wheeze in my chest.

"Really, really, sick of it," she blasted on. "What is the matter with you?"

"I'm having a hard time breathing, actually."

"Are you on drugs now, Michael?"

"I'm not Michael. Michael is gone!" I gasped with difficulty.

"Who are you then, smart guy?" she said, chewing an olive, and sucking the last drop of her martini. Cigarette ash fell to the floor like snow.

"Head and neck check, M-16, check, ribs, blood, damage. I can't breathe. Is this my final breath? Incoming…"

"Michael, what the hell is wrong with you?"

I gasped, choking for one final moment of clarity.

"I'm Jimmy Crane. Call me Jimmy Crane."

ACKNOWLEDGEMENTS:

It's with deep gratitude for the wonderful support by the team at Luminare Press, Patricia, Kim, Claire, Melissa and, especially, Molly Martin. My sisters, Cathy and Laura for the late nights and, my deepest thanks to my partner in crime, Cyn.

I hope you enjoyed *Spiral*,
Book I in *The Crane Trilogy*.

Check out Chapter 1, "Dead Man's Curve,"
of Book II, *Flux*, along with upcoming events
and release dates at jmfisherauthor.com

www.ingramcontent.com/pod-product-compliance
Lightning Source LLC
Chambersburg PA
CBHW032059050726
47590CB00001B/340